# Unsportsmanlike Conduct

A Single Mother Sports Romance

Ella Haines

LIBRA LIBROS LLC

# Contents

# Author's Note About Content Warnings

**See list of content/trigger warnings here on my site at www.EllaHaines.com/Triggers**

The list is also found at the end of the book through the table of contents

**WARNING**: will possibly contain plot spoilers by nature of disclosing – proceed as you are comfortable

# Blurb

**A neurospicy single mom. A search for her adopted son's dad that jeopardizes her custody agreement. All the while, spending time with a sexy professional athlete who never dreamed he'd love playing pseudo step-dad to two adorable tots.**

**

Exhausted single mom, Megan Lowell, faces a life-altering choice: should she seek out her adopted son's biological father? The only lead she has is that he's a player for the Springfield Spartans football team. But what if pursuing this path puts her custody at risk? Despite the heart-wrenching possibility, she turns to Danny, her incredibly sexy yet forbidden friend on the team, to discreetly inquire.

*

Danny Parker, All-Star wide receiver and media sensation, is America's heartthrob. He's charming, witty, and dangerously attractive. He's always been clear about his aversion to parenthood; he can't afford distractions from his career. Yet, as he gazes into Megan's eyes, he senses a familiar desperation, reminiscent of his own mother's struggles. He's determined to help her find the missing puzzle piece even if it means confronting his demons and questioning his lifetime anti-fatherhood rhetoric.

*

But when they find her son's father...Danny and Megan have to deal with the sack of a lifetime. Will they recover or will the turnover cost them more than they could have ever imagined?

# CHAPTER ONE
# August 25, Thursday
## Megan

"Ava! No biting your brother. Teeth are for eating. No, honey, we use gentle hands. No jumping on him, either. Babies don't give piggyback rides!" Megan Lowell rushed to save her ten-month-old from the weight of his three-year-old sister. Once enough space was put between the two tots, she dashed to the fridge to grab their already-prepared lunch boxes so she could stuff them in their daycare bags.

Surely, Ava couldn't remount her brother in the thirteen seconds it would take to grab their lunch boxes...

Wrong.

A wail echoed out in the small but pretty apartment and Megan whipped back around to see Ava interrupting Theo's play with more cowboy practice. She hurried back to the crying almost-toddler and confused little girl who just wanted to play with her baby brother.

"Ahh, honey. No climbing on the baby, remember?" It was just easier to refer to him as a baby...she probably always would.

Megan let out a tired sigh as she settled on the ground next to them, giving them loads of snuggles as she stared blankly at the opposite wall.

Man, she couldn't wait till Theo was older.

Famous last words.

After five minutes, Ava left to do something else and everyone was happy once more. Megan seized the moment and hurried back to the kitchen and tried grabbing her lunchbox from the fridge.

A wail from Ava had her whipping around.

What now?

Ava's face was ruddy with unexploded anger. A little, chubby fist went wild as she tried to pull one of her favorite toys out of her little brother's mouth.

Megan's shoulders slumped.

God, it never ended.

Megan rushed over and calmed the simmering volcano. "Shh, baby. I have your toy. Theo didn't know that he shouldn't chew it. Babies are still learning. See? Here it is." She solved the hostage situation and scooped up Theo, swaying him for a moment before turning and buckling him in his walker.

There. Maybe that would buy her some time to get shit done. Maybe.

Walkers weren't exactly 'supported' in the mom community, but Megan had learned Theo liked the motion and...well, she had to do what she had to do. It's not like she kept him in it unattended or for hours at a time.

This was a game of *survival*.

Parenting two kids within two years of each other? Not for the weak of heart.

Ava climbed up on her Montessori-style kitchen stool and started into her bowl of strawberry yogurt.

Good. That would keep her busy for a minute.

Megan dashed around the house to make sure she wasn't forgetting anything for the day. More wipes and diapers for each kid for daycare? Check. Lunches and bottles? Check. Washed crib and cot sheets? Check. Extra clothes for school? Check. Her work laptop bag?

Not check...

She surveyed the area and approached the table where Ava was singing a song from *The Greatest Showman*, albeit in broken English. Was her laptop bag around the corner?

As she peered around the corner, Ava gave an animated arm gesture and sang the crescendo of her song.

Ava's elbow knocked the still-full yogurt bowl off the table and it went flying, splattering the ground at Megan's feet.

Megan beat back a sigh, conscious of the little girl's big, worried eyes on her.

"Sorry, Mama," Ava babbled in her sweet, high little voice.

"It's okay, Ava girl. It's easy enough to wipe up. We just need to be careful, right?" Megan waited for the girl to nod and then she offered Ava her hand so they could use some cloths to wipe up the mess together.

Surreptitiously, Megan glanced at the clock.

Fuck on a fucker. She was going to be so fucking late.

She took a deep breath and held it as they worked together to clean up the mess. Every instinct inside her was telling her to have Ava step away rather than wasting time letting her smear it everywhere in her attempt to help, but Megan fought it back. Barely.

Work would be fine. It wasn't the end of the world. It would all be okay.

Everything would be okay.

The pressure on her chest grew, suggesting that things would not be okay.

It would all be okay.

She let out big breaths quietly, trying to channel her anxiety and stuff it down.

Megan needed to get her shit together and channel her inner Elsa.

It didn't work out great for Elsa, but it would do in a pinch.

Apparently, her exhales weren't quiet enough because Ava's little blonde head swiveled in her direction, and she looked sad again.

"It's okay, honey. It wipes up. I was worried I got yogurt on my work clothes, but I have this t-shirt over my work shirt, so I can just pull this off and be good as new. After I change my pants, that is." She tried her best to ease her daughter's worry. Ava was staring at the mess with a quivering lower lip, clearly upset she spilled her breakfast. The little darling was quiet and emotional, and like Megan, didn't like making mistakes.

The two kids might be adopted but they were still very much like Megan.

As she tip-toed through the leftover yogurt splashes on the kitchen floor, Megan's eyes flicked back to the clock. Megan would clean the rest up later.

Shit, shit, shit.

"Okay. It's fine. It's just yogurt, we can clean this up tonight. No problem."

Ava cautiously stepped over, doing her best not to step in the yogurt, but her little socks still landed in it anyway. Her little arms reached up and Megan scooped her up, swaying gently.

"But for now, going to go into Mama's room and pick out some new pants. Then, we're going to go straight to school. *Really* quick. Okay, team?"

Breathe.

Megan bent to place the little firecracker on the worn and scratched linoleum so she could escape to her room for a quick change of pants. Ava's legs climbed higher until they were horizontal to the ground. There was no way Ava was willingly going to be lowered to the ground. Not without a battle.

Breathe.

Megan looked at Theo wandering around happily in his walker and took a second to center herself. Her 'fight-or-flight' response was easily triggered lately. When she asked her doc for a different anxiety med, her doctor stared at her hard before chastising her with, "It would work if you remembered to take it."

Well, screw her then. Remembering to take her laundry list of pills every day wasn't as easy as her doc made it sound. Iron supplements, vitamin C, vitamin B12 Complex, daily multivitamins, fish oil, prescription anxiety meds, ADHD meds, birth control...some of which upset her stomach if she took them all at the same time. Forgive her for forgetting to pop the rest before bed or during their chaotic dinnertime ritual.

Megan scanned the apartment, counting items to distract from her rising panic. One couch, two stools, three pictures on the wall, four...

The apartment wasn't anything special, but it was home. Megan had shared the apartment with her cousin, Starla, for several years, both not having the means to upgrade. They didn't have too much in common, but family trauma had a way of bonding people.

They had escaped to Springfield as soon as they turned eighteen. Working odd jobs and seeing each other rarely, they both lived their own lives. Megan worked her way through an accounting degree, thanks to scholarships and her knack for football stats. When Megan graduated, she was tempted to find a new place to live, but Starla wanted them to stay together. So when they got the new, still modest apartment, they made it nice in whatever way they could, separate in styles but still united.

Shortly after they got the new apartment, when they were twenty-four, Starla announced she was pregnant, and Megan was there every step of the way. Supporting, comforting, and encouraging.

Only judgmental in the privacy of her own mind.

The idea of having Megan adopt the baby occurred to Starla during one prenatal checkup.

The pleas began and Megan couldn't say no.

After Ava was born and the waiting period was over, Megan and Starla signed the papers with the help of Megan's lawyer friend, Bianca Staylee. It happened so fast, from day one, Ava was Megan's, and no one would ever know differently.

Both Megan and Starla agreed, *no one* from back home would know the truth.

When Starla announced she was pregnant again a year-and-a-half later, Megan wanted to choke her.

Hadn't she ever heard of a *fucking* condom?

Something about this time was different, though....

Starla had always been wild, whereas Megan had been calm. Starla was outgoing, whereas Megan was an introvert. Starla was carefree, and Megan was cautious...and anxious...and OCD. And...

But after having Ava, Starla got hooked up with a crowd that was worse than usual.

A crowd that was a little wilder than even Starla's 'wild'.

So, when she told Megan she was pregnant, something about her was off. And it wasn't just the coke making its way through her system. She was shifty about it. Depressed. Anxious. In fact, Starla continued to party while pregnant. Which she had never done when pregnant with Ava.

Megan wanted to beat her senseless. Week after week, she confronted her cousin about alcohol and drug use. All to deaf ears.

Once again, Megan accepted Starla's request to adopt the baby. But concern seeped back in when Starla started immediately talking about not even wanting to see him after he was born. She even made comments about finding a new place to live.

Who was the father? Why was this time so different?

The shock had flooded her.

Holy crap, had someone raped her cousin?

Her cousin's desperation to not want to even look at the baby and her talks about moving out made more sense if that was the case. It's not like Starla was ever home that much anyway and she tried not to be around when Ava was home. But to outright not even want to meet the baby?

Something was up.

Megan agreed to adopt this one on the condition that her cousin be truthful with her about whether she was violated.

Starla had turned green and vehemently swore up and down that she was not raped. Not by a long shot. She defended the guy passionately; he was great, smart, hard-working, *good*. When Megan asked her why he wasn't involved, Starla had gotten all cagey and said she didn't know how to get a hold of him. Megan let it lie, thinking she'd have more time for questions later.

She didn't.

Miraculously, Theo was born with no complications from Starla's poor choices.

In a daze, Megan signed the papers again. And after a little flourish of her pen...boom! She was a mom of a two-year-old and a newborn.

Sweet baby Jesus, it felt like yesterday, not months ago.

And not long after that, Starla overdosed and died, leaving Megan with nothing but boxes and unanswered questions.

Theo started fussing as he stared at Megan, still swaying with Ava. Ava clung tighter, no doubt sensing that she was going to be put down to soothe the fussing baby.

Breathe.

Megan trudged over to free Theo from his captivity. After a couple of small grunts to share his displeasure, Theo mimicked his sister and snuggled close to his mama's shoulder.

All was forgiven if Mama didn't put him down. But Mama had to put him down to put new pants on...

Megan braced herself for the cry fest that was about to happen if she lowered them to the ground.

On each hand, she tapped her pointer fingers and thumbs together rapidly, channeling the nerves out of her stomach and out through her hands. Megan's stomach tensed further as the children clung to her, expecting a flood of cries as soon as she set them down.

Nope, not able to handle the big emotions this morning. Not when she was already riding the edge of a panic attack because of being so late.

"Okay, then," Megan mumbled as she shifted them slightly onto either hip. "We'll all go together."

With slow, tired steps, she marched down their messy hall with the worn carpet. Decorating the dark hall was Ava's artwork, taped at waist height so Ava could admire it whenever she toddled past. Megan couldn't stop her smile as she remembered how proud Ava looked when Megan hung the first one up. It had become their tradition. Though they were running out of wall space.

As Megan picked out new pants, she tried to think of a way to remind her bosses how lucky they were to have her and to please not fire her for being late again.

She was failing at work.

She was failing at being a mom.

She was failing at everything.

It was easier when it was one kid. Now she only had half, probably less, attention to give to each. Neither kid was getting the attention they needed.

Megan was dropping balls left and right.

Speaking of balls...Megan didn't have any.

Sure, the kids had some incredible pseudo-uncles. But that didn't replace having a dad.

Ava's dad was a dead-end. Megan would sell a kidney before she told that asshole he had a daughter.

But Theo's...

Megan could stop the questions from rattling around in her mind.

After she successfully loaded herself up like a camel, she slogged her way out of the apartment and to her car. Megan chatted with her children as she loaded them into the car, avoiding thinking about how late she was.

Even knowing that nothing good was waiting for her at the office, she wouldn't trade the nuggets nestled in their car seats for anything in the world. They were *everything*.

But *holy crap on a cracker*, she needed some freaking help.

# CHAPTER TWO

# August 25, Thursday
## Megan

"Everyone should be present and ready for the meeting with Spartan management next week as it is crucial to our firm. I know we're adjusting to this period of transition, but we need to rally. Let's be ready to represent Galloway, the Spartan team, and their business interests."

The stale conference room was filled with head nods and manly grunts.

Transition?

One of the partners fucking *died* last week.

Guess that was a type of 'transition…'

Megan dipped her head to the notepad in her lap and pinched her lips so as not to chew them out for being so cold.

If William Galloway and the Spartans chose to work for her outdated and sexist firm, she'd make sure she had quiet words with William's daughter, Lexie, expressing her concerns for his mental health. A person couldn't walk down the halls here without being beaten with the toxic masculinity that reigned supreme.

What Megan wouldn't give for a new job.

But the time wasn't right. Like always.

Money was tight enough as it was, and her bosses would try to blackball her quicker than TMZ reporting a nip-slip

In the predominantly male conference room, Megan couldn't help but ponder the dynamics at play. On more than one occasion, management had been heard saying that women were distracted in the workplace and they preferred male staff. To her knowledge, no one ever publicly accused them of sexism. She was their affirmative action hire, the one that said, "We support women".

Yeah, right.

Megan yearned for a better environment, where merit triumphed over gender. She believed in challenging the status quo, fostering diversity, and advocating for equal opportunities.

As management dithered on about how they needed to suckle at the 'Spartan Teat' next week and be on their best behavior, she couldn't stop her disgusted scoff. Luckily, no one seemed to notice.

Megan would slash William's tires before she let the owner of the Springfield Spartans football team come to this terrible firm.

As the meeting adjourned, there were handshakes and slaps on the back doled out left and right for winning this important introduction next week. Noticeably absent was any attention towards her. They all liked to pretend she didn't exist. Unless they had a more progressive client come in, then the firm executives paraded her out like the trophy she was.

God, this place sucked. Why couldn't she have found a better firm when she was looking for a job so many years ago?

"Megan. A moment, please."

Megan jolted and whipped her head towards where the managing partner still sat at the head of the dark wood table. She eased her body back down into her chair and looked around at the men now eyeballing her, wondering what she did that would demand such a one-on-one.

Sure, she was late that morning. Again. a quarter past eight was still hardly anything to sneeze at. It just wasn't 7:00.

But the kids had rough drop-offs.

She broke into a slight sweat as she waited for the room to clear. Two of the other managers stayed behind as well.

Crap.

"Megan. We wanted to talk to you about your performance lately."

Her stomach curled into knots and her hands fisted.

"As you know, last month, we verbally issued you a warning about your time off from work."

Megan opened her mouth to defend herself. The kids were sick with the flu. What the hell was she supposed to do?

"We're here today to deliver a formal, written warning."

On the heels of a staff meeting? They didn't even want to schedule a separate time to do this shit?

One manager slid a paper on the table over to her and she reached out and slowly dragged it across the dark table to her, half not believing this was even happening.

"This formal acknowledgment is meant as an incentive to improve your performance, attitude, and commitment to the firm."

Megan looked down at the stiff page with the firm's antiquated emblem emblazoned on the letterhead. In Latin, there was some stupid phrase about being united in manhood. Blech.

After a quick scan, she raised her eyes to look at the managing partner.

"Bob, like I said last month, I'm unsure what performance issues have arisen. I'm hitting my billable hour goals, exceeding my realization ratios on all accounts, and even clocked forty hours of overtime last month alone. Again, I have no issues with my direct supervisors or subordinates. Please tell me what exactly you're writing me up for, as this letter is vague and offers no direct feedback."

She used to be meek and circumspect but learned it was a sign of weakness to these men.

Now she was more direct in her communication style.

She wasn't considered weak now.

However, now they considered her a bitch.

This firm and its staff were the definitions of shitholes.

"This warning states you're deficient in several areas and that you'll no longer be treated as an individual contributor but will be moved into a probationary position until further notice. If your attendance can't be improved..."

She tried to stop herself from rolling her eyes, failed, and sucked in her breath. This was ridiculous.

She looked at the other three men in the room and saw each of them wore a face of solidarity and disappointment.

"Bob," she fought the urge to toss his ever-present coffee in his face. "My kids were sick-"

"Again?" His mocking tone set her on edge.

She ground her teeth before smoothing out her expression. "Yes, again. Daycare is a cesspool. When one kid gets sick, they all get sick. And with the daycare's rules, if they are sick, they can't come back in until they are fever-free for twenty-four hours. Like I've told you all before." She leveled a look at the men and took a risk. "Go home and ask your wives. Or ex-wives. Whatever. Daycare kids get sick. Ask them how often your kids were sick when they were little. You'll see I'm not lying. Hell, I can even get a note from the daycare if that's what this has come down to."

One manager shifted and looked to the others.

Finally! Someone saw reason!

"You know, maybe she's right." Megan felt a surge of relief, until... "Maybe we should ask for confirmation letters from daycare saying that the kids are excluded until a certain date."

Megan stiffened. She was being tongue-in-cheek when she suggested that. Obviously, she could provide it if she needed to, but that wasn't the point. Where was the freaking trust? She worked 80 hours a week for these people for four months a year and this was how she was being treated. What the hell?

Not to mention, was this even legal? Wouldn't FMLA have a case here? Regardless, she wouldn't poke that bear. She could only push them so far.

"Fine. I'll get you a freaking letter." She slapped her hands on the table and pushed to stand, but was stopped by a harsh grunt from one of the other dickhead managers.

"Language," he bit out.

Straight up, last week she heard him refer to one of his clients as "a giant fucking idiot who wouldn't know what to do with two tits to rub together."

She bit her lip to stop her vicious reply.

Megan simply leveled a 'really?' look at him before nodding to the remaining men. When no one else stopped her exit, she stomped from the room and back to her small office.

Ass. Holes.

In the past, her one relief at the firm was her boss and mentor, Stuart Bleeker. He was a partner and oversaw some personal tax and ran a small forensic accounting umbrella at Smith, Tatum, and Doug, CPA. He cushioned her from the poisonous snakes that he was partnered with.

*Was* being the operative word.

He died last week from an unexpected heart attack, and she was left without her one supporter. The one reason she didn't hate every single second she was at work.

When Megan put in for time off to attend his funeral...she was denied.

Freaking denied.

They said they had too much of a backlog of work and too many others had already requested it off. Plus, she "didn't have any vacation left."

Assholes.

All of them.

She tossed her 'written warning' in the recycling bin in her office and threw herself down on her swivel chair. As she logged into her computer and waited for the various programs to load, she pulled out her phone to check her kids' daycare app.

She was greeted with a picture of them eating snacks together, and then a general update on their diapers and meals for the day so far. Then she saw a note saying Theo had a watery bowel movement and a slight temperature. Not enough to be sent home, but they would keep her updated.

Knowing her lackluster daycare, they would probably take his temperature right after a nap when he was the hottest and use that as an excuse to send him home. They were perpetually short-staffed and seemed to always find a reason to send her kids home. And wouldn't you know? There was no price break on sick days. So even when they kicked her children out of school, Megan was still paying an arm and a leg for their services. Several times she picked up the kids just to get them home and have them act perfectly fine.

However, as much as their tendency to send the kids home frustrated her, there was such a shortage of daycare openings, she was grateful she at least had a place to send them. She certainly didn't have anyone else to rely on.

Clearly, work wasn't going to accommodate a flexible arrangement for her.

And her friends all had kids and lives of their own.

She let out a sigh and put her phone back on the desk with the screen up so she could see if the daycare sent another notification. It was the weirdest thing. When she was with them, she sometimes couldn't wait for them to be put down for bed. But when they were asleep, she just wanted them to be awake. She might not be their biological mother, but she had the postpartum hormones and the hot mess part down pat.

A chime sounded on her calendar, reminding her of Stuart's appointment she'd volunteered to cover. When he died, the managers combed through his client list and snatched up the heavy hitters as quickly as they could. They left the no-names and unknown referrals to the bottom feeders, aka Megan.

She pulled up their office manager's notes on this new client intake and gathered the notes she had prepared yesterday. She assembled everything in their firm's onboarding folder and made her way to the smallest conference room. Hopefully, this meeting went better than her last.

# CHAPTER THREE
# August 25, Thursday
## Danny

Danny Parker tapped his foot idly while skimming the generic magazine he found on the side tabletop next to him. He regretted turning down the receptionist's offer of water a few minutes before because the subterfuge was stressing him out. He kept his baseball hat low despite his desire to take it off when inside the nice office; his mother would chew him out right now about manners. But so far, the disguise worked. No one recognized him.

Maybe accountants weren't big football fans?

"Mr. Smith? Megan will see you now. Just follow me. Are you sure I can't get you some water? Coffee?"

Megan? He was supposed to meet with Stuart Bleeker.

"I'm fine, thanks" His mouth answered for him again, eager to not draw attention to himself. An excessive amount of pictures and certificates lined the hallway toward the conference room. Every few feet was a portrait of a different man in a tailored suit, posing stoically with a slight frown on his face.

Did women even work here?

On each side of the hall were stately offices with large windows, not only facing the interior hall but also out towards the city. Furnished in dark woods and maroons, each room looked the same. The little wall space they had was adorned with certificates, awards, diplomas, advanced certifications, and even a few notable newspaper clippings.

The receptionist let Danny into a conference room that seemed excessively large for the one-on-one meeting. There was a solitary woman sitting alone at the head of the table near the door.

Ah, women did work here.

Her blonde head was down as she flipped through some documents. On the table next to her was a manila folder and pen, ready to be used.

She also had two glasses of water sitting on the table.

Thank god.

The clear liquid sent a pang through him-he wished it was vodka being offered instead. He beat back the usual and intrusive thought.

He stilled as he forced his eyes away from the cups.

Oh shit. He knew her!

The accountant had a low ponytail, thickly framed glasses that were trendy years ago, and a black business suit. Her shoes were made for comfort and practicality, not style. Even her nails were kept trimmed and didn't have a drop of polish on them. From what he could see, the only thing that spoke to a possible louder personality was the dazzling jewelry she had on. Deep sapphires in each earlobe with a halo of diamonds around the oval shape of the stones, and a matching ring and necklace.

She was a far cry from the supermodel he had seen gracing various Spartan functions, bringing the house down with Spartan heiress Lexie Galloway.

How was this even the same woman?

Her eyes were still on the documents in front of her as she stood. "Mr. Smith, thanks for coming in. How are you?" When she looked up into his face, her entire body jolted, and she gave a sharp inhale.

Busted.

Clark Kent set the bar too high. The secretly sophisticated and seductive fox of a woman in front of him could clearly see through his comic book disguise of wearing reading glasses and a hat.

The receptionist was already back down the hall, completely unaware she just escorted one of the Springfield Spartans' crown jewels into the conference room.

The Spartans moved to Springfield, Massachusetts fifteen years ago, bringing wealth and prosperity to the area. A couple of other flagship sports teams followed and now Springfield was a hub of sports, nightlife, and business. At the time, there was concern that the professional football team would be too close to Foxborough to offer up any kind of success. However, William Galloway, the owner, was a billionaire renewable energy tycoon who was determined to make it work. And he did. The team had made several Super Bowl appearances in its short tenure and was on track for another stellar season.

Despite her shock and obvious recognition, Megan extended her hand and gripped his in a warm handshake that threw him off kilter.

How did he not know that Lexie's femme fatale friend from her notorious book club was a CPA? The guys on the team would add that to their fantasies if they knew that she had the looks, the party gene, *and* the brains.

Actually...when was the last time he saw her out bringing in the 'last call' from the various bars?

It had been a bit...

He shifted and caught a hint of her perfume. It took a minute to place it, but she smelled like the lavender garden at his new house. He had transplanted some from his childhood home; it brought back memories of calm and peaceful times.

Danny inspected her as she did the same. He broke the silence. "You don't look like a Stuart."

Her dirty blonde eyebrows climbed up and she shot back, "Just about as much as you look like a Josh Smith." She inspected him in a challenge, waiting for him to fess up.

"About that..."

He scanned her pretty face, but he kept getting drawn back to her big, wide eyes. The shape of them was unique. They tilted inward in the most dramatic and unique way, just the barest tilt. Her unique green eyes with her pearly white skin, rosy cheeks, and dirty blonde hair created a jaw-dropped effect. He couldn't help the quick dash of his eyes to her left hand.

Empty still. Nice.

"I have a rather delicate matter. And I didn't want it to get out that I was meeting with anyone from your office. My current accountant doesn't have time and suggested Mr. Bleeker."

Megan gave a small nod, her face still confused, and waved toward the chairs. As they sat, he continued to watch her. Her nose sloped down in an adorable way that made him want to take a tiny nibble of the tip. Danny should have felt embarrassed by how much he was studying her, but she was giving her own appraisal of him if her darting eyes were anything to go by. Megan's confident and unashamed inspection of him excited him more than it should have. It had been a long time since a woman had been so...direct with him.

Her head cocked to the side and the intelligence there...the cunning...the no-nonsense...it shot right to his dick.

Jesus. Down boy.

She shifted slightly and he could tell that she had recrossed her legs under the table. Megan wet her lips and placed her hand on the table. Her fingers down her delicate hand arched. "So, to start. I'm sorry about changing up your meeting on you, Danny." She said his name softly and Christ.... Her saying his name shot to his dick as well. "If we had known we were meeting with you, I'm sure one of the other partners of the firm would have rearranged their schedule to make sure they could be here." She paused, clearly searching for her next words. "But, um, Mr. Bleeker passed away last week. Suddenly. And things are a little up in the air right now."

Oh.

Danny sat back at a loss on what to say to her. She was matter-of-fact, but there was a flicker of sadness in her eyes. "I, uh, I'm sorry." He paused, inspecting her closer. She did look a little tired. Gorgeous, but tired. "How are you guys still in the office this week? You guys aren't closed or anything? Wasn't he one of the partners here? I'm sure the clients would understand if you all needed some time off."

He was surprised to see her carefully modulate her reaction to his questions. Not looking like a woman who lost a beloved boss, but looking like an employee that was told to repeat a company line.

To be fair, she looked like she was sucking a lemon to do it.

"Yes, he was a partner here," Megan started slowly. "It was very sudden. It was a heart attack. The office is in transition. Again, I'm deeply sorry that one of the other partners couldn't be here to meet you. They always try to prioritize meeting high-profile clients personally." She looked down and then back up. Her look of uneasiness was gone. It was now replaced with a chastising look. "They don't usually come to us under a pseudonym. Josh Smith certainly wasn't associated with anything to do with the Springfield Spartan organization."

He raised one shoulder in recognition of her comment but didn't say anything else on the topic. "Please extend my condolences to the team here. When are the services?"

The gorgeous woman across from him chewed on her lip again looking like she was biting her tongue. "This afternoon actually," she started flipping her pen on the table, dropping one end down, picking it up, and then letting it slide through her fingers, so the other end hit against the table.

Drop, lift, drop, lift. Danny had to force his eyes away from watching the pen glide through her pretty fingers.

Then her words hit him, and he stiffened. "What?"

She looked out the windows across from Danny and avoided making eye contact.

"Yeah, it's this afternoon," she mumbled.

"You guys aren't all there?"

She pinched her lips together and kept her pose, staring out the window. She then looked back at him. "Well, there are too many clients counting on us, we can't all just disappear for a few days." She said it with a hint of an attitude that had him cocking an eyebrow. Feisty Mouse wasn't drinking the company Kool-Aid. "Management decided we couldn't afford to have a bunch of staff on vacation and not working right now."

He looked at her, eyebrows raised and his expression showing his disbelief. "Vacation? It's not like you'd be going surfing. It's a funeral. They didn't give you time off to go to your dead boss's funeral?" He felt bad at his bald analysis of events, but...come on.

"Well, they were going to give us time off if we put in the vacation request in time, but I didn't have any more time left over. So..." The muscle on her cheek twitched and she gave him a look that showed she agreed with exactly how he felt before she forcibly smoothed her expression out.

Why would his CPA suggest this ass-backward firm for this project? It was a shit hole.

Drop, lift, drop, lift. The pen moved faster on the table.

Megan then visibly rallied herself and placed both hands on the table, one over the other, and changed her expression, clearly trying to move on so she didn't go out and start ranting at her bosses.

Which, from having seen her around, he could absolutely picture her doing.

God, she'd be a vision all fired up.

"What can I help you with, Mr. Smith?"

He jerked back to the now and let her close the door on that dangerous topic.

"It's a bit of a complicated matter really, but I need someone to help my mother with her finances."

The CPA sitting across from him blinked and cocked her head.

"So, you're not even here for you, but for your mother?"

He nodded.

"She doesn't have her own accountant?"

"This is where it gets tricky. My mother and father separated years ago," he started slowly, choosing each word after careful thought. "I saw a statement on her counter the other day with a couple of her retirement balances; they didn't seem right. I know what she pulls out each year for her required minimum distributions and I roughly know how the market has performed over the last several years, but something just doesn't quite add up."

"Have you talked with her financial advisor?"

He nodded. "She has a lot of different accounts, not all of which are managed through a financial advisor. Some are just sitting there stagnant from old employment. I started trying to trace the amounts. A thousand withdrawn here. A thousand deposited there. The dates weren't working and there were too many ins and outs. That leads me to assume my father still has access to the accounts somehow or there's something I'm missing. I'm not able to tell from my quick looks. I don't have the time to really dive in, not that I'd really know what to look for anyways. And my mom refuses to look at any money accounts. She said it tends to disappear when she looks at it." He smiled softly as he remembered his mom's favorite phrase to him. "If my dad's involved, I don't know how or what the gross amount of withdrawals is. There are too many ins and outs in all the accounts to follow. And her accountant...also works with my father...unfortunately."

Megan had started scribbling furiously on a scratch pad when he started talking, now she looked up, her green eyes almost luminescent as she looked at him. "Is your dad a beneficiary or co-owner of the accounts?"

"I don't know. Does that matter?"

Megan nodded. "It's nice to know more than you need to, rather than not enough. They're legally divorced?"

"Yep."

She made another note. "When did that happen?" She peppered him with more interview-style questions, and he felt a weight lift from his chest as she worked through her questioning.

Clearly, she knew her shit.

He watched her take illegible notes on her legal pad and was surprised at how messy her handwriting was. For someone as put together as she was, he would have thought her penmanship would be pristine.

"Is this something you guys would be willing and able to look into?"

She hesitated, set her pen down, and gave him a level look.

Shit.

"Usually no." Light pink blossomed on her cheeks, and it took him aback. When was the last time a woman blushed around him?

"But I think your name, your real name," she amended, "will make the management team more inclined to take on this job. Even if it's not necessarily something we would normally do." She rolled her lips to the side and raised an eyebrow. "Can I go to them and also say you're planning on using us as your new accountant as well?"

She gave her an apologetic look like she didn't want to ask the question.

He shook his head.

He thought he caught a "don't blame you." Louder, she said, "It might have helped your case if I could have said we were doing it for a long-term client. They might just do it for the hourly rate plus any goodwill it might bring us with any people associated with the Springfield Spartans." She shrugged again. "I really can't tell you for sure." she tapped her pen on the scratchpad and brought it to her lips. "Who does your mom's taxes? Would you be able to get us copies of her prior-year tax returns, her monthly statements for each of the investment accounts, as well as the tax return backup? I don't see how we would be able to complete this job without all that information."

Danny nodded. "Yeah, we can get you all of those documents." He then hesitated and Megan shot him a small frown, clearly sensing something amiss. "So, about the tax returns..."

She slid the pen slightly to the side, so it was now in the corner of her mouth. And then she chewed on the end cap absently, the little dents already in the cap showing that it was a common occurrence for her.

Something about the pen sitting between her lips shot a jolt down to his dick and he felt himself twitch.

She raised her brows, waiting for whatever issue he was going to admit to.

"She hasn't actually filed in a year...maybe two." Megan gave him a droll look that had him smiling huge. "My mom is not a numbers person. She does all these little jobs throughout the year but is terrible about recordkeeping for them. I've tried but I get so bored sitting there and making spreadsheets. I've offered to hire someone to do it for her and then she gets pissy with me."

Megan widened her eyes at him and then closed them as she shook her head, clearly disappointed in the pair of them.

The pen sliding along her pink lips caught his attention and he stiffened again.

What was the matter with him? It was a freaking meeting with an accountant, not a trip to the strip club!

One meeting with a woman with glasses and a business suit and he was getting ready to hand over a tie and ask her to take him to her red room of pain?

Jesus.

He shifted and forced his eyes away from her mouth.

"Would your mom consider coming to us for tax prep going forward? Usually, management likes to see continued relationships rather than one-off projects."

That was a thought.

"My mom's CPA has been doing her taxes since she was 25. She would very much benefit from having someone a little more with the times to do her taxes. I.e., someone who knows how to prepare tax returns on a computer. And personally, I'd like to get her a preparer who doesn't have weekly beers with my father."

"A little independence goes a long way, sometimes." The woman across from him chuckled low and smoky.

It sounded rusty, like she didn't do it much.

The members of the team had dubbed Lexie's book club ladies the Book Club Hotties. They were the fantasy of every guy on the football team. All the women were straight bombshells.

Megan especially. Movie star gorgeous, wickedly intelligent (assumed, given her occupation), and clearly a blast to be around if the uproar that surrounded her at charity events was anything to go by. She was the whole package.

He wondered if he should ask her what her thoughts on Wonder Woman were and if she had ever been seen in the same room with her.

He couldn't stop the slow smile from stretching as he looked at her.

She kept her eyes down like she could sense his perusal, and her ears pinkened with her blush.

Interesting.

She raised her hands and placed them on the notepad in front of her both "Okay, I think we have all we need. Everyone at the front desk has your actual contact information. It's not contact information for some real Josh Smith somewhere. Correct?"

He felt his smile soften. "No, that's my actual contact information. Do you want to exchange numbers here now? Just in case."

She shook her head, looking at his chin and mouth rather than meeting his eyes.

Worth a shot.

She shook her head again with a small smile and looked back down at her paper. "I'll give this to the partners in charge and see if this is something that we take on. I can't promise it would be done with any kind of expediency." She paused. "Unless, of course, you wanted to pay for that perk." She gave him a face that said she didn't recommend it, so he shook his head.

"There's no immediate rush. She hasn't filed for long enough now that a few extra weeks won't kill anyone."

She nodded and continued. "So, if the partners decide they do want to take this job on, I expect we'd be able to jump into it in a week or two." She shrugged. "But I'm just a cog in the machine here, so I guarantee nothing." She gave him a wry smile filled with camaraderie and long-suffering.

He nodded and shot her a wink. "Thanks for the heads up."

She nodded and clasped her hands in front of her. The attention brought his eyes down, only to blink when he saw what looked to be white frosting on the outside of her arm, up to her elbow. He felt his head cock as he looked at it, wondering if that was a supreme patch of dry skin or if she rested on a huge section of whiteout. His moment of inattention caught her eye, and she twisted her arm to look at what he was looking at.

"Shit," she mumbled and hurriedly tried rubbing up the arm with her opposite hand. Her speed increased when she realized that it was not doing anything to whatever was there. She looked up at him with a horrified expression. "I'm so sorry. That's yogurt. I'm sorry. That is so unprofessional." She covered it with her hand and looked at him. "There was a snafu this morning before I came into work, I thought I wiped it all up." Her face was blazing red, and you could almost feel the heat radiating from across the table. "Is there anything else I can help you with?" Her voice squeezed out.

He saw a small glisten of sweat form on her forehead.

Was she always so high strung or were her bosses here that uptight and assholes about a little bit of yogurt on her arm and sleeve?

Given that they were making their employees use vacation time for their boss's funeral... maybe they were that big of dickheads.

A voice in his head tried to tell him it wasn't his problem but a part of him wanted to offer to help. To fix something for her. The ragged but determined look in her eye struck a chord in him. It reminded him of his mother growing up: the drive, the tenacity, the bark and bite. It was as familiar as breathing.

The sexual awareness though...was certainly interesting. He couldn't say that he'd ever been attracted to the mama bear look before, but on Megan? It was alluring.

An urge welled up and demanded that he try to help, but with Megan, he had a feeling that he'd get shot down quicker than an unidentified aircraft floating over DC.

He sat back and clapped his hands together. "Alrighty then. You'll be in touch?"

Still covering the dried yogurt, her cheeks still bright pink, she gave a terse nod.

They both rose and wandered to the door. As they arrived, her hand shot out and waited for his resulting handshake. He clasped her long, delicate fingers in his own and he felt fireworks explode in his gut and tingles prick along his skin. He held her hand for one heartbeat too long...and then another.

Part of him rejoiced in the fact that she didn't seem to be letting go of his hand either.

She stared up at him, several inches shorter than his five-foot-eleven frame even with her low, no-nonsense heels. He was hypnotized by the way her glossy lips parted in a soft 'oh,' showing her big, gorgeous pearly whites behind them. Her small, upturned nose and striking, big green eyes made him want to find an artist to paint her, thereby locking in her beauty for all time.

She was just a pretty person.

The tingles transformed into something more carnal as he stared down at her. Finally, she blinked and jerked out of his hold. Megan wiped her hands on her pant leg as if he had cooties.

Danny felt the smile spring to his lips, but he tempered it. If he smiled at her like he wanted to, with full sexual awareness, it would send her running for the hills.

People didn't go into accounting because they liked risks.

He forced his expression away from the 'I want to eat you' smile to a smile that said something more like 'I would enjoy sharing a drink with you and talking to you over a plate of hors d'oeuvres.'

He misjudged just how tough she was though.

Instead of blushing pleasantly at his flirtatious smile, she cocked her head and studied him openly. Her eyes admired him as a smile teased her lips. But she kept it professional.

Man, what if he could get her to break that rule?

Damn, the thought of being able to get her to break that rule nearly had him daydreaming.

She gave him one last admiring look, her lips curved in a sexy smile. Then she gestured to the door and led him out.

Danny was sure any CPA or financial adviser could've helped him, but right then, as he stared at the woman in front of him, he was hit with a warm feeling blooming in his chest. He could have called any time in the last few months and met with Bleeker. Instead, he had uncharacteristically found excuse after excuse to postpone a meeting.

After saying quick goodbyes, Danny watched her retreating form.

*Maybe* divine intervention did exist.

When he couldn't help his eyes from dipping to her delicious ass, unable to be hidden by the plain black pantsuit, he changed the subjunctive of his earlier thought.

Divine Intervention *absolutely* existed.

He had to force himself to break his stare with her apple-shaped bottom, as it swung left, right, and left down the hall.

He'd never left a meeting with a CPA so intrigued and entertained.

# Chapter Four

# August 26, Friday
## Megan

"Theo, honey, take a breath. Ava, baby girl, please stop throwing your cup."

The kids looked at her with expectant expressions, waiting for her to fix all the wrongs in the world.

They'd be waiting for a long time.

She blew a raspberry into the air while staring into their beautiful blue eyes. Starla had pitch-black hair and equally dark eyes. Combine those dark eyes with her snowy white skin tone and her cousin was a striking individual. She was gorgeous and always had this confidence Megan envied.

Starla's and Megan's moms were sisters and they were equally beaten down by life...and the men in it. Megan never knew her dad was—though, she did have a lot of different 'dads' in her youth. Her mom was constantly looking for that 'special someone.' Usually, the guys were toxic as fuck.

Starla? Starla's dad was always around, and given how awful he was...they both had wished, many times, that he wasn't. The man would con, fuck, or fight anyone, it didn't matter who. The man was simply...deranged...and Megan prayed to God that he never came looking for her or realized that Theo and Ava were Starla's.

Their family being broken, unhealthy, and toxic left different scars on them; scars that manifested and healed over differently.

That Starla and Megan escaped that life was something Megan was immensely proud of.

The kids had nothing of Starla in them, neither looks nor personality, and Megan didn't know if she should be grateful for that or mourn it.

"Who is your daddy, my baby?" she whispered to Theo as she started poking various ticklish spots on the kiddos. Their squeals of laughter caused her to smile.

Theo grabbed one of her fingers and pulled it to his mouth, clearly feeling the need to gnaw on something. Ava smiled at her, patiently waiting for the next round of tickles. Megan wiggled her free hand before going in for a sneak attack on her armpit. The little nugget roared with laughter and thrashed on the plush carpet, her little fingers grabbing at Megan's hand and wrist.

"You're not fooling me, missy," Megan said. "I know there's a little imp hiding underneath all that angel."

Theo twisted her finger just enough that when he chomped down with his gums, it caused Megan to wince.

Kid was teething early.

"Okay, darling, let's get you chewy before I lose my finger." Megan pushed up off the floor and wandered to the fridge, grabbing a cold silicon chew toy from a basket there. She brought it back to the little boy and plopped back down on the ground with them.

Looking into Theo's beautiful face, she asked quietly, "Does your dad even know about you? Does he know he has a perfect child out there somewhere?"

Theo ignored her, focusing on the cold teether. Ava wandered off to the corner where some books were waiting.

"I wonder what he's like." Megan reached forward and tenderly stroked Theo's fuzzy hair. "He must be gorgeous. Just look at you."

Theo swatted her hand away, still focused on trying to chew a hole in his toy.

"Are you saying you don't want me to touch you? Or no, you don't think he must be gorgeous?"

She waited for an answer that would not come.

She watched her children play and babble at each other and her heart felt ready to burst. She might not have birthed them, and they came to her via an unusual route...but they were her kids through and through. Even their personalities were like her own, giving her a compelling argument of nurture versus nature.

But still...

They deserved a dad. Or at least a consistent male figure in their life.

And she certainly didn't have time to date and vet out any good men nowadays, so it wasn't coming to them in the form of a stepdad. Most men heard 'single mom' and ran for the hills.

It reminded her of a Brad Paisley song.

So, because a dad stand-in wasn't coming from her finding the love of her life, the best she could do was uncles for them.

But...was that truly *the best* she could do?

Ava would never know her biological father...but Theo...

If Megan could find a clue about who his father was, maybe at least one of her kids could have that puzzle piece provided for them as they grew up.

At the very least, if his dad wasn't a terrible human being like Starla claimed, wouldn't he want to know he had a son?

If Megan were in his shoes, she absolutely would.

Then again...she wasn't the type to have random sex with strangers and never talk to them again. Mostly because she'd want to make sure that no unintended consequences arose...but that was just her.

The 'right' thing to do would be to search for him. To at least let him know he had a son.

She stilled.

What if he wanted Theo?

Was her adoption ironclad? Could he fight it and gain custody of Theo? Bianca had pulled strings and completed everything so fast. What if someone didn't cross a T correctly and the bio dad took Theo from her?

Or...maybe he had more right to Theo than she did? He would be his father, after all...

Was her selfishness preventing Theo from knowing a loving parent? A parent who had more rights to him than she did?

Was Megan willing to take that risk?

Could she risk losing Theo to some guy who contributed nothing but an orgasm to make him? What if he was a schmuck?

Her stomach rebelled and a snake twisted low in her belly.

Breathe.

She rolled her shoulders and alternated squeezing her fists, fighting the anxiety that had formed. She hadn't even decided what to do yet, and she was already stressing the consequences.

Doing her best to ignore her churning stomach, she pushed through and got the kids ready for bed, her movements on autopilot. Even her smiles and laughs with them felt wooden. She wouldn't lose Theo tonight, regardless of what she decided, but naturally, she couldn't shake the impending feeling of doom.

After they were down, she dragged her weary feet to the kitchen. After countless nights of lullabies...she had Pavlov-dogged herself. As soon as she sat in that freaking chair with the lights off and the noise machine on, she was immediately ready for bed. It was a battle of wills every night to leave the kids' bedroom and rally enough that she could either get some work done or do regular household chores. Things that she absolutely could not do with the kids hanging underfoot.

She hauled open the fridge and searched through the sparse contents. The toddler food was plentiful. Adult food? Not so much.

A late dinner was better than none, right?

Megan eyeballed the leftover eggplant parmesan and grimaced. That was probably spoiled by now. She scooped that out and tossed it on the counter to serve as a visual reminder to throw it in the trash.

Her life was full of the need for visual reminders now. She used to be able to keep a mental checklist. Now? Now, she needed visual cues.

How far she had fallen.

She checked another Tupperware container. Nope. Also, bad.

Megan opened a third container...not *bad*, per se...but she also wasn't in the mood for pasta. She added those to the counter as well and shuffled over to the cupboard. Maybe some cereal?

Damn. Slim pickings.

She meant to pick up more before grabbing the kids from daycare tonight, but work ran late.

Megan took a deep breath, held it, and counted to three before letting it out.

Did everyone feel like there was a four-thousand-pound weight just sitting on their chest all the time?

Probably not.

She poured herself a bowl of whole-grain Cheerios, splashed in some milk, sliced up some bananas and dropped them in. She paused as she noticed the wine bottle on the second shelf of the fridge. Wine and Cheerios. The dinner of champions.

Megan poured herself a glass, grabbed her bowl, and headed into her bedroom. She plopped down at her desk and pushed her work stuff to the side. Megan would tackle that after their book club meeting.

Megan pulled up the video link for their late-night meeting and started wolfing down her cereal as the screen loaded.

Her girls were already on and chattering away.

Lexie Galloway and Jen Medina argued about eye color in men, citing Hollywood heartthrobs as examples. In a surprise twist, Lexie, in her dark goth-meet-steampunk style, was arguing for blonde-hair-blue-eyed hotties. In a further twist, she was giving them bonus points for being goody-two-shoes.

Chloe Aloyan had her chin resting in her palm and was staring at the screen with a patient yet disinterested expression on her face, her dark hair falling around her in thick waves.

Rose Catcher, with her red-orange hair and freckles, had her twin boys curled in her arms, nestled tight but still managing to whack her with matching Sophie the Giraffes.

Between Rose and Chloe, there were two sets of twins. Jen and Lexie made sure they never shared the same drinks with the two women in case the 'identical twin-ness' gene rubbed off on them.

Goons.

There were other members of the Book Club Hotties, as the group had grown over the years. But the five of them were at its core and stuck to the assigned schedule with much more religion than their new recruits. Case in point, only the five of them logged in that night.

"If Julie was here, she'd back me up," Jen declared with confidence.

Lexie snorted. "Please."

"There's literally a phrase for tall, dark, and handsome."

Chloe puffed out her cheeks, clearly trying to stay awake.

Megan unmuted herself by pressing the spacebar and chimed in with a cheek full of Cheerios. "Are we actually going to discuss the book or not?"

Both Jen and Lexie stiffened in affront and turned their fiery personalities onto her.

"We are!" they protested in unison. Then they both started talking at Megan, stressing the connection between the two possible love interests in the book.

Megan took a deep breath again. It was going to be one of those nights: Jen and Lexie bickering like sisters over which guy would be better for the book heroine for the full hour.

"If you could be any Disney princess, who would you be?" Rose interrupted to ask. She sat back with a satisfied expression on her face when both Lexie and Jen fell silent and contemplative.

All bow before the master.

Damn. Megan would have to remember that one.

"I'd be Moana."

"Bitch, you're crazy if you don't think Elsa is the best," Lexie fired back to Jen.

"I'm partial to Vanellope von Schweetz," Rose added.

"I definitely think I would be Belle," Chloe said.

Megan grinned when it was her turn. "Dory?"

They all laughed, but she was only partially joking. The attention span and forgetfulness thing...Pixar was onto something there.

She paused, wracking her brains quickly for a better match. "Dude, I don't know. Some of them are awesome..." She thought for a minute more. "I think I'd probably be Megara."

"Megara is technically not a Disney princess."

"Says who? Anyway, maybe not in the traditional sense," Megan allowed. "But she should be. Think about it. Her nickname is Meg. My nickname is Meg. She has one use for men. I have one use for men. She's sure of herself. She has a dry and caustic sense of humor. I'm known to be full of trusting rainbows and butterflies all the time."

The chuckles turned into outright laughter.

After receiving pretend hat tips, Megan took a sip of her wine, pleased with herself for upsetting the status quo. She also wondered if she should write to Disney and ask for Megara to be instituted as an official Disney Princess.

"Okay, time for our mental health check-in. How's everyone doing?" Lexie's eyes moved as she checked each person's individual section on her screen. "Everyone's okay? Nothing's happening at work, home, or otherwise? Love lives are good?" Her ice-blue eyes moved as she looked over her monitor and then looked back up at the camera. "Ladies, roll call. I need some verbal confirmation that everything's going all right and no one is drowning. Drowning is silent, as the mamas in our group frequently tell me."

Man, when did Lexie become a mother hen? Usually that was Jen's job.

"All good."

"Same here."

"Same."

They paused as they waited for Megan to chime in. She had a mouth full of cheerio-infused wine and tried to swallow as fast as she could. "Yeah, I'm fine. We're fine." The stuttering belied the truth.

"Meg," Chloe said softly. "What's going on?" She certainly didn't look ready to fall asleep anymore.

"Nothing. Well, not anything more than usual," Megan amended. "Kids might be getting sick again. Work is full of assholes. Men suck. The *uszh.*"

"Here, here," Lexie raised her drink to the camera.

"What happened at work?" Rose asked while leaning forward toward the screen.

"Nothing any different than usual. They're just being dicks about the kids being sick so much."

"They're little *and* go to daycare. Of course they're sick all the time!" Chloe protested.

"I know," Megan agreed. "But try telling *them* that."

"I could take you on part-time as a bookkeeper if you needed something to hold you over while you found a new job?" Chloe suggested slowly.

The amount of stress that would add to her friend's already crazy life. That was a whole lot of nope.

"No, I'm good. Thanks. I'm keeping an eye out for any openings at the local firms that might work with me and the kids' arrangements. There's such a shortage of daycares right now, so I can't afford to push my luck."

So...she was stuck.

Think positive.

Okay, she was stuck *for now*.

"I'm fine. We'll get through this. It's just a rough month. Or ten."

"Do you need help with childcare?" Rose asked. "I could try to take the kids for a little bit some days?"

"Same," Chloe said.

"Same here," said Jen.

Lexie also gave a nod.

Megan's cheeks burned. God, how she hated this for herself and her kids. She wished she could give them more stability. "Yeah, I might have to take you up on that. The only issue is the kids being sick."

She immediately saw the other moms retreat. Yeah… No mom wanted to bring a sick kid into their home and risk getting their own kids sick. Not fun for anyone.

Megan sighed. "Yeah, like I said, I'm fine. I'll let you guys know."

They all eyed her dubiously, and she waved them off. "Onto the book," she encouraged before taking a gulp of her wine.

"Wait," Lexie halted them. "Did you decide what you wanted to do about the search for Theo's bio dad?"

It had been something she had been chewing on for the last few weeks.

Megan bit her lip and searched for the right words. "I'm still thinking about that."

Chloe said softly, "If he doesn't know about him yet, then he deserves to know he has a child out there somewhere."

"Fuck that," Lexie chimed in. "You know the type of guy that your cousin was banging. They are not the type of guys you want hanging around those kids. He was in it for a quick and dirty orgasm, and he got it. Can you imagine what would happen if he wanted Theo?"

Megan wanted to vomit. Hearing her very own fears said out loud by someone else cemented it for her.

Jen said, "Slow your roll. He might not be that bad. Meg's cousin could clean up nice when she wanted to."

Chloe scoffed.

Rose said, "That's true. He might be a perfectly nice guy with a bit of a horn dog past. Regardless. Is that really our choice, or should I say *your* choice, to decide whether he gets to know he has a son?"

Rose's reasonable question made Megan want to reach through the camera and choke her. She didn't want 'reasonable!' She wanted people on her side, telling her to let sleeping dogs lie so she didn't risk losing her son.

But... Theo was also his, whoever *he* was.

Ava's dad was a nonstarter—that man would *never* know Ava existed. Megan knew him and he was the scum of the earth. But Theo's dad? Maybe he was great.

Maybe this unknown dad had other kids. Maybe her little nugget had half-siblings out there. Maybe Theo would have a stepmom who adored kids. Maybe he'd be a father that could provide Theo with opportunities that Megan never would be able to. Maybe he'd take Theo to gymnastics or swimming. Or teach Theo how to tie a tie.

Megan's heart hurt.

The kids had men in their lives. Great men. Fantastic men. The best men. But none of them were their dads. Megan just didn't feel like she was doing them justice. The mom guilt was hitting her hard. She should be providing them with more opportunities and experiences. She was failing them.

Just then, Brandon swooped into view behind Rose and grabbed the two imps that were getting bored sitting in their mom's lap. He leaned down and swept a loving kiss against his wife's neck and then rubbed his large thumb against the apple of her cheek. He said something to her that her muted mic didn't pick up and she smiled happily up at him.

Megan's heart thumped.

What she wouldn't give for someone to just share a night with. For someone other than the girls to share her day with, to talk about the milestones of the children, to lament about work with, to watch a movie with.

Scratch that! Just for someone to watch the kids so *she* could watch a movie.

But alas, the last few dates she had been on had been depressing and nonstarters. The first one ran for the hills as soon as he found out she was a single mom. The second was good enough for a slam, bam, thank you, ma'am. She called up the second whenever she got depressingly lonely, but the sex felt empty. Emotionless. Mechanical. It got the job done but there were no fireworks. Sure, she was tired and overwhelmed all the time, she really didn't want nonstop fireworks to add to the mix, but a little extra something shouldn't be too much to ask.

In fact, she had more sparklers erupting on her nerve endings simply by holding the hand of Danny Parker and staring up into his beautiful eyes. She had never noticed before, but his eyes had blue on the outer edge and turned greenish hazel around the pupil. It was stunning.

He was stunning.

Megan hung her head and looked down at her keyboard.

God, she needed to get laid. A good lay. One with heat. Passion. One that reminded her she wasn't just a mom and wasn't just an unappreciated employee. She needed a lay that reminded her she was a *woman*.

After she got a full night's sleep, that is.

Priorities.

As the book club hotties transitioned into discussing their latest read, Megan had to get up to soothe a fussing Theo. When she got back, she poured herself another glass of wine and settled in.

A third glass and she was feeling silly about being stressed about everything.

She didn't drink much, so she didn't have much tolerance. Hence why she was buzzed after three glasses of wine. She had never gotten drunk while at home with the kids before. It seemed unsafe. But the alcohol in her brain told her not to worry about it; everything was fine.

It was hardly likely that this night, of all nights, was going to be the one with an emergency.

Despite what her sober brain usually thought.

After she signed off from their video chat, she wandered over to her cousin's somewhat packed-up room. She pulled at some drawers in her dresser and dragged over an empty tote. She collapsed on the floor next to them and started looking through the things.

"Trash. Keep. Trash," she mumbled as she sorted through the myriad of items.

She sorted through some more paperwork and found a thick envelope with Theo and Ava's names on it. Megan stilled. She didn't remember seeing this before. The envelope was sealed.

Her stomach tightened and her heart rate picked up. Despite a small part of her brain telling her it wasn't her business, the alcohol fueled her on. As she peeled a letter out of the stuffed envelope and unfolded it, her heartbeat started raging in her ears. Megan's eyes raced down the letter, line by line, horror infusing itself into her very being. She felt a lump form in her throat and her eyes burned. Her sinuses caught fire, and she sniffed hard, trying to get control of herself as she read the letter, her hands shaking so hard she kept losing her place. The wine eyes didn't help.

Her cousin, Starla, in all her infinite, damaged wisdom, had killed herself.

The police had ruled it an accidental overdose.

Reading this letter...it was a suicide.

What the hell was thinking?

Megan pushed to her feet in a fury and the second envelope stuck inside the first tumbled out. She bent down and savagely ripped it from the floor.

What next? A letter from the president saying, '*Thank you for being deep-cover CIA for the last seven years. Your country thanks you for your service*'?

"Dude. What was she thinking?" Megan said as she ripped open the new envelope and found a thick stack of Benjamins.

A thick stack.

Megan's jaw dropped.

Oh *fuck*.

Megan dropped the cash on the floor and took a step back, horrified, as the bills fluttered haphazardly to the ground.

Fifty-two Pickup was nothing compared to the mess in front of her.

How much *was* that?

And what did it have to do with Starla's suicide?

Megan took another step back, her body vibrating with rage, fear, and confusion. What the hell was her cousin caught up in? And why hadn't Megan fucking noticed? Was it her fault for not seeing the signs? Not picking up on the cries for help? For not being there to help prevent it?

Mixed emotions burned a path to her gut, unrelenting in its pain.

And that freaking letter! It was full of vague messages like "it was a mistake" and how Starla "regretted it terribly." She wrote about how she never wanted to be a mom but knew that "Megan would be a better mom." How she "loved them but didn't want them as her kids." She said she hoped Theo got his dad's smarts and good attitude toward life. Starla said he still didn't know about Theo, but he was a good guy, so they should be confident in that. Then, in the next sentence, she said to never contact him because it would ruin his life.

What the fuck did that mean? Ruin his life? What the hell?

Talk about fucking up the kids.

When was Megan supposed to be reading this fucking lovely Dear John to them? When they were kids? Teenagers? Adults?

What the fuck?

And seriously, was the guy married with kids of his own or something? How would the addition of Theo into anyone's family 'ruin' anyone's life?

Megan raged. Silently, of course. Megan decided to move past the suicide part and focus on the more actionable part of the note.

Her cousin wasn't right in the head. Megan knew that. But the entire letter basically told her children they were a grievous mistake and Theo would ruin his father's life if he knew him. What kind of message was that?

The alcohol fueled the fire burning in Megan. She continued to stomp in short, jerky steps at the entrance of the room, careful not to disrupt whatever blood money was on the ground.

If bio-dad was such a great guy, how would Theo's existence ruin his life?

Megan fought the urge to crumple the letter.

Did the kids have a right to read this when they were older? What purpose would it serve? Was it her job to destroy it? To save them from this hurt? Or was it her job to give it to them when they were ready? Was someone ever ready for this drivel?

God! Why didn't parenting come with a guidebook? Accounting had guidebooks! It made everything easier! Usually.

The only sweet part of the entire letter was Starla's sign-off. She wrote, *"I'm sorry I wasn't the mom for you. I know you have questions, but Megan will take much better care of you than I ever could."*

Well, at least she was right about that.

The woman writing this letter was *not* in a place to be raising children. Megan shivered as she leaned hard into the door frame.

How did she not know?

How could she not see how much her cousin was struggling?

She hung her head and sucked in a sobbing breath.

"Shit."

She rubbed hard at her eyes and tried quelling her shaking body, counting, and focusing on the good in her life. She thought of the two kiddos in the other room and reminded herself that Starla must have loved them, or they would have gone into the system rather than to Megan. Megan would always do whatever it took to care for them, to provide for them, to give them opportunities that she never had.

They were still her babies. And always would be.

The thought had more tears rushing to her eyes, and she sniffed again.

Shit.

She allowed herself one minute to wallow, her buzz a thing of the past. Megan then slid down the wall to the floor, where she had dropped the poisoned apple of an envelope.

Did she call the police? And say what... *Hi, I, uh, found a wad of cash in my cousin's belongings, and oh, by the way, also a suicide note.'*

Megan thumped the back of her head against the door frame as she looked up to the ceiling.

"Shit."

She didn't know what she wanted to do with the letter or the cash, but she didn't need to decide now. Maybe she'd ask the kids when they were older if they wanted that little piece of Starla.

Putting the cash back into the envelope for later inspection and detective work seemed like the only thing she had the headspace for right now. Regardless, she didn't need to make that decision right then.

Oh, man. What if Starla was a hooker and Theo was from a John? Megan's head whipped to look down the hall at the kids' shared room.

Megan shifted to her knees, trying to minimize her contact with the bills. Should she be wearing gloves?

As she folded up the letter to put it in the envelope with the second envelope of cash, something fell out of the bigger envelope.

Great, another goodie.

Megan stared at the small picture on the floor.

This couldn't be good.

Unease prickled at her skin. Slowly, Megan bent down and picked it up. She stilled as she saw the picture up close.

A team picture of the Springfield Spartans.

At the top, Starla had written two words.

*Theo's dad.*

# CHAPTER FIVE

# August 27, Saturday
## Danny

"Daniel. Fucking finally!"

Danny's shoulders slumped as he cursed himself for answering his phone. But his deadbeat father had called three times in a row and that didn't normally happen. Against his better judgment, he wanted to make sure things were okay. He never knew what kind of shit his dad got into...or could rope his mom into by association.

"Hi, Dad. Everything all right?"

"Of course. Why would you ask that?" His dad's voice was too loud.

Great. He was drunk.

Danny sighed and looked around his too-large living room. When he got his first big paycheck from professional football, he made some stupid choices. Fast cars, presents for women, ridiculous watches, and other statement pieces. One of which was this stupid house. Too big for just him. It was a home, not a bachelor pad. It didn't reflect his lifestyle choices at all. And every time he came home, he was reminded of that. The only good thing was that it was down the road from his mom's house so he could run over and help her out when she needed it.

Danny closed his eyes and prayed the answer was no. "Do you need a ride?"

"No, no, no. Nothing like that. I'm just here at the bar with Pokey and Boomer and we were watching Sports Center. We saw a segment on you, and I wanted to call and check-in."

Danny would bet they saw a segment on him. The Spartans had just given him a whopper of a contract extension. He had more money than he even knew what to do with at this point, and now the extended contract money? Jesus.

Was he honestly sitting there, internally bemoaning having too much money? He shook himself and focused on his dad.

"Oh, gotcha."

Silence.

A small cough and some coaxing words in the background.

Right. Now they were getting to it.

"I also wanted to ask. Do you have any tickets for this season for your old man? You know how much I love watching the games."

Danny ground his teeth. If his father loved his wife and kid half as much as he loved football, Danny's life would have been a lot easier growing up. The shit his poor mother had to eat to make ends meet because she fell in love with an asshole...

"I don't think so, Dad."

More whispering on his dad's end.

"I know there are box seats reserved for family; what about those?"

This time, Danny sighed. He'd been down this road before. A lot.

He thought back to the last time his father had come to a game. The Spartans hadn't played well against New York, losing by two touchdowns. The team had come out flat and slow. No one could really explain it, though everyone blamed the loss on the fact that the offensive line couldn't protect the quarterback.

The last time his dad and his cronies attended a game, they'd caused a scene that required security intervention. Danny later assured staff they were right to escort them out.

Okay, time was up on the phone call limit. Before things started getting nasty, Danny had to end it.

Cut off his dad completely or give him one ticket to shut him up?

"I might be able to get you one ticket."

"You can't do that, Danny," his dad said, his voice still loud. "It's no fun going to a game solo."

That wasn't true at all. Going to games solo could be a blast. Danny had done it loads of times. Usually when he was growing up, his dad got so drunk in the parking lot that he passed out during pregaming and never made it to the game itself.

"Dad, you're a grown-ass man. If you want to go to a game alone, or with a bunch of other guys, that's fine. But if you want more than one ticket, you'll have to get your own."

"My own boy is a star player and you're telling me to go scalp tickets? Are you fucking shittin' me right now, boy?" His dad's voice lost its cajoling edge and turned nasty.

Right on schedule.

Danny felt his own temper flare. "Look, I'm trying to help out here, Dad. I'm not going to get a bunch of tickets so you and your buddies can go and cause a scene. So, take the one ticket, or go buy your own damn tickets. Or don't go at all. I don't fucking care."

His mom would be chewing him up and down right now for his language, but washing out his mouth with soap just never seemed to work.

His dad started in a hate-filled rant, cursing out Danny and insulting everything from his personality, looks, skills, and performance on the field.

Fuck, his dad was a real winner. And the prime reason why Danny was never fucking having kids. His dad's toxic bloodline ended with Danny. Full stop.

Especially once Danny learned he had his father's taste for alcohol. No kid needed that gene passed down.

"You don't understand a thing about life, do you?" His dad's sour and gravelly voice rasped over the phone. Danny heard more swearing in the background.

"Sorry, Dad. I can't help."

"Fuck you, Danny."

"Yeah, right. Fuck me." Danny bit out. He hung up and slammed his hand down on the side table. He closed his eyes again, feeling the rage build up inside of him. He breathed in a deep breath and then slowly let it out. Danny dropped his head against the too-homey couch, letting his arms fall to his side.

Fuck.

Why did he even bother answering? Why did he try at all for this asshole? He was a jerk and a loser. Only out for himself.

Mom.

Danny absently cracked his knuckles and thought of his mom.

His darling mother taught brats like Danny her entire life. She rotated preschools and private elementary schools for his entire childhood, following where he went to get the parent-teacher discount but still send him to the best schools she could. They moved all over New England as he grew up, his father's job requiring frequent moves. Then when his father lost his job...and didn't care about finding a new one, the drinking began in earnest.

Once they divorced, Danny and his mom settled in northern Massachusetts near the New Hampshire border. He was drafted out of college and had to move a short way away to New York, but his mom stayed in Mass, migrating to Springfield. After a couple of years, he moved mountains to get 'back home'. He would have been good with either Foxborough or Springfield but ultimately, he was relieved it was Springfield. It was clearly the organization for him.

His mom had managed two jobs for Danny's entire life. He didn't remember a time when she wasn't working like a dog for some company or another. After his parents divorced and it was just them, his mom kept the family afloat by working as a teacher during the day and then cleaning on the nights and weekends. As he got older and more expensive, she needed to find more ways to afford his camps and hobbies, so she started an at-home daycare during school breaks. Danny grew up knowing that school vacation wasn't really 'school vacation.'

Instead, it was 'help entertain the kids because mom was starting to look a little ragged'.

Luckily, he enjoyed it; playing with the kids was never a chore. Danny never had any siblings, so he used that opportunity to play pretend. As he got older, it got less and less cool to play with the babies during his vacations. But his mom always looked so damn tired he always made the time to help when he wasn't working. When the rest of his friends were going on off-roading trips through the woods outside of the city, he was choosing to stay home and offer his mom whatever help he could.

When he got into college, his mom retired from teaching and instead expanded her cleaning business. She was making a killing at it. But then, the crazy lady decided she missed the kids and started tutoring and babysitting again. His mom was not a restful woman. She didn't seem to know what to do with idle hands.

He got that from her.

Idle hands meant a drinking mouth. He learned he needed to stay busy.

Now that he thought about it, he needed to call his mom and make sure she was being good about getting her records up to date for her tax filings. It was too late in the evening now, but he added it to his mental to-do list, and he'd give her a call tomorrow.

He was also hoping that he'd have an answer back from the enigmatic Megan Lowell on whether her firm would be interested in taking on his mom's project. Sure, it had only been a couple of days, and it was the weekend, but when he called on Friday and revealed his real name, the receptionist had been more than happy to take a message to one of the partners. Shortly after, he received a phone call personally assuring him that they'd be discussing it this weekend. He knew the project wasn't going to be fun. But hopefully, his name and money would grease the wheels.

The perks of being a superstar athlete.

Danny's current CPA didn't want to do it, and his mom's current CPA was either inept or dishonest, but also, after meeting Megan, Danny didn't want anyone else.

A smile tugged at his lips as he thought of calling Megan. She seemed so put together and composed, yet her frantic rubbing of the yogurt on her arm gave a hint of an iceberg of idiosyncrasies.

And the direct yet faint blushes she gave him during their meeting?

Not as composed and indifferent as she liked to pretend.

His fingers itched to see just how far her embarrassment would extend.

Generally, he had a rule not to mix business with pleasure, but it had turned out all right for a couple of his teammates over the last few years. And he couldn't get Megan out of his head.

If her firm didn't want to take on his mom's project. Well…

His smile turned wolfish.

He could be very convincing. Everyone wanted something, and *he* wanted Megan Lowell.

At least for a time. By the heavy weight of her gaze when they said goodbye, he'd bet she wanted the same as well.

What was stopping them?

# CHAPTER SIX

# August 28, Sunday
## Danny

"How are you feeling this morning, mother dearest? Want to go on an early morning jog with me? I've heard this neighborhood has the most eligible older bachelors." Danny sat on his uncomfortable kitchen stool, twisting it rhythmically back and forth as he watched the world wake up on the slow, Sunday morning.

"Don't be a turd. It's way too early for your cheer." Danny heard her coffeemaker brewing in the background. "And I wasn't born yesterday, Danny boy. I've seen a few lovely ladies start to make their way to the front yards in the morning, wearing their not-suitable-for-public robes. You buying that house and doing your 'runs' has brought down the class of our neighborhood. We pray for you every Sunday at Church. For you *and* your shenanigans." A pause and he knew what was coming. "You're welcome to join anytime, you know."

Danny grinned as he brought his own coffee to his lips, sipping carefully.

"Appreciate the prayers, Ma. But I don't know *how* I'm at fault though. They're just early morning runs. Nothing scandalous."

"Don't talk back to your mother. I know exactly what they are."

He chuffed out a small snort but otherwise didn't argue. She wasn't entirely wrong. The neighborhood had some hotties. Not that he'd do anything about it.

Shitting where he ate? Nope. Not for him. Ever.

"What do you have on tap for today?" his mom asked after she took an audible sip of her own coffee.

"Got to head to the stadium after my run to review some film. And I need to see if I can scrounge up some tickets for Dad and a couple of his buddies."

He heard her deep sigh on the phone. "You don't owe him that, my sweet boy."

He was thirty-one; hardly a 'sweet boy.'

Danny let out a tired breath. "Yeah, I know, Ma. But if I don't do it, he's going to call me every day until I finally say yes. I'm being preemptive and saving myself the headache."

"If you cave, he's going to continue to do this to you. Every single time he needs a ticket."

Danny looked up to the ceiling. She wasn't wrong.

Time for a topic change. "What do *you* have on tap for today?"

"Apparently, I have bookkeeping homework from my bossy son. Though, I still don't understand why I can't have Charles do it. Vincent vouched for him. Vincent even said *he* could do it for me if I gave him access to all the accounts."

Danny's gut tightened. "No, Mom—"

"I know, I know. But he's been my accountant forever, I hardly think he's untrustworthy—"

"No, Mom," Danny repeated, his body still tense. Everything about the situation just made him nervous. Something about the guy....

"Yeah, yeah. Fine. So that means I have a fun-filled day of opening all the mail from the bank from the last decade and sorting it so I can do some stupid, boring bookkeeping."

Decade!

At Danny's horrified silence, she gave a small chuckle. "Not really a decade, Danny. Goodness gracious, relax. I thought you were the lighthearted of the two of us."

Holy fuck, Mystery Megan might never talk to him again if the firm took this on.

"About that, I think I found someone to dig into things and reconcile everything for you. And to take care of all your late filings. I'm just waiting to hear back from them."

Staring at his boring backyard, Danny bet Megan's wouldn't be so plain. Even in her professional wardrobe, he'd seen her party side. The woman could throw *down*. No one who had a wild side that could rival Lexie would allow themselves to have a boring backyard. She'd have fire pits, games, stonework, and maybe a hammock. Lights and lanterns. Not this...*blah*, that he had.

His mother's squeal brought him back to the present.

"Oh! That's wonderful. I'll stop opening the envelopes now then. Oh, thank the Lord."

"What? No, Mom. You still have to open the damn envelopes and sort them so they can do their jobs. You can't just give them unopened envelopes and have them sort it for you." He dropped a soft "Jesus" under his breath so she couldn't hear. He rolled his eyes as he shook his head at his feet.

"Language," she said brusquely. "One day, when you have kids, that mouth of yours is going to get you in trouble."

"We've been over this. Don't hold your breath."

"No one who loves kids as much as you, *can't* not want them."

"Sure they can. I'm here, aren't I?"

She harrumphed but otherwise didn't engage further.

Danny shook his head and looked up to the lofty ceilings.

His mom.

Loved her to death but the woman just couldn't see reason about some things.

Mostly finances and children.

He couldn't try any more than he already had to convince her grandkids weren't in her future, but hopefully, he'd at least solve the blind spot in her finances. A certain feisty CPA who looked like a damn wet dream come to life and smelled like a fresh flower garden under a hot summer sun was the answer to his non-existent prayers.

Megan and her firm were probably overqualified for the job. But the one good thing he got from his father, the king of con artists, was the ability to be persuasive. So even if Megan's firm shot him down...maybe Miss Meg would be interested in a little side hustle.

He could certainly make it worth her while.

# CHAPTER SEVEN

# August 28, Sunday
## Megan

"Hello?" Megan whispered into her phone as she slipped out of the kids' bedroom. She prayed they stayed asleep and didn't wake at the sound of her answering the call.

"Megan?"

Why did that voice sound familiar?

"Yes?"

"Hi. It's Danny."

She blinked and stopped before she officially entered the kitchen. "Danny who?"

"Danny..." A pause. "Danny Parker?"

Oh shit! Megan darted a hand to her hair and smoothed it down before tugging at her wrinkled shirt.

It was a Sunday! Why was he calling?

"Oh. Yeah, um, hi. Hello. How are you?"

What the hell was he doing calling her freaking cell phone? How did he get her number? She was going to fucking kill their intern if he had been giving it out to people.

"Nice to see I made such an impression." She could hear the smile in his voice, so at least he wasn't offended.

"Yeah, sorry about that, I was sneaking out of the kids' room so I couldn't really hear. What's up?" She resumed her entrance to the kitchen and started putting away the remnants of their dinner: sliding the noodles into the Tupperware, wiping up the spills, and putting drinks into the fridge.

Then, after that was cleaned up, she needed to do meal prep for the week.

Fucking hell, she was tired.

"Did I catch you at a bad time?" His voice came out somewhat brokenly through the phone as she had wandered to a corner with poor reception.

Megan walked back to a better spot and leaned against the counter, mind whirling at the million things she needed to do.

Crap! She forgot to wash the kids' crib and cot sheets for daycare. She pinched the bridge of her nose.

"Megan?"

She mentally refocused and forced her eyes on a clean patch of kitchen floor that wouldn't get her itching to clean it up and multi-task.

"Yes, sorry, I'm here. What's up?"

"I wanted to reach out and ask if you would be personally willing to take on the job I met with you about last week."

Megan felt the air still around her.

"What?"

"I got a phone call from some guy at your office this afternoon telling me they weren't interested in taking on the job for my mom. No hard feelings and all, but they didn't feel like it was a good fit for their staff and resources. No biggie. But I'd like to work with you if you're willing. Just from our short meeting, I think you'd be well-suited to deal with my mom. She's great but can be stubborn."

Like her son, apparently.

"Danny—"

"And obviously, I'll pay you what you want. But I think making my mom feel comfortable with all this is the priority right now. You discussing the importance of timely bookkeeping and reporting would go a long way for her; I think she'd find you easy to talk to."

Crap.

"Danny, I'm so sorry, but I'll tell you right now, if the firm said no, then they won't change their mind. She's not their ideal client and with my boss's death..."

A beat of silence and then Danny started again, his voice still way more energetic than he should be at eight on a Sunday night.

"Oh, yeah, no. I totally get that. I'm not talking about the firm. I'm talking about you. You personally. Outside of your job. A side gig. For you to report taxes on or not." He gave a chuckle at his joke.

Megan blinked and looked up, breaking her mental promise from before to not let her eyes wander and tempt her to get distracted.

"You want me to do this on the side?" she clarified.

"Yeah," his voice was too chipper, it made her tired just listening to it. Danny would get along great with Theo. Theo was a night owl as well. Little terror.

She smiled and remembered Theo rubbing peas on his face from dinner and how hard he had laughed. Megan looked over to the highchair and saw the remaining mess resting there, waiting for her. She stepped towards the highchair to clean the mess before stopping herself.

Phone call first.

Then clean-up.

She needed a higher dose of focus medication. Motherhood demanded it. She made a mental note to call her doctor, though she'd likely forget.

"So?" Danny's voice sounded a little less confident after her prolonged silence.

Crap on a cracker. She was a mental fucking disaster.

Focus, girl!

"Yeah, I'm so sorry, Danny. I'd love to help you, but I really can't. I have a noncompete at work and I'd get in big trouble if they decided to come after me for violating that. I don't have the funds to fight that battle and it's not like I have another job waiting for me if I pissed them off and get fired. Not many places want a single mom of two toddlers. Especially one who doesn't have a steady daycare or a babysitter on standby. I'm sorry, but I can't help." She added an afterthought, "Plus, I don't even have someone to watch the kids while I helped her. They'd have to come too, and I *promise*, that would mean no work would get done."

"You have kids?" Something odd was in his voice and she tensed. Maybe he didn't realize what she said when she picked up the phone.

"Yeah, two," she said tightly, her defenses up and ready.

"Okay..." he said slowly and then paused, the silence heavy. "What if your bosses said it was fine?"

He wasn't going to say anything about her having two kids? She tried to relax but her body was already tensed for fight or flight mode, and it didn't seem to want to ease up.

She sighed and shook her head. "Danny, I still wouldn't have any place to send the kids. I'm so sorry. I can try to give you some names of some local bookkeepers and CPAs that might be good fits for you if you'd like. Heck, even Chloe might take your mom on if she needs help that bad. I'm sure Kenny or Lexie could convince her." Chloe had her own bookkeeping firm — it would be a logical choice.

"Chloe's a sweetheart." He paused. "And my mom would steamroll her into a pancake." He waited for a beat again. "But if you did have a place for the kids?"

A laugh burst out. This guy. He was like a dog with a bone. She wiped at the small tear that gathered in the corner of her eye. "Yes, yes, sure. If my bosses were cool with it, *and* it was a world where I had childcare, I'd love to make some extra money and help you out. So, if that alternate universe ever pops up, let me know."

Danny gave his own soft chuckle into the phone and Megan felt small tingles dance down her cheek and neck at the low timbre. The man was endearing, persistent, and delectable. Too bad, he was the definition of a good-time boy. Not Future Mr. Megan Lowell material.

"I'll see what I can do." The low promise in his voice caused the small tingles to travel... south.

Oh, dear.

Shock rippled through her at the burn of arousal. Huh. Who would have thought the sexy playboy would be the one to wake her sleeping dragon? Interesting...

Danny continued in that subdued voice. "Until tomorrow, darlin'."

Wait, what?

Before she could say a word, her phone beeped, signifying that the call was over.

As she cleaned the kitchen and made lunch boxes, Megan waffled between anxiety and excitement. It'd been a long time since a man intrigued her.

Danny was stimulating. Unpredictable. Megan didn't 'do' unpredictable.

Yet, something about his capriciousness...it was intoxicating. Refreshing. Invigorating.

What was 'tomorrow?'

Megan found herself falling asleep with a smile on her face. For the first time in a long time.

# CHAPTER EIGHT

# August 29, Monday
## Megan

Megan fought to keep her eyes on the screen in front of her. She had slept like absolute crap last night and Ava had woken up with a runny nose. Megan snuck her into daycare anyways, knowing her boss would lose his ever-loving mind if she missed another Monday for 'the snivels'.

All night long she was plagued with the same nightmare: Theo growing up and hating her for keeping him from his dad and phantom siblings. Dream Theo screamed at her that it wasn't her place to deprive him of knowing his dad and never spoke to her again. Even Ava cut her off.

Then Megan got old and died alone.

So, yeah, the message was delivered *and* received from the universe.

She needed to find his bio dad. Or at least try.

How would she even start? All that she had to go on was a stupid picture of the Spartans' team photo from last year, most of the men wearing surly and ridiculous frowns.

Well, all except a few. Like Danny. Danny looked like he was having the best time of his life during the photo. Had she ever seen a photo of him frowning? The man was sex, optimism, and confidence in a bottle.

Looking at the kids' photo — Danny could connect her to the players subtly.

She could ask him to show her cousin's photo around and see if anyone recognized her.

Would asking Danny be unprofessional? She considered asking her friends on the team instead. But what if one was Theo's father?

The risk of finding out that one of her friends was Theo's father was too icky.

She'd rather go through someone she didn't really know, someone like Danny, who could poke around in a subtle way that could filter her from learning if one of her friends slept with her cousin. In the Ick Factor game, she'd prefer to deal with Danny. Danny was much prettier to look at than asking her friend Jen, who worked with the team, to subtly ask around.

Plus, he was entertaining as all hell. Danny's always-positive voice was vastly different from the negative mental voice that always nagged her. It was refreshing just listening to him speak. It was like his energy was transferring itself to her.

When she closed her eyes, she could almost imagine his woodsy leather smell.

Her shoulders slumped. She couldn't. Megan couldn't ask Danny to help her do this if she wasn't doing something for him in return and there was no way she was going to get the okay to work on his project. Her bosses were not that flexible. And if she wasn't doing the job for him, she couldn't ask him for a favor. He owed her nothing. Life was full of give and take and Megan didn't want to be a 'taker.'

If she couldn't give him something in return, then she wouldn't ask him for this.

An unfamiliar burning started in her sinuses. She wasn't a crier, but damn if she didn't feel tired, defeated, and pulled too thin.

As she closed her eyes and tried centering herself, she was interrupted by her office door being thrown open unceremoniously. She opened her eyes and tried to keep the scowl off her face, not knowing whom she'd find barging into her office. A giddy intern stood there, quivering in excitement.

"Megan, Danny Parker is here to see you." The kid was coming out of his freaking skin with how much his excitement was vibrating him.

Megan's stomach clenched. She didn't think she'd actually *see* him today!

She wasn't even wearing her good underwear!

## CHAPTER NINE

# August 29, Monday
## Megan

If he had any passing appreciation before, it'd be gone after he saw her with undereye circles and blotchy skin.

Not only that, but Megan was also nowhere near mentally prepared for the impromptu meeting and didn't relish the idea of letting Danny down. Despite her spunky outward demeanor, she was innately a people-pleaser. He was just so stinking *nice*, it felt like kicking a puppy to let him down. When he called last night asking her to personally take on the job, she wanted to help. Danny had been nothing but nice and he clearly adored his mom. It sucked to let them both down. It sucked to let anyone down, her bosses hadn't beaten that out of her...yet.

But there was no way her bosses would let her do it, there was no point in even asking.

A tall frame appeared in the doorway behind the intern. Danny sauntered into her office, past the starstruck intern, oozing energy and sexiness.

"Mr. Parker, come on in," she said dryly, giving the intern a dry look. Megan made a mental note, that she was sure to forget, to talk to him later about not escorting clients to offices without letting the employees know first. Luckily, she didn't have any client information strewn about, but she could have.

Megan stopped herself from reaching out and shaking Danny's hand. The remembered tingles that erupted after the first time didn't need repeating. It wasn't healthy to tease her almost non-existent libido.

Instead, she gestured at the seat across from her desk and gave him a nod. "Please, sit."

He gave her a wide smile. "Planning on it." Danny relaxed in the leather-bound chair, looking completely put together and utterly gorgeous.

She matched his comfortable pose by crossing her legs under her desk and folding her hands on the desk in front of her.

Might as well get this over with.

"Mr. Parker—" Megan began but was quickly interrupted.

"Danny, please, Mr. Parker is my father." He shot her a ridiculous wink that had her smiling despite herself at the most cliché line ever.

"Danny—" she amended.

Danny interrupted again. "Also, some doughnuts are in your conference room. The kid up front took them. I didn't know what kind you liked, so I bought ten of everything."

She cocked her head at him and gave him a small smile. "You didn't need to do that. Plus, bribery doesn't work on me." When he looked like he was going to interrupt her again, she rushed to say, "But thank you. I'm sure the whole office appreciates it." Megan leveled a look at him that had him grinning and closing his mouth, giving her a nod as he accepted her demand for silence. "I thought a lot about your request. And I don't think it would be appropriate for me to take on this job. And frankly, I also don't see how my bosses would allow it even if we were in a world that afforded me additional childcare options." She gave him a sympathetic smile, hoping he could read her regret and genuine desire to have helped him.

Danny stared at her with a patient expression, his eyes warm and crinkled in the corners, a hint of a smile on his lips as he waited for her to finish. When she was done outlining all the reasons she had mentioned the night before, he sat forward, resting his elbows on her desk and clasping his hands together.

"I hope you don't mind, but before I came back here to talk to you, I cleared it with one of your partners, just to be sure it wouldn't be an issue. They said that they would be perfectly fine with you taking on this job for me on the side.”

Megan blinked and stiffened at the overstep. “Excuse me?”

“If you want,” he said quickly, starting to look a little uncomfortable. Like he finally just realized the gaffe he had made. “I mean, you said if the universe aligned…I just wanted to make sure they had no qualms about you accepting the position before I formally offered it.”

He pulled out an envelope and placed it on the table in front of her.

The last envelope she picked up had a Pandora’s Box worth of issues inside of it. She wasn’t all that amped up to pick up another surprise envelope…

She stared at it with apprehension.

“I even had my lawyer draft up a document for them to sign, saying they accepted all the terms and they did not find anything wrong with them. Just in case they ever came back later, and tried to tell you that you breached any,” he used finger quotes “‘professional duty.’”

Holy crap. Pretty boy *got shit done*. Why was that such a turn-on?

Her empowered feminist side should be rampaging over this overstep. Instead, the fickle bitch was fanning herself in the corner and purring ‘Mommy like.’

Ho.

She looked down at the envelope and prepared herself. Megan unfolded it and scanned it, aware of Danny’s eyes watching her.

Was she breathing too loud? It felt like she was breathing too loud. Was she doing too many belly breaths? Did it look funny having her belly expand and not her chest? She took a breath with her upper lungs but when she felt her chest push out, she chastised herself for the stupid move. Hell, now it looked like she was trying to get him to look at her tits.

Shit, she was a dumbass. Focus.

Megan redirected her brain on the words in front of her and stilled, forgetting her worries about her breathing style. She looked up at him with wide eyes.

"We *just* spoke last night—"

Danny gave her a proud smile. "I'm a professional athlete. I have a lawyer on retainer. If I need something by nine am," Danny shrugged again, "I have it by nine am."

Wow.

She gave him incredulous eyes and looked back to the papers in her hand. Sure enough, one of her firm's partners signed on the dotted line saying that they were declining his business and that they were one hundred percent comfortable with Megan taking on this project and *any* projects that Danny would offer her in the future. They signed that there was no conflict of interest or violation of her non-compete.

Holy crap, what did he say to the managing partner to get him to sign this?

She didn't know how legally binding that contract would be if the firm ever decided to push it. But, again, wow.

Mr. Parker knew how to *get shit done.*

Yes, Daddy.

She raised an eyebrow in appreciation as she continued scanning the pages. She stilled when she came to a particularly interesting clause. "You seriously included a section about giving me babysitting so I could accept?" She raised her eyes to his dancing blue, somewhat green, ones.

He shrugged, sat back in the chair, and crossed his ankle on his knee, the absolute picture of confidence and coolness. "My mom was a teacher for years and I'm no stranger around a diaper genie. Hardly an inconvenience to offer up." Another shrug. "Kids are great. And it helps my mom."

He pulled his pretty eyes away from her and looked around our office. His eyes caught on the one picture she had of the kids. Danny paused and looked at it for a heartbeat, cocking his head slightly.

"Cute kids."

The firm partners thought that having more than one family photo was distracting in the office. Hence why Megan was only limited to one eight-by-ten photo of her with the kids. If it was her choice, she'd have pictures of them everywhere. A good reminder why she was even still here in the first place.

She felt her lips curl into a soft smile as she also turned to look at the picture. "They're my little imps," she said softly, pulling her eyes away. She expected to see him still looking at the picture. Instead, he was looking at her, his head tilted, his eyes assessing.

"Do they look like their dad?"

Oh, how to answer that question?

They certainly didn't look like her cousin, so she nodded.

"Yeah, I guess."

Danny looked back to their picture "Are you guys still together?"

Oh...that was where he was going.

Interesting.

It *shouldn't* be interesting. Especially if she was essentially going to be working for him on a side project for a little bit. But a little flirting never hurt anyone, and she was having a dry spell. Might as well embrace the good vibes and feel good about herself while she could.

"I believe that's outside the scope of this meeting." Her words were knife sharp but she made sure to add a small smile so he could read the teasing in her words.

He grinned bigger and his white teeth basically glowed when surrounded by his dark facial hair. Give him two arm shields and he'd be fighting Thanos' army in Wakanda.

Man, he was sexy.

She caved under his nosy and waiting look. She chuckled and shook her head softly before giving in. "Fine. No, their dads are not in the picture."

Maybe, one day, she'd tell him about their history. But they weren't there.

His smile turned winning, and she shook her head again, trying to bite back her smile. Megan looked down at the pages in her hand and kept scanning, it seemed safer than staring at the handsome and charming man across from her.

"I honestly didn't expect you to get the okay from my boss," Megan said in a soft voice, raising her eyes and darting a quick look at the door. "Therefore, I wasn't really prepared to honestly consider it. How soon do you need an answer?"

Danny lowered the wattage of his smile into an easy grin. "End of the week?"

Megan sighed and looked through the papers some more, already knowing she was probably going to accept. The pay was good, she'd have a leg to stand on when she asked him for some help finding Theo's father, and...there were babysitting hours included. If nothing else, it would break up the long weekend days where she was trying to find something to do with them.

He interrupted her mental musings by leaning forward. A whiff of warm leather met Megan's nose and she instantly felt like jumping on a Harley, donning some tassels, and running away.

Down girl!

The man wasn't even wearing any leather for goodness' sake.

"So, what do you think?" Danny had a mischievous smile on his face and was clearly sensing his victory.

Megan nodded absently but otherwise kept scanning the document, looking for something she might have missed.

Movement caught her attention, and she looked up. Danny had sat back and was giving her a steady look. "Really? It was that easy?

Just throw in some babysitting hours and your boss's sign off and I won you over?"

Megan gave him an embarrassed grin. There was a line in the contract that promised that not only that he or his mother provide childcare when she was working on this project, but they would provide a couple of extra hours per month for the two months when she could be somewhere else.

Grocery shopping solo? Yes, please.

Watching a movie?

Taking a freaking nap?

Or, less attractive, catching up on work...

All possibilities.

"It's not just babysitting hours you're offering, it's a chance for me to not be on diaper duty or in charge of feeding them for a meal. It's a chance at...freedom."

It sounded awful, there was no way around it, but it was honest.

And she was burnt-the-fuck-out.

Danny tilted his head back and let out a roar of a laugh, unphased at the idea of disturbing anyone in the large office. His tanned hand came up and grabbed at his chest as he quieted down to chuckles.

Sexy as hell chuckles.

She fought back the way his laugh made her stomach clench.

Crap, she liked making him laugh *way* too much.

"You have no idea how nice it is to have an hour or two here or there only having to worry about yourself," she sniffed with attitude, hoping to elicit another deep smile from him despite her inner voice saying to leave it alone.

Sure enough, he laughed hard again and patted the armrest twice with the palm of his hand. As he calmed, Danny looked at her, smiling while shaking his head. "Can I have that back for a sec?" He held up his hand asking for the papers. He leaned forward, taking a pen off the desk in front of Megan, once again blessing her with a small tease of a delicious deep leather smell.

She handed over the pages.

His handsome face sobered in concentration as he scratched out something on the pages in front of him. He then scribbled something else next to it and did a flurry of initials. He handed it back to her, Megan braced for whatever ridiculous clause he added and prepared herself to beat back the chuckle. No sense making it too easy for the guy.

However, she wasn't prepared for what she saw.

He threw in an amendment to the contract. A big amendment.

One weekend day of babysitting per month, for the next four months.

Her heart started pounding. This was too good to be true and the cynic in her raised her sour head. Maybe his mother was a nutjob. Megan pursed her lips and looked up at him, studying him carefully. "You seem to have turned out... fine. So, I imagine your mother is a competent caretaker. But I want to meet her first. This is a lot to decide right now without even having met the woman."

"Of course. I don't need an answer now. Come by this Saturday and meet her."

This man was completely unflappable. Hell, he would have been a perfect politician. Despite not seeming... slimy enough.

"I reserve the right to back out of this anytime I feel that it's not working out for my kids," Megan warned him again, starting to warm up to the idea. His confidence in the arrangement was taking root in her despite her better judgment. Babysitting? From a reliable source? Eeek! "A meeting is necessary. And maybe a trial run. Trial runs are always a good idea for anything important."

His thickly bearded face grinned deep at his victory.

His mother must have the patience of a saint to have raised such a self-assured man.

Megan sighed and folded the papers to put them in her purse. "Saturday? I'll swing by her place in the morning, and we can all meet and see if the kids like her."

Danny eyed her, now with a distinctly not professional look. "Sounds perfect."

Did his voice get deeper when he said that?

He nodded over toward her purse. "Her address is on those documents and she's free any time after nine." He slapped his hands on his thighs and stood up. Megan thought he was going to walk out without saying anything else, but he turned back in the doorway. His eyes combed over her face, searching for something. "I appreciate this. Thank you," he said in a surprisingly somber tone. "She means the world to me, and I don't like people jerking her around. And I like you. I...I trust you not to do that."

Megan gave him a solemn nod and tried to force her eyes to stay on his face and not coast over the long muscular lines of his body. Her eyes got away from her for just a moment, and when she brought them back to his face, a devilish grin pulled up one side of his mouth.

"See ya Saturday, darlin'. We'll get this trial run started."

He shot her a wink and took off down the hall towards the lobby.

Technically, she was supposed to be escorting him throughout the offices for security reasons, but she found that she couldn't move.

One, *he* was going to be there on Saturday? Was he going to be there for all the visits?

Her heart beat faster.

And two, why did the way he called her 'darling' make her want to pant and climb him like a tree? Her libido had been dormant since bringing Theo home. And one handshake from Danny had woken it up? Was that really all it took? A lightning-in-a-bottle football player that was one hundred percent *not* her type. She wasn't looking for a good old boy. She needed a guy with staying power. One that wanted to play Daddy.

Scratch that.

She didn't *need* a man at all.

But having one certainly wouldn't hurt. At least a man for some temporary...Biblical purposes.

If she were to take this job, that man couldn't be Danny.

The hard part would be convincing her recently re-awakened lady bits about that.

## Chapter Ten

# September 3, Saturday
## Megan

As the sun began to rise over the quiet suburban neighborhood, Megan pulled her car to a stop in front of a quaint white house with a well-tended garden. The place exuded a sense of warmth and coziness, and Megan took a deep breath, trying to calm her nerves. She wanted to make sure she got a good vibe from Danny's mom, and more importantly, that her kids would feel comfortable here.

The house had a charming porch adorned with potted flowers, and the soft scent of blooming flowers filled the air. Megan noticed several cheerful wind chimes hanging near the entrance, swaying gently with the light breeze. It seemed like a place where laughter and happy memories were cherished.

As she stepped out of her car, the sound of birds singing in the trees and the distant hum of the city greeted her.

Megan's apartment was on the outskirts of the city. But even so, this was a step beyond that. Hell, it even had a chicken coop with chickens milling around. She never thought of Springfield as a city. Not like Boston or New York, but seeing this tiny bit of country here... it shocked her. She never really had much thought to the fact that her kids didn't have their own yard.

Now?

Just another thing she wasn't giving them.

Megan took a moment to adjust her outfit, brushing imaginary wrinkles off her shirt, and smoothing her hair.

She unloaded the kids and brought them up to the front door, babbling to them and reminding them what they were doing. Ava's speech therapist had told her to narrate their actions whenever possible, so it was second nature now. Hell, she even mumbled to herself at work.

Before she could even lift Ava to ding the doorbell, the door swung open, revealing a warm and friendly woman with kind eyes and a warm smile.

"Hi, you must be Megan. I'm Nikki, Danny's mom. It's lovely to finally meet you."

Megan returned the smile, already feeling an immediate sense of comfort. "Nice to meet you too. Danny spoke highly of you."

"And these must be the two sweethearts Danny was telling me about," the woman sang out while kneeling down agilely in front of Ava. Megan twisted so Theo on her hip could also see Nikki. Nikki pulled out two identical toy cars and held one out in each hand to the children. "I bet you like cars," she said in a playful voice. She placed the durable car in Theo's tiny palm and his fingers reflexively closed around it. Ava released her death grip on Megan's pants and was *all* about getting her dimpled hands on her new present.

Nikki stood and met Megan's eyes. "They're adorable, just like Danny said."

Megan smiled "Thank you. They're not always this sweet though."

Nikki waved her away. "Oh, this age is all about stranger danger. They'll warm up in no time. Come on inside. I got everything cleaned up."

As Megan stepped inside, she was greeted by a cozy living room, adorned with family photos and colorful decorations. The room felt inviting and lived-in, a place where love and laughter were abundant. The scent of fresh coffee filled the air, making her feel even more at ease.

As Nikki led them into the kitchen, Megan detected the smell of warm savory muffins, and it made her belly rumble in a way that had Nikki looking at her with a small frown.

"Did you remember to eat breakfast this morning?"

Megan shook her head. "Had some coffee at six when the kids woke up."

The woman gave her a motherly look and then waved her into a kitchen chair. "Come on, I'll make you something. Here, snack on a muffin while you wait."

Megan accepted the muffin while also giving a soft chuckle "No, no, you don't need to."

"Nonsense. I know how hard it is to eat with children needing you nonstop. If nothing else, you can grab a bite to eat while the kids are occupied, and you can get off your feet and enjoy a nice breakfast with no one hanging on you." Nikki leveled her a look that had Megan smiling.

"Do people usually say no to you?"

"Not if they know what's good for them," the older woman replied with a smile.

Megan heard a clunk and soft swear. She whipped around to the corner where a plumber was working on his back underneath the sink; one knee bent, his torso deep under the cabinet.

"Language," Nikki snapped out as quick as lightning. This was clearly a common occurrence.

Megan's eyes scraped down the plumber's long body.

The man's stomach was muscular, and his thighs were thick, testing the limits of his work jeans. Three inches of skin showed from where his thin t-shirt had rolled up above his jeans and a dark happy trail traveled from his belly button down below the waistband of the Hanes boxer briefs he proudly wore.

Damn. She really needed a leaky faucet.

Megan took a deep breath and caught a hint of the man's rich smell mixed in with the coffee and muffins. Almost a combination of leather and earthy forests. Delicious.

Damn, she needed to get laid. First, she was salivating after Danny Parker, and now this poor, unsuspecting plumber.

She hadn't realized she was so hard up for a good orgasm. She wasn't one to usually objectify men but here she was. Wondering what was at the end of that happy little trail. She turned to blow kisses at Theo happily on the ground next to her to distract herself.

A warm piece of toast with bacon and sausage was set on the placemat in front of her. Then a matching plastic plate was slid next to it.

"In case Ava wants some, this way she won't steal yours," Nikki explained with a wink.

She bustled back to the counter where she was now breaking apart a blueberry muffin into a toddler-sized bowl.

Megan sensed movement and looked back to the plumber, just in time to see Danny's head pop out from under the cabinet with a groan. He smiled at her before redirecting his attention to Ava driving her car along the lines on the floor by his feet. He gave her an even bigger smile and wiggled his fingers in a friendly wave.

"Hey there, cutie," he said softly. He modulated his tone just enough to smooth out the rumble of his normally deep voice.

Ahh, that was sweet.

Ava looked up at him with big blue eyes and paused, not quite sure how to react. They stared at each other for a moment, neither moving an inch. Ava caved first, moving her arm just enough for her car to drive along his jean-clad shin.

Theo continued to chew on his fist while gripping his new car in the other hand.

Careful not to startle Ava, Megan didn't react to Ava's abnormally warm welcome.

Her little nugget didn't normally let people into her circle of trust so easily.

After a couple of quiet interchanges between Danny and Ava, Danny was given some hidden signal it was okay for him to move his leg, Ava's new racetrack, and stand.

When he finally stood, Ava's motives were clear when she pulled on his pants leg and demanded "up" in her soft, little princess voice. Ahh, it was all just a hustle so she could climb Danny Mountain.

Megan couldn't blame her.

Danny's eyes were glued to Megan's princess and there was no surprise on his face there. Apparently, Mr. Parker was experienced with children. He squatted down smoothly and opened his arms.

Ava climbed into him, nestled snug, and started driving her car along his chest and shoulder. Without any outward reaction, Danny stood again, settled her on his chest, and started organizing things on the counter. A wrench moved here, and a pipe part moved there. All the while swaying and bopping absently with Ava curled close.

The man was clearly no stranger to toddlers.

Something about that gave Megan warm fuzzies.

But also...

"What are you doing here?"

Danny turned and gave Megan a confused look.

"Huh?" Ava's hand wandered up and rubbed at his closely trimmed beard. "I told you I was going to be here..."

"Well, yeah. But I didn't think that you'd actually be *here*."

"I said I was."

"Yeah, I know you said you were going to be, but I thought it was more of a figure of speech."

He shrugged. "You can pretty much take that as a life lesson: when I say I'm going to do something, I do it." He looked down at Ava, who was now using her tiny fingers to try to pluck whiskers from his cheek. "What do you think, darling? Do I keep the beard, or do I shave it off?"

Obviously, the toddler said nothing. But Megan felt oddly tempted to ask him to leave it to see just how thick it could come in. Already it was looking impressive.

She thought back to all the cars on the street and the driveways and didn't see anything an All-Pro wide receiver would drive.

"What do you drive? Where's your car?"

He paused his movements at the counter and gave her a serious look. "Oh, I live here. Mom drives me wherever I need to go."

Oh...

Ick.

Her heart sank, overwhelmed with disappointment, causing her to freeze, at a loss for words.

How did she even respond to that? Also, maybe this wasn't the healthiest relationship to introduce her kids to...

Danny's handsome face then broke out into a grin.

"Just kidding. No, I don't fu—" he paused and visibly bit his tongue. "I don't live here. I  live about five minutes that way." He pointed in a vague direction behind him out the kitchen window. "I just walked over."

Oh, thank Hera.

The relief that washed over her was downright refreshing. To know he didn't still live at home with Mommy? Yeesh.

"Jeeze, you looked like you were going to need a barf bag for a moment there."

"There was some concern."

"I could tell."

Nikki walked up to him with his own muffin on a plate, after she lovingly set it on the table next to his tools, she then hauled off and slapped him on the shoulder. He laughed and swatted her away, clearly used to her reprimands.

"Stop teasing her. Did you realize when the last time was that she got a good night's sleep?"

His easy smile and bright eyes immediately faded, and he whipped around to face her, concern evident.

His mom continued, bustling over to Theo, and scooping him up with ease. "Having two kids under two is exhausting. Give her a break. Plus, she doesn't even know us that well yet. Give her some time to get a read on you before you give *her* grays as well."

Even though it wasn't two under two anymore, it still felt…accurate.

His eyes were still on her, clearly still concerned that she was suffering somehow.

She waved his concern away. "I'm fine. Just not quite awake yet."

He squinted at her as he read her lie, but didn't push, which was appropriate given that they knew each other for all of five minutes.

He barely even knew her; how could he read her so easily?

"Do you want more breakfast?" Nikki's soft voice asked as she swayed gently with Theo, cooing down sweetly at him.

Megan gave a blink and looked down at her empty plate. How long had it been since she ate without having to share her food? Yikes.

"I'm good, thanks! It was delicious, thanks for warming some up for me."

"Nonsense. Danny made it this morning and brought the extras over. Hardly a big deal to warm it up for you. I'm only glad you took a minute to sit still long enough to eat it. I remember that phase of motherhood well." She peeked up from over Theo's dusty blonde head. "Not that you processed eating it enough to actively enjoy it."

Busted.

"Don't worry, there'll be plenty more meals coming your way. Also, I'm sure Danny could take you to a couple of great restaurants when I'm watching the kids to give you a nice meal and a break. Have you been to Versailles? Danny took me there a few months ago and it was divine!" Nikki looked back down to Theo. "You're going to be a little towhead like your sister, aren't you?" She looked back up at Megan. "Were you a blondie too?"

"They're actually my cousin's biological kids. I adopted them at birth. So even though I was a blondie and they have coloring like mine, she had raven black hair."

Megan felt Danny's attention zero in on her.

Nikki's eyes held compassion as she looked at Megan. She nodded kindly and looked back at Theo. "I love my little blondies, don't I?

Yes, I do. Let me go show you some pictures. You can see Danny with all sorts of cute hairstyles. Did you know blonde hair is perfect for dying all sorts of silly colors?" The woman wandered from the room, still babbling softly to Theo's blinking blue eyes.

Megan couldn't stop her soft smile at the grandmotherly behavior. She'd never had that for the kids before. Or for herself, for that matter.

"She loves kids," Danny said softly from across from her. He had pulled up a seat and was now letting Ava drive her car along his face and head.

"I see that."

"She's pis— angry, at me for not wanting kids."

Megan's friends went through infertility treatments for years, there was no way she was making a flippant comment to him about how it would maybe happen one day for him. You could never be sure what a person was going through.

"She can snuggle with Theo and Ava whenever she wants. They'd love the extra attention." That seemed like a good response.

Danny leaned back in his chair and inspected her, his heavily lashed eyes coasting over every inch of her face, causing a tingling sensation to erupt everywhere.

The intensity of this man...wow.

Plus, the well-worn tool belt resting low on his hips?

If he didn't have the raw talent to be a professional athlete, he certainly would have made for a successful plumber. Housewives all over New England would find themselves with lots of leaky faucets that need fixing.

Megan included.

Megan's gaze lingered on Danny's rugged appearance as he leaned against the counter, his well-worn tool belt hugging his hips. Her heart fluttered at the sight of him, and she fought to suppress a blush creeping up her cheeks.

She didn't know exactly what he earned as a wide receiver combined with his various endorsements, Megan would be hard-pressed to say that he wouldn't bring a greater income as a contractor.

"How's the trial run going so far? Have we passed your test?"

Megan gave him a droll look. "You have two kids in a city with very few friends and you tell me how you'd go about vetting people to watch them."

He held up his free hand, the one that wasn't securing Ava, and put out the fire. "Hey, no judgment. I completely agree. You don't just drop your kids off with anyone without meeting them first. Though, I would have thought I'd have more clout than your average Joe off the street given that we know each other, somewhat."

Megan chuffed out a laugh. "In the barest sense of somewhat. For all I know, you have handcuffs in this house to chain the kids to once I leave."

"Oh, I have handcuffs, but not child-size," he said in a deep voice, his eyes dancing across her face.

The tingles erupted again and spread like fire, prickling and tickling her skin. Megan shifted in her seat.

"You're flirting with me? Here? In your mother's kitchen? With my kid on your lap?"

He shrugged good-naturedly. "I'm not dead, and you're hot. What's the harm?"

Megan rolled her eyes. "You know it's just in good fun and I'm not actually open for business."

"Lady, I knew you weren't open for my business as soon as you mentioned you had kids. But a little flirting never broke anyone's heart, and you look like you could give a good flirt."

"Once upon a time," she sighed wistfully, smiling sweetly down at Ava, now driving her car on Danny's forehead. "But I'm completely rusted out now. They don't even do parts for my model anymore."

"Nah, you don't need new parts. Just gotta use 'em and they'll oil themselves right back up."

She eyed him. "Is that so?"

"Yup." His smile was blindingly confident.

They stared, silently assessing each other. Danny no doubt wondered if Megan would take that little step toward reclaiming herself as a woman. Megan was fighting with the idea of flirting with a man who was going to be paying her to work on his mother's finances and who was going to be watching her kids in the future.

"Seems messy," she said after a moment.

"Trial run?"

She shook her head and looked down at her feet, hiding her smile. This guy.

As she was about to retort, Nikki wandered back in, a sleeping Theo in her arms. "So, do you want to get started?"

Megan gave her a nod and carefully avoided meeting Danny's eyes. Megan followed Nikki to the adjoining dining room where stacks of papers lay waiting.

Megan glanced at the stack of papers on the table, her eyes widening as she realized the enormity of the task ahead. Her mind raced with the implications of untangling Nikki's financial mess.

Jeez Louise, what did she sign herself up for?

Nikki gave her a rundown of her finances and Megan cringed. Not only did the sound like a lawsuit waiting to happen but it also sounded like her financial advisor for several of her accounts might know more than he was letting on.

"So, I started pulling my bank statements to see if I could start doing some bookkeeping because I haven't been keeping track of anything this year. But I know my shortcomings and I always make sure to keep all of that stuff in its own bank account at least. All of my cleaning gigs, tutoring, piano lessons, babysitting. I have the dates and amounts put on the calendar, but if it was cash...I didn't deposit it. Oh, I know, I know. I let things slip. I've just been so busy. Plus,"

She whispered as if imparting a state secret. "I don't enjoy it. I hate numbers. My CPA said he'd do it, but Danny threw a fit, and then my CPA recommended a local bookkeeper, and Danny once again threw another fit, so here we are."

From the inelegant snort Danny let out as he settled on the floor with Ava, it was clear he didn't think that scenario played out the same way.

"These are my tax returns," Nikki grandly pointed to a stack of still-sealed envelopes.

The woman had never even opened them; Megan tried to hide her wince. Oh, holy guacamole.

Babysitting. Babysitting. Babysitting.

Not to mention a roundabout route to finding Theo's father.

She needed to focus on the benefits...not the headache this project was going to be.

When Nikki left to go grab some documents, Megan sat down, pulled over a notepad, and started compiling her thoughts.

As she scribbled, the hair on the back of her neck stood up and she felt fine prickles on her back. She paused her messy notes and took a slow breath, concentrating on the warmth hitting her ears. She turned her head the barest amount and saw Danny sitting up, Ava reading a book in his lap, her car abandoned on the floor by his hip. Danny's bright eyes were on her.

Yeesh, he was handsome. Especially when that cocky smile came over his face...like it was right then.

Damn him.

Megan shook her head at him, fighting the odd blush that threatened to take over at being caught peeking at him.

What did she have to feel embarrassed about? He peeked first! Focus!

She turned back to the paper in front of her and literally *felt* his smile widen.

After rereading the same line four times, she slammed her pen down and turned to see him still watching her.

"You," she commanded. "Look somewhere else."

Danny's smile lit up his face, revealing a set of perfect, pearly-white teeth that dazzled. "Why?"

"Because... you're distracting me."

"Oh?" Danny's right eyebrow climbed a bit.

Megan fought the flurries in her belly.

"You're paying me a ridiculous amount of money to do this. It would be in your best interest to not distract me and let me focus. Plus, it will grant you freedom from Princess Ava's clutches a bit sooner. Get you back to your fantastical life."

"Please tell me what it is about me that's distracting. I want specifics."

She rolled her eyes. "You clearly own a mirror."

He grinned unrepentantly.

*Was that a freakin' dimple?*

Megan's heart pounded, and her cheeks warmed as she watched Danny's confident grin. She couldn't believe how effortlessly he charmed everyone around him

"You watching me while I work is a distracting sensation. That's all."

"Do you need some help over there?"

"God, no. Stay away."

She wouldn't be able to focus at all if he came any closer.

Not with him looking like porn fantasy come to life.

Judging by how his smile turned somewhat wolfish, he seemed to have read her thoughts.

Crap.

He shot her another wink and went back to reading the board book in front of him. The man was a first-class flirt through and through.

Yet she was falling for every tease.

Hook, line, and sinker.

Each forbidden, sexy smile had her heart skipping a beat like she was fifteen at a high school dance.

Megan was no blushing virgin. She was a strong, intelligent, and empowered woman that certainly didn't need some man to swoop in and rescue her.

She had her own tool set. Thank you very much.

Yet...she couldn't stop her eyes from darting over and looking at the toolbelt that he had shucked and left on the floor in the kitchen. That tool belt had seen some miles.

What other things could a guy like Danny fix?

Her eyes snuck back to him, where his deep voice was rumbling over the silly words on the pages. Megan fought back a toe curl.

Well, he could fix a broken libido, that's for sure.

She hadn't felt this ready to go in months. Maybe years. He hadn't even touched her.

Hell, her kids were in the room and her eyes dropped down to where his long, strong hands were holding the book.

What would they feel like on her?

Megan's eyes crawled up the veins on his forearms, and she had to swallow and beat back the urge to fan herself.

When did thick veins become a turn-on for her?

She wanted to trace every one of them with her tongue.

A matronly chuckle had her ripping her eyes away. Coming from a side room, Danny's mother approached with Theo still snoozing on her shoulder. On the other shoulder, she held a tote bag full of documents.

She smiled kindly at Megan. "You're not alone. He gets that a lot." She said it with such tired comradery, it was hard to feel embarrassed for being caught staring at the woman's son.

She plopped the tote down and pulled up the seat next to Megan.

Never one to beat around the bush, Megan looked at the woman and asked, "Did you create him in a lab?"

Nikki laughed and immediately started patting Theo's bum to soothe him from his startle reflex from her initial outburst.

The baby startled easily, but even so, the burst of laughter was loud.

Then again, would Megan have expected anything else from someone who was related to Danny? The man was made to live loud. Clearly he had to have learned that joy for life somewhere. As she watched Nikki's eye sparkle with mirth, it wasn't hard to see where Danny got his zest for life.

"I sometimes wonder the same thing." the woman chortled out in between 'shhs'. "If he didn't look so much like his father and his father's family, I'd wonder if they switched him at the hospital. I always thought he was too clever to be mine. And way too outgoing."

Both women turn to look at the man in question, who was eavesdropping shamelessly.

"Shame you're so ugly," Megan remarked drolly to him.

Danny gave her a pathetic nod while he nodded agreeably.

Dork.

"So, what do you need from me?" Nikki asked.

"Nothing right now. Just getting some notes down. I'll circle back with you once I have a list of questions."

As she got up to leave, Megan stopped her. "I might have to run to my car to get my laptop."

Nikki nodded. "Of course, that's fine. Danny and I have the kids. They're good."

Megan gave her a small smile and looked at the snoozing Theo, and giggling Ava.

Yes, they did certainly seem to be 'good.'

•  •  •  •  •  ●  •  ●  •  •  •  •

As Megan closed her laptop, she let out a big sigh. There was a lot of stuff going on here. And she wasn't so sure that Nikki's financial advisor and her accountant were competent…or ethically pure. She needed to finish looking at all the statements and tracking everything, but she had a sinking feeling. Also, there was a bit of scope creep happening. Her accountant didn't set up her books properly and Megan's OCD wouldn't allow it to stand. Megan found herself reclassifying and reorganizing everything in the files. Combine that with everything else Danny wanted her to do, and this was a project that was going to take many hours and certainly wouldn't be wrapped up on a single Saturday morning.

Earlier, Danny dragged an old highchair from the basement and Nikki furiously cleaned it before setting Ava into it. Danny and Nikki were now in the kitchen, happily feeding Ava in the highchair and giving Theo a bottle.

Crap, she really should be working harder on weaning him off a bottle. Another thing she was failing at.

Ava was having the time of her life if the laughing Megan heard this morning was anything to go by. Clearly, her chick had found her new best friend.

Actually, the excitement wasn't reserved for just Ava.

Nikki and Danny seemed to be enjoying themselves just as much.

Who would have thought that a professional athlete could find so much joy from three hours of babysitting? She had heard his deep, open laughter all afternoon. Just being around a man who was that in-tune with his feelings had her all fuzzy and buzzy.

The guys at work were not overly outward with their emotions.

Sort of like her.

Shocker.

As Megan packed up her stuff, she double-checked her notes. She added some last thoughts and slipped out to her car to put her bag away.

When she hustled back inside, Danny's loud, silly voice blasted out. He was coaxing Ava to eat.

She walked into the kitchen. Ava was proudly eating peas with Danny. Even miss stranger danger was drawn to Danny. People wanted to make him happy. His energy was magnetic.

Nikki bounced over to Megan.

Man, she wanted Nikki's energy level when she grew up.

"How is Ava eating peas right now?" Megan couldn't hide her shock. Her shoulders naturally tensed as she remembered the countless dinners where Ava had pushed her plate of peas away, refusing to take even a single bite.

The woman laughed. "I have a way."

Danny chimed in from his seat in front of Ava's small toddler chair. "It's true. She does. Somehow, her vegetables always taste better than everyone else's."

Nikki beamed with the compliment and shot a wink at her son.

A wink that had Megan double taking.

She assumed Danny's winks were a trait he picked up in high school or college. Or whenever he realized just how gorgeous he was. She never thought that maybe he got the saucy wink from his mother. As she looked at them now, she couldn't help but notice the similarities between the two.

Despite Nikki saying that Danny favored his father in the looks department, in the bright lights of the kitchen, there was no mistaking that her beautiful features were there in her son.

Megan shook her head as she watched Ava reach out with her tiny fingers and delicately pluck a single pea off her tray and place it gently in her mouth, all the while, smiling big at Danny.

Megan's eyes widened in amazement as she watched Ava happily munching on peas under Danny's watchful eye. He had an uncanny ability to coax even the pickiest eaters into trying new foods. That or Danny's pure beauty was enough that not even a three-year-old could resist trying to impress him.

"What do you think, kiddos? Are you coming to my next home game with Mama?"

At her name, Ava's head whipped around the room trying to find her. When she located her, Ava let out a half squeal, and her legs started kicking.

Theo's head tilted slightly in Nikki's arms as he peered around for her, but otherwise, didn't move from his snuggly cocoon.

"I don't know if Mama is up for bringing two small kids to a professional football game. One, because I'm certainly not going to buy a ticket for each of them. And two, that would be ridiculously hard to manage." She gave him a sorry smile. "But we always watch from home, promise."

Danny gave her a big smile. "You don't need to buy a ticket, I can get you some in the family box seats. That's where Mom always sits. It's a lot quieter and more temperature controlled. They even have toys and private bathrooms for the families. It will be fun, not stressful, promise."

"I'm not so sure Theo and Ava would be able to last the entire football game, it might be a waste of some tickets."

He waved her away. "No worries, experiences are usually times well wasted. You should at least try it." He paused and eyed her in a challenge. "A trial run."

As she was about to decline again, she hesitated. The team hadn't changed that much in the last two years. Maybe, she could bring a picture of Starla and ask some of the family members if they recognized her. Maybe it would be a lead.

But first, she needed to talk with Danny.

# CHAPTER ELEVEN

# September 3, Saturday
## Megan

"Hey, Danny? Can I talk to you for a quick second? I have a…request of you." Her words stumbled out slowly, the uncertainty in her voice echoing the way her hands nervously twisted together and twirled her ever-present. She paused, searching for the right words, as if plucking them from the air one by one.

Danny looked over from where he was making silly faces with Ava. At her change in tone, and upon noticing her wringing hands, she could see his body tense and his face sober.

His eyes darted to his mother, and they exchanged a fleeting, indecipherable glance—an unspoken language they seemed to have. Then, with a solemn nod, he gestured for her to follow him.

He led them into the living room, shoulders hunched, and steps heavy, his usual exuberance dampened to a mere flicker. Each footfall seemed to echo like a heavy sentence being pronounced on his way to the gallows.

Jeeze, what did he think she was going to say to him?

Once they were out of earshot of the children and his mother, he looked out the window for a moment before turning back at her, a reserved look on his face.

A wave of unease washed over Megan, and her stomach tightened into a knot of anxiety, as if trying to warn her of the weighty conversation ahead.

She had never seen him look so serious, resigned even.

Danny took a breath that had his large chest expanding before bringing his blue eyes to hers. "How much do you need?"

His voice came out in a near-whisper, so low that Megan had to strain to catch every word, as if the weight of the request was too heavy even for sound.

His right arm went behind his back and started digging out his wallet. Danny pulled a couple of blank folded checks out of a pocket there and patted his body for a pen.

Megan's body jolted with shock, and her mouth opened and closed wordlessly, like a fish gasping for air, her mind racing to process the unexpected offer.

Danny found his pen in his chest pocket and used his wallet to form a writing surface as he wrote out her name, not meeting her eyes.

"How much money do you need?" He repeated, his body stiff as a board.

Good gravy. How many times had people hit him up for money?

Megan couldn't stop herself. Her trembling fingers reached out tentatively, gently touching his wrist, where she could feel the rhythmic pulse beneath his warm skin.

"Danny, I'm not asking for money." It was such an energy shift, it felt like she was being punked. But unfortunately, in her heart, she knew that wasn't the case.

People with success? Others always wanted a taste. There was always someone asking them for something.

Her stomach revolted with guilt—was she any better than those 'takers?'

He stiffened even more, if possible. His eyes rested on her hand that was still touching his skin, and then looked up at her, his eyes searching.

"What?"

Though her brain was telling her the right thing to do would be to release his hands, Megan couldn't make herself do it.

Instead, she curled her fingers around his and continued to look into his bright blue-gray eyes.

"I don't need money, Danny. I'm not asking for money. I just wanted your help finding Theo's dad."

With the way he was looking, it was probably best to cut right to the chase.

His only reaction was a blink and a small tilt of his head as he looked at her.

"I'm sorry, what?"

Without meaning to, she rubbed her thumb across his knuckles, expecting to feel the same calloused hands from when they first met.

Yikes. The tops of his hands were silky soft.

How could some parts be velvet, and other parts be so calloused and strong?

That was...intriguing....

Megan refocused herself.

"I don't need money from you, Danny," she said softly and looked back towards the kitchen. "Theo is my cousin's kid whom I adopted when he was born. His dad was someone from the Spartans from two seasons ago, but I don't know who. My cousin never told me. She had some demons..." Megan trailed off, not knowing what else to say. The knowledge that her cousin's death was intentional, rather than an accident still stung. "Theo deserves to know his dad. And his dad deserves to know he has a son out there, especially one as awesome as Theo."

Danny's taut shoulders lowered and absently his thumb started making slight circles on her fingers still holding him.

The topic of conversation wasn't particularly sexy...yet a bolt of lust fired through her at the contact anyway.

He was like freaking acid. She got high just from touching him.

"I just figured with you being on the team, you could maybe ask around, show her picture to some people and see if anyone recognized her. Then we could go from there. That was all." She looked up into his face and tried to communicate with her eyes that she wasn't trying to take advantage of him. At least, not financially.

Her gut still squirmed at using him, even in this somewhat benign way.

Megan's tension eased as Danny's guarded expression softened, understanding crossing his features. Crisis averted.

"Okay," he dragged out. "So, you just want me to ask around? That's all?"

"Exactly. I wanted to know if maybe I could give you a picture of her. And you could show it to some of the guys on the team and I could reach out to any that recognized her. She had so many notches in her bedpost, it was basically whittled down to the size of a toothpick. But I'm hoping it made her memorable enough that one of the players recognizes her. And then from there…" Megan trailed off and then shrugged, at a loss for what to say next. "I guess we could do a DNA test if he agreed. I haven't got that far yet."

Danny cocked his head and squinted at her. "Are you sure you want to go down this road?" His piercing blue eyes darkened with concern. "Some of the guys on the team are fantastic and some…well…not so much. You might find that the guy isn't even on the team anymore. Or your cousin could have lied. Ultimately, you are opening yourself up to the dad coming back and saying that he wants Theo. Are you willing to risk that?"

All good points that she'd already debated ad nauseam. It didn't make her heart hammer any less though. Was she sure? Absolutely not. Did she owe it to Theo and this mystery dad to try? Probably…maybe.

She swallowed hard past the lump in her throat and tried to project confidence. "I know." Her voice was a weak squeak. "And it's absolutely a concern and something I've lost more sleep about than you can imagine. But I just can't shake the fact that I'm not being fair to Theo for robbing him of that introduction. And I'm not being fair to this guy, whoever he is, who has a super awesome son out here and doesn't know it."

"Meg," he paused, and she felt a thrill shoot through her at the nickname. Her friends called her 'Meg', but coming from Danny? It was *way* different.

"Theo is awesome. That's my point. Have you checked into the legalities on if this guy wants to have him full-time? Can he take him from you permanently?"

Megan felt her whole stomach clench and the all too familiar elephant sat on her chest making it hard to breathe. She closed her eyes for the briefest moment trying to calm her thoughts and emotions.

Breathe.

The chances of losing Theo were small. What guy would just strip a baby away from the only mother he'd ever known? And from his sister?

No one would do that...right?

Megan looked up at Danny, hoping her expression hid her terror at the thought.

"Yes, but what if Theo wants to know someday? What if he hates me for never finding out when I had the chance? Rosters change all the time. This could be my only good chance. And..." She whispered the concern she had yet to speak aloud to anyone else. "I would fight tooth and nail for Theo, but at the end of the day, doesn't a dad have more claim than a mom's cousin? And if this guy was a great dad? How could I deprive Theo of that?"

Her eyes watered, and a lump formed in her throat. She looked away, trying to compose herself as conflicting emotions tugged at her heart. Megan breathed through the sensation of being ripped in two. Her guilt and sense of obligation to Theo versus her desire to keep Theo all to herself and not risk losing him.

She looked back at Danny and saw his normally cheerful face was somber and understanding.

"Wouldn't you want to know?" she whispered. "Wouldn't you want to know if you had some kid out there? A super awesome kid who spent his whole life wondering who his dad was. And what if he never had any opportunity to find out because his aunt slash adoptive mom waited too long to get him answers?"

Theo's dad might try to take Theo from her and would most certainly have the resources to do it easily. But he probably wouldn't... right? But those same resources could benefit Theo and give him a well-provided childhood and endless opportunities.

Danny tipped his head back and stared blankly at the ceiling, giving her scenario the consideration and weight that it deserved.

"Yeah, I guess if you wanted to do it and wanted to figure it out, you'd have to do it now. It's only going to get harder and harder as the roster changes year after year and memories fade."

He sighed, the sound blending with Ava's and Nikki's laughter from the kitchen.

Megan nodded, her mind racing with uncertainty. 'I know...DNA testing might not even be necessary. Maybe I'll just make a list of the players who recognized her and just keep their names somewhere. Give Theo the list when he's older or something. As I said, I haven't quite figured it all out yet." She gave him a sheepish smile.

Danny raised an eyebrow at her. "And what am I supposed to be giving them for a reason of 'do you recognize this woman?'"

Megan winced. "I haven't got that far yet."

Danny sighed, running his fingers over the scruff on his cheeks.

"Damn, woman, you've given me a hell of an assignment. I'd rather you just ask for money; it seems less dangerous. I'm tempted to say 'no' just to save you from all the potential heartache."

Well, that was one way to get rid of the guilt. Refusal of participation from the man who was supposed to help her.

But that was a copout.

She still had other ways to access the team. She owed it to Theo to at least try. So even if Danny said no, she'd have to go those other routes, even if going through Danny was the... cleanest.

She needed to buck up and...

She stilled as she looked up into Danny's face.

There was nothing but rage and frustration there.

Oh, *fuck*.

# CHAPTER TWELVE

# September 3, Saturday
## Danny

Danny saw the truck haphazardly park halfway up on the curb and jar to a stop. He then watched as his father jolted out of the vehicle and gave a stagger step before righting himself, pulling his shirt straight, and focusing on walking a straight line towards the house.

Ava wasn't exactly a chatty three-year-old, but she sure as shit didn't need to hear the words that were coming their way.

Neither did her pretty mother.

"Stay inside," Danny bit out.

Her lovely eyes were wider than usual as she looked out the window where his dad just stumbled a step before righting himself again.

"I'll come back in when he's gone."

Her big eyes looked up at him, searching for something. She gave a small nod and straightened her shoulders as she looked out the window again.

As he turned to leave, her soft hand rested on his forearm.

Fire shot through him.

Hot damn, the woman's touch was electric. Every fucking time she touched him, he wanted to take her back to his place and do X-rated things with her.

"Will you be okay?" Her voice was quiet, and her eyes were on him again.

In a hurry to get this scene over with, he nodded and turned to go. But not before holding her hand in his own for a second longer than necessary and giving it a soft squeeze. His calluses were probably uncomfortable to hold in her soft palms.

After making sure the front door was latched and locked, Danny marched down the steps, steeling himself for the forthcoming scene.

"What's up, Dad?" Danny's whole body tightened in anticipation of the upcoming fight.

"Can't a man come home every now and then to see his goddamn wife?" His father's Boston accent was still strong despite the nomad lifestyle his father had lived.

"Yeah, but now's not a good time, Dad. All right? She's got people over. Plus, you're not married anymore, so I don't think that applies in your case."

His dad's eyes went immediately to the house over Danny's shoulder. Even the damn man's neck craned as he tried to see through the windows of the house. When Danny shifted slightly, breaking his view, his father shifted in response to inspect the cars in the drive and on the street.

He immediately clocked the small, yet nice crossover parked on the road.

"She got herself a fucking guy in there?" he barked out, his face growing ruddy. He took a couple of steps towards the house and Danny reached out, careful not to touch him, but clearly indicating that he would if needed to.

"Not a man. Jesus. calm down." He lowered his hand when his father stopped moving towards the house. "It's a woman she's helping out."

He didn't want his dad to know shit about Megan. It felt wrong to have his shitbag father even know about Megan.

The protective gut clench was...unfamiliar.

Interesting.

"Helping out how?" his father still eyed the house suspiciously.

On his heavy exhale, Danny caught the familiar smell of liquor.

Fuck.

"She's helping a friend who's going through a tough time, Dad. Give her some space."

"Your mother babysittin' again?"

His interest didn't bode well.

"Don't know. I just know she's helping out my friend for a little bit."

His father's eyes flashed to him when he said the word 'friend.'

Shit.

"Your friend?" His father made finger quotes. "One of your special ladies?" His expression changed to a leer and his skin crinkled. "The kids yours?"

Danny stiffened, not able to tell if his father was trying to piss him off and get him going, or if he was being sincere.

"They're not mine," he bit out. "She's not that kind of friend."

Though, the idea had some merit.

"Good. You'd be a shit dad."

Danny tried not to wince at the insult from his own trashy father.

Steve's face turned shrewd, so Danny continued feeling the need to defend himself. "Just to be clear, if they were my kids, there's no way in hell that they'd be going through what they're going through." Danny narrowed his eyes on his father. "And as far as I know, there are no little Parkers running around."

His father shrugged, completely unapologetic. "I hear things. I know you get around. Just wanted to ask if I had a grandbaby somewhere."

Drunken asshole.

His days of sleeping around willy-nilly were over, along with his other reckless choices fueled by alcohol.

"I don't give a fuck what you hear. I'm telling you."

There was a fine line between shit-giving and outright fighting with his father. As Danny matured, the line became blurrier.

His father had a warped view of reality. If you couldn't give back what Steve dished out, he viewed you as weak.

Like a shark, you did not want Steve Parker to view you as weak. He'd fucking eat you.

However, the old man also had a fuse. And Danny had never quite mastered how to read how long the fuse was on any given day.

Hence, their joyous and loving relationship.

"As you can see, Mom's busy right now. Maybe try calling later. But right now, I need you to go."

With the way his father stiffened, his fuse was lit.

Fucking hell.

"Excuse me," his father hissed, leaning into Danny's face. "You're telling me to leave my own fucking house?"

Danny's fingers dug into his palm, itching the clock his old man.

However, it was a strange feeling knowing that his father wasn't beneath filing a lawsuit against him.

He hoped Megan hadn't witnessed any of this.

Danny refused to look.

"You divorced her years ago. This isn't your house anymore."

Steve's bloodshot eyes glistened with rage, and he closed the distance, his thick Boston accent escalating in anger. "Who the fuck you think you are, kiddo? Get the fuck out of my face before I make you." His father placed his hands on Danny's chest and shoved him.

Steve wasn't a small man, but Danny was used to being pushed around. He sure as fuck wasn't going to give the old man a chance to smell blood in front of a house that had Theo, Ava, and Megan in it.

"Don't make me call the cops, Dad," Danny said with a sigh. "Take a walk. Or, just get in the car. Or better yet, let me call you a ride, and just go someplace to cool off."

Being told he was drunk was an explosive trigger for his dad.

Implying that he wasn't a better driver while drunk?

Jesus shit, Holy Christ.

Upon hearing the implied insult, the drunk man's eyes blazed with anger, and he slurred his words as he lashed out with a venomous retort, his fists clenched and his demeanor volatile and unpredictable.

"What the fuck did you just say to me, Golden Boy?" The wobbling had stopped, and now his father was unnervingly still as he stared at Danny.

Danny glanced at the house and noticed a curtain shift. Hopefully, it was his mom. Megan certainly didn't need to see this shit.

He sure as fuck didn't want the kids to see, or hear, whatever his deadbeat father was about to drum up either. Even though Theo was probably too young to understand.

Danny tentatively slid his hand into his back pocket, the action once again carrying an unpleasant, almost repulsive sensation. If he thought it was painful thinking that Megan wanted money? This was worse.

When would he stop caring? What would it take for the remaining shred of loyalty to his father to be stripped from him?

Clearly, it would have to be something serious.

"How much do you want, Dad?" Danny quietly combed through the bills in his wallet. "What will it take to get you out of here?"

His dad's ruddy and irate face turned sleazy. Downright slimy.

Fucking winner.

"Not *that* kind of friend, you say?"

Danny stiffened at the implication. "Not that kind of friend," he repeated, staring down his dad. "But even so, she doesn't need to see or hear whatever shit you're about to spew."

His dad's hungry eyes took in the bills. His hands darted forward and ripped a handful out of Danny's hands.

He let the bills fly out, all of them. Whatever. Fuck it. Take it all.

If that's what it took to get the drunk away from there, it was worth losing a couple hundred bucks.

He was more than willing to give Megan whatever money she needed when he thought she was asking earlier. He had assumed she needed the money given her comments when they discussed his mom's job. Helping her find Theo's dad wouldn't be too much of a hardship.

However, even though he was willing to give her whatever she needed, the thought that she was going to ask him for money when she hardly even knew him felt wrong. It didn't match what he thought he knew of her from their brief time together.

But then it made him nervous. She was proud. Independent. How bad did things need to be to ask essentially a stranger for money?

So, then those worries bounced around his head as he made out the blank check. When she assured him she didn't want his money, the wave of relief that washed over him was… different.

Asking him to help find Theo's dad…

That was heavy shit.

She was opening up her life to him in a way that felt out of character and very vulnerable.

There was trust there.

A power given over to him.

That felt significant.

Meg was trusting him to handle this in a way that wouldn't result in her losing her little boy. That trust?

Fuck.

He sure as fuck wasn't going to let her start to lose confidence in him by seeing some shitshow fight with his dad.

Yeah, seeing his father storm off down the road to a friend's house with a wad of cash in his hand was shitty.

But the trade-off? Well worth it.

The opportunity to help a single mom who needed a helping hand? A helping hand that could have made his mother's struggle a little easier when he was growing up? A helping hand at possibly finding a father figure for a little boy who was going to have some questions about his father as he grew up? The opportunity to possibly present a child with a worthwhile father?

The number of times he prayed that his mother would sit him down one day and tell him his father was not actually his father? Innumerable. That his real father was just a guy making his way through town, and in a moment of passion, his mother strayed. And boom. Danny was conceived. Unfortunately, that wasn't the truth.

But he knew what it was like to wonder. To wish.

Was having a deadbeat father better than none?

As he stared at his father's wobbling, retreating figure, he had to wonder...

But he'd do his best to make sure that little Theo would have as few questions as possible in a way that brought about the least amount of heartache. Not only for Theo.

But also, for his beautiful, strong-yet-worried mother that couldn't seem to catch a break.

# CHAPTER THIRTEEN

# September 5, Monday
## Danny

Megan texted him a picture of her cousin later that night and Danny practiced his lead-in speech all Sunday.

"Hey, can you take a look at this pic and let me know if this girl looks familiar?"

"Hey, check out this girl on my phone, do you know her?"

"Hey, have you slept with this chick? Cuz, if so, you might have an adorable light-haired little boy looking to throw the pigskin with you."

None of them felt 'right.'

Just looking at the picture of Starla, he could see small similarities between her and Megan. But that might have only been because he was looking for them and spent a lot of time watching Megan when she wasn't looking. He had seen Starla around at a couple of parties but couldn't recall seeing her shackled up with any one player.

It should have made things easier that Theo didn't look anything like Starla. Danny was going on the theory that Theo must look like his dad. Danny combed his mental roster to see if he could see any of his teammates in Theo's pudgy baby face. Dead-end.

Theo had more in common with Nikki than any of the men on the team. That too-trusting look. Sometimes, he thought he saw a similar look on Megan's face, but it always disappeared in an instant. He didn't know what life had brought her to the city and away from her family, but it certainly wasn't a happy one.

That made him sad. She had the wit and humor to be fun-loving and light. Instead, there was this weight on her that he could see sapping the life from her soul.

Could have been her family, her job, single parenting, a number of things really. Whatever it was, something inside him was demanding action in helping her when he could.

She needed a knight, and he was feeling the need to find a place at a round table.

•••••••••••

As Danny walked into the gym on Monday morning, he was met with the smell of sweat, overpowering cologne, and the tang of rubber mats.

Ah, home.

He eyeballed the men in the room, wondering how he should go about this.

Keep it subtle so as not to alarm or piss anyone off...or make a team announcement?

Immediately, he scratched the idea. There were a couple of scumbags on the team that had no business being a parent but thought they did. If they knew they had a kid out there, they'd fight for him just for the sake of taking what was 'theirs' and then toss him away.

Nope, subtle was the way to go.

And if he got down to those final few guys that didn't deserve to be parents...well, he'd discuss that with Meg if it came to that.

He really hoped it didn't.

Christ, that'd be terrible for Theo.

Danny saw their young buck quarterback in the back of the room, doing some work on the bike in a slow, lazy manner.

Perfect. Ryan was still doing his warm-up.

Plus, if Theo was Ryan's, he'd be a lucky SOB. Ryan Cole was as good as they came.

"Hey, Ryan, got a minute?"

Ryan looked up from his phone and popped an earbud out.

"What's up?" Ryan's bright blue eyes looked surreal in his summer-tanned skin. The kid really should be a model and not a football player. The women loved him.

Hmmm. Did Megan love him too?

"I have a pic I want to show you." Danny held out his phone. "Do you recognize her at all?"

Ryan gave it not even half a second before he was nodding. Danny's gut squeezed. "Yeah, definitely. She was always hanging around the parties when I started on the team. Haven't seen her in a bit though. Why, what's up?"

He hated to ask; it was none of his fucking business.

But he had to for Megan and Theo.

"You ever hook up with her?"

Ryan looked up at him with wide eyes. "Dude, you trying to trace a breakout?" The younger man gave a meaningful look towards Danny's crotch and Danny took a hasty step back.

"No!"

Ryan didn't look convinced.

"Just trying to figure out who she might have...entangled herself with on the team."

Ryan's dubious expression didn't change but he nodded and resumed a faster pedaling pace. "She didn't seem like 'good' people if you know what I mean. She was always pushing drinks and more handsy than was appropriate, even for some of those parties. Which is saying something. Don't know, bud. Can't say I remember seeing her tied up with anyone in particular. Just a hanger-on."

Danny nodded and knew the type all too well. There was a period in his life when Danny hit the bottle a little too hard. He knew exactly the kind of woman that Ryan described. The ones that always had a fresh drink in hand and *somehow* it was always the guy's drink of choice. It made it easier to constantly drink if your groupies kept you well-lubricated all night. Hell, there was one night that Danny got so drunk, he woke up naked in his teammate's closet with a floatation device around his waist and a swimming mask on. As humiliating as that was the following morning, it was the wake-up call he needed. He had been stone-cold sober ever since. Thinking of his father, it was probably true what they said about alcoholism running in bloodlines.

As Danny walked away from Ryan, he didn't know whether to feel relieved or disappointed.

Theo couldn't have done better than Ryan Cole for a dad. And if Starla really was the...not super awesome type...chances were that some of the other good guys on the team wouldn't have spent time with her either.

Fuck on a fucker.

• • • • • • • • • •

After a team meeting in one of the classrooms, Danny braced himself up to ask another of his more circumspect teammates. One who would keep the conversation quiet.

The men filed out, one by one, their considerable frames making the large classroom seem tiny. The maroon and navy coloring of the floor and walls was drowned out by the bodies now taking up every free inch as they all patiently waded from the room, jostling each other good naturedly.

Danny didn't know if he hoped that Kenny would say he recognized her or if he dreaded the thought that Kenny recognized her.

The drama of Kenny finding out he had a secret love child while he was planning a wedding to the love of his life...

One surprise child was more than any man needed to experience. Three? Well, that might just kill Kenny.

Kenny was engaged to Chloe of the infamous Book Club Babes. Therefore, Kenny absolutely knew Megan. There was *a chance* he'd not know Megan's connection to Starla. Maybe. If he didn't know Starla, that would make all this so much easier. But if he knew her...by having Danny ask Kenny, it meant that Megan didn't need to ask her best friend's future husband if he slept with her cousin.

Fucking hell, this was going to get messy.

"Yo Kenny, you got a minute?"

Kenny paused on his way out of the classroom and approached Danny where he leaned against the wall. Kenny picked up on the privacy vibe that Danny was projecting. Silently, they gave matching nods to their teammates as the others filed out of the classroom.

When they were finally alone in the spacious classroom, Danny took a deep breath and—

Something different came out instead. "How are Chloe and the girls?"

He was a chickenshit.

How Megan was planning on doing this before he came along, he'd never know.

Kenny's eyes narrowed as if he knew that Danny was just delaying.

"Perfect, but you didn't shanghai me after a team meeting to ask me about them." Kenny's eyes narrowed and the brown patch in his blue left eye seemed more pronounced as he stared Danny down.

Shit.

Well, all right, here goes nothing.

"I have a weird question for you, man. And it's kinda on the DL."

Kenny's body grew stiff, and he pushed up from the wall. "What's up?"

Danny swallowed and unlocked his phone. Starla's picture was already loaded up, ready for this moment. He handed his phone over to Kenny.

Kenny looked confused. "Megan's cousin?" He nodded down toward Danny's phone. "Why do you have a picture of Starla? I didn't think she was your...type."

Danny grimaced.

Well, Kenny knew her connection to Megan. On the plus side, he didn't seem to think much of her, so chances were they never hooked up.

Kenny also had another thing right: Starla was *definitely* not Danny's type.

Back in the day when he drank too much? Maybe. But luckily, Starla was only vaguely familiar to Danny, at best.

"Yeah, no, she wasn't my type. I'm just doing something for Megan."

Kenny's face grew more confused.

"You know Megan?" Kenny handed the phone back and raised his eyebrows at Danny, clearly wondering how they were connected and how far that extended.

All it would take was Kenny telling Chloe that Megan and Danny were talking. And then all the Book Club Babes would be all over playing matchmaker for them.

When he waited for the shiver of revulsion to dance down his spine and it didn't come...

Huh. Interesting.

He wasn't looking for anything long-term, especially with a single mom. He sure as shit wasn't looking to drag children into the mess of his life. Danny wasn't the type of guy that he'd want any child to look up to. He'd made too many mistakes. Had too many demons.

But for a little warmth on those cold New England nights?

Megan was an absolute fox.

If she was looking for a fun time and that was it? No strings attached? Heck, she'd be the perfect candidate. Smart, funny, sexy, kind, not likely to fawn at his feet.

A woman who actually busted his balls for a change.

That suddenly sounded glorious.

Kenny's expression darkened at Danny's continued silence.

"Dude. What the hell is going on? Why do you have Starla's photo? And how long have you and Megan been...talking?"

Danny looked up into Kenny's now-worried face.

"Relax. We're not fooling around. I met her through her work, and we got to talking. My mom watches her kids sometimes." Not quite a lie. "She wanted help figuring out who on the team her cousin...dated. And I offered. Stop stressing."

Kenny frowned and opened his mouth to say something more, when their resident Quarterback coach popped his head around the corner.

"Great, Kenny, I was looking for you. I want Ryan to do a couple of runs..." John trailed off and stared at them, finally taking in the mood of the room. He stepped fully into the room and crossed his arms. "Everything okay?"

Jesus. So much for keeping this quiet.

Before Kenny could say anything to get Danny in trouble with John's fiancé, Jen, Danny held his phone out and spoke quickly.

"Just need to know if you recognize her?"

Danny bounced lightly on his feet as he waited for John to hand the phone back, shooting a dark look at Kenny to keep his trap shut.

Kenny just pressed his lips together in a secret smile and turned to wait for John's answer.

"Nope, nada. She looks familiar as fuck but I couldn't even tell you her last name." John looked down at him. "Who is she? Baby mama and a paternity suit?"

Danny ripped the phone out of John's hand.

"Why does everything think I knocked someone up?" he grumbled as he stuffed it into his back pocket.

Kenny and John shared a look that had Danny unable to control his outburst. "It's not like I slept with anyone with a pulse! Jesus. You act like I was a sex addict! So I...explored. I don't anymore."

"Yeah, cuz now you're old as shit."

"Boring too."

"And ugly."

The two men kept at it, their smiles growing bigger as they heaped their shit on him.

"Assholes," Danny grumbled, fighting back his own grin now.

Well, seemed like Megan didn't need to worry about Jen and Chloe's men being Theo's father.

The beginnings of a headache started to form. This was going to get complicated. Their book club was incestuous with the Spartans' team at this point. Shit.

Danny slapped his hands together to get their attention. "Welp, I'll leave you to it."

John looked confused, no doubt wanting to know more about why he was quizzed about the girl on Danny's phone. Comparatively, Kenny's expression turned to knowing and satisfied.

Ah, hell.

"What?"

"Nothing." Kenny had a stupid smirk on his face. Like he knew a fucking secret,

Pinpricks danced along Danny's spine. "What?"

Kenny's smile deepened and he pushed his lips together in a shitty attempt to hide it. "Nah, nothing man. I just know that look you have on your face."

John stilled even more and whipped around to inspect Danny closer.

Fucking busybodies.

"What look? There was no look."

He had no look.

Kenny outright laughed and clapped Danny on the back, moving his slightly to the side.

"Ahh, the things we do for women. No worries, bud. Secret's safe with us." Kenny gave him an inkling of a frown. "But whatever happens, for the love of God, just let me get married before you do, all right? Chlo will have my balls if yet another couple gets married before we do."

Danny heaved a breath and gave Kenny a look.

Marriage? Was he fucking kidding?

Kenny started laughing harder while John looked on with an amused, yet puzzled expression.

Luckily, John wasn't the chatty type. But he'd for sure be bringing this back to Jen.

Shit.

"For the love of God, don't tell me it's a book club hottie." John groaned as he realized what Kenny was teasing about.

"Babe," Danny corrected in a grumble.

That threw Kenny into another round of laughter. Without another word, he slapped Danny on the shoulder and left the room, somewhat dragging John with him.

His laughs echoed down the halls back into the classroom where Danny was rubbing the back of his neck.

Well, shit.

# CHAPTER FOURTEEN

# September 6, Tuesday
# Danny

A day later, the sound of joyous giggles sprinkled with intermittent crying echoed in the air along with the scent of disinfectant and rubber.

*Just like home.* The comparison to the guys at the gym at work had Danny biting back a laugh.

The red, blue, and yellow walls were a bright change from the Spartans' darker and subdued color scheme. Danny ambled along the edge of the gymnasium, looking for the female that he hadn't been able to get out of his mind since their official meeting just a week prior.

His fingers played with the folded sheet of paper as he scanned the people scattered about. Uncomfortable tingles spread over his skin as the crowd started to scan back.

Busted.

Danny gave polite nods but kept a determined and focused look on his face to waylay any people, any fans who might try to stop him and interfere with his current goal. Over the years, he learned that if he looked distracted, people were less likely to approach him.

Like an addict, when he heard the low, sultry chuckle of the woman in question, his head whipped in her direction and his heart started thumping just a tiny bit harder.

Danny found her crouched low by a balanced beam, tiny hands in each of her own as she eased Ava across it, Theo strapped to her chest in a carrier, snoozing away.

The media was going to have a shitstorm when they saw him going up to a single mom at a kid's gymnastics class.

Somehow, he couldn't find it in him to care.

He wanted to put her mind at ease as soon as he could and this was the only time she had available.

Danny approached his targets and studiously ignored the weighty silences followed by frantic whispers behind him.

Almost immediately, he was hit with Megan's warm, floral scent.

Heaven and Hell.

How could *looking* at her make him want to undress her with his teeth, but *smelling* her made him want to cuddle up on a porch swing and talk about what puzzle they were going to do next?

"Hey there, gorgeous," he said with an easy smile as he crouched down.

Megan cut him a look and rolled her eyes. "Please."

He smiled bigger. "Excuse me, Miss Meg. I wasn't talking to you." He then turned to face Ava. "I was talking to you. How are you doing, sweetheart?"

Ava beamed at him and ran the three steps to give him a big hug.

Apparently, he made an impression.

Megan let out a soft chuckle and his body hummed.

Score one for Danny Parker.

He then peeked around and into Theo's sleeping face. "Hey there, handsome," he whispered. His cheek looked so fat and squishy that Danny had to stop himself from reaching out and touching it.

Or pinching it.

It was fucking adorable. So adorable, Danny wanted to just grab hold of his little cheek and pinch...hard. Fuck. What was the German saying?

Zum fressen gern haben? Something about something being so adorable that you just wanted to eat it?

Yup. Pretty much.

"Here's the list of guys that are no-goes so far." He offered the folded page to her.

Her head jerked and she tentatively reached out to take the piece of paper. Her beautiful face looked terrified when she peeked back up at him before unfolding it.

Hell, even her hands were shaking as her eyes rapid-fire scanned the names.

Her shoulders lowered with the depth of her sigh.

"Thank fu—" Her eyes darted to her daughter, "fun-loving Santa." Megan looked back up to him. "You asked this many on the team already?"

He gave her a cocky grin. "I told you I'd help, and I'm an overachiever."

Megan gave him a funny smile before she looked back down at the sheet of paper.

Her shoulder sagged.

What did that mean?

Relief? Upset?

She didn't make him wonder long.

"Thank god Kenny didn't recognize her."

Oh.

"About that..."

She stiffened.

"Some of the guys did recognize her but none of them copped up to sleeping with her." He grimaced and forced out the last bit. *Like a bandaid.* "At least within the last few years."

She jerked so hard little Ava lost her grip on Megan's lowered right hand. With a small scowl, the little princess marched away and tried to make her way onto the small foam block next to them by herself.

"Some of the guys on this list *slept* with her?" Her voice got high and tight at the end.

It was adorable. Even if the topic wasn't.

Danny nodded reluctantly.

She gave him a ridiculous look that had him biting back a smile. "Don't tell me who unless the timeline matches," Megan grumbled while giving an absent pat on Theo's rump.

"Went without saying."

She was tough, but she was still adorable. And she'd probably hate that he thought that.

Freaking adorable.

Now rubbing Theo somewhat compulsively, she added quietly, almost to herself, "At least, John and Ryan are also off the list."

Now it was Danny's turn to grimace. "Yeah, about that..."

Her shocked eyes flew to his and the straight horror he saw there caused a weird bubble to dance in his stomach. Without being able to stop the sensation from rising up, Danny threw his head back and laughed. This whole situation was so *fucked*.

She gave him an incredulous and nervous expression, clearly waiting for his moment of insanity to pass. As she watched him, her eyes caught on the hand he had placed on his chest while exorcising his laughing demon.

Her expression went...soft.

Well, hello.

Danny sobered and reluctantly looked around, all too aware that he had drawn attention to them.

Once satisfied that there was still an appropriate amount of space between them and the other caregivers at the little tykes gymnastics class, he took a step closer and lowered his voice to stress his sincerity.

"Nothing like that. Theo isn't one of theirs. They recognized her but nothing from a *Biblical* sense."

She whooshed out a breath and watched Ava jump off the low balance beam a few feet down from them. She had clearly given up on the foam block when Megan didn't help her up.

Danny continued. "But Kenny may have an idea of what I was doing. Asking around." He clarified.

She blinked.

"John too, possibly. They definitely gave me the impression they knew I was asking for you, and they know we're friendly outside of our occasional run-ins at events." Danny shrugged. "Not sure what that means for you and the other ladies but if it's going to get you grief, I wanted you to brace. Not sure what their feelings are on the matter."

They better be fuckin' supportive. Megan was risking it all by doing this and trying to do the right thing.

If they weren't...well, Danny would have a few fuckin' words with them or their men.

They'd be supportive when he was done if they weren't already.

"Ah, hell," she groaned before widening her bright eyes. "Shit! I mean, crap!" She covered her mouth and closed her eyes in horror. Megan dropped her head forward and shook it side to side in defeat. Her plump pink lips brushed softly against Theo's peach fuzz.

Danny couldn't stop his smile.

What a hot mess.

"Luckily, I don't think she heard you."

Her only answer was a soft groan that translated to 'She didn't hear me *this time*, next time, I'm screwed.'

Fuck, she was a hoot. A gorgeous, smart, caring, hoot.

Once she got herself back under control, she peeked up at Ava who had now wandered over to a slightly taller balance beam. With a burst of speed that had the professional wide receiver impressed, Megan basically teleported to Ava's side, giving her space, but not *too much* of it.

Fucking hell she was quick.

Without even missing a beat, she turned back to him and seemed surprised he hadn't followed automatically.

"I, uh, had discussed finding Theo's dad with the girls. To a...mixed response."

Danny followed good-naturedly and twisted his lips into a wry smile. "I can imagine. I can also imagine how scary all of this is.

Trying to do what you feel is right versus what you feel is *right*, ya know?"

Her pretty eyes turned appreciative. Somehow showing something warm and...grateful.

Megan pinched her lips together, nodded at him, and turned back to watch Ava cautiously navigate the beam.

But not before she reached out and warmly squeezed his forearm.

Just once.

One gentle squeeze.

But that was enough.

She had crossed the divide.

Initiated contact.

And just like that, he was hard as a rock.

At a fucking kids' gymnastics center with over a dozen of people around.

Fucking hell.

Danny scratched roughly at his beard to avoid fidgeting but even so, he couldn't shake the buzzing on his skin.

He tried focusing on his breath, but it only further resulted in inhaling more of her soft lavender scent.

Lavender was supposed to help project calm and tranquility.

It certainly wasn't fucking working for him.

And, after knowing her for more than five minutes, it clearly didn't work for her either.

The woman was made to be wild. Reckless. Fun-loving and impulsive.

Instead, life had forced her into a corner that left her little room for choices. She was riding the ride of her life, not driving.

And a woman like her? She was made to drive.

As he studied her while sucking in her scent like an addict, he was struck with a thought.

Maybe he could also help her with that...maybe he could help her drive. Just a bit.

Hell, why not?

"I have a question for you."

She looked up at him, her green eyes open and listening, but still...dark and tired.

Damn, Megan needed to get a nap.

She was still gorgeous. Fair skinned, like she never saw the sun, with light pink lips and the cutest pert nose. She looked like a model for Barbie. She was stacked to perfection, even with the tired eyes.

Her bosses were complete assholes, how could they not see her running on fumes? He barely knew her and he could see life weighing on her.

"Hmm?"

And that simple vibration also shot straight to his cock. Fucking hell, what was it about this chick?

"What do you feel about dropping the kids off with my mom this weekend and going out to dinner with me?"

She blinked and turned around to look behind her, feigning a search for another person who he must be talking to.

"Brat."

She turned back to him with a grin on her face. "I'd like to get back into your mom's financial stuff actually. Just got her Power of Attorney and some other documents that the investment advisor was stonewalling me on. So, I want to jump back into it if I can, so I'm not sure a dinner date is in the cards."

"Stonewalling? It's only Tuesday. You emailed him at most four days ago, two of which were not business days."

Megan, the scamp, waved him away. "I have ways as well. I'm *also* an overachiever."

He smiled as she threw his words back in his face. "Touché."

The barest smirk teased her lips but otherwise she remained impassive as she turned back to watch Ava. Absently, she swayed back and forth, like she wasn't even aware she was doing it.

"So, the good thing about dinners is that they happen at dinnertime. Not earlier in the day. So, you can still work yourself to death with my mom's stuff, but then after, you need to eat. The kids would already be there with her and that would leave you free to be my plus one."

Megan opened her mouth and he pulled her in for a quick one-armed hug to disarm her. He squeezed tight and kept his eyes on Ava, not letting her get a window of opportunity.

"Perfect, it's settled. Wear something comfy."

Danny sensed her watching him but ignored the touch of her look. Instead, he released her and crouched low, helping Ava climb through a small foam tunnel. Ava smiled big at him and babbled something completely incoherent but adorable, nonetheless.

Danny never wanted to be a dad, not his calling, but that didn't mean he didn't think kids weren't cute as fuck.

As he rolled, raced, and crawled around with Megan and her kids, he felt the stares and subtly, and sometimes not-so-subtly, pointed phones in his direction. No doubt, Megan would be fielding some questions as soon as the Springfield gossip chain got started.

But the good things about Megan, unlike his other women, were one, she didn't want the attention, but two, the woman was tough as nails. No way would a little media attention scare her off.

But she was perfect for what he had in mind on Saturday.

# CHAPTER FIFTEEN

# September 7, Wednesday
## Megan

"What the hell do you mean you guys are closing Theo's classroom on Fridays? You're a daycare; you can't just close. Parents have to work!"

Megan felt her stomach seize and a headache started to form.

The daycare director in front of her was unphased. "Have you watched the news at all? Daycares everywhere are in crisis. Staffing is impossible to come by, and everyone is sick, teachers *and* students. With the current staff-to-student ratios, we're trying to stay afloat until something changes. This is the best we could come up with. Heck, half the days we're at the bare minimum for ratios."

Megan could hear her heartbeat in her ears and her hands started to tremble. "Look, I get you're in a tight spot, but I need care. I need daycare for my kids. I *have* to work. I'm a single mom with no family to call on. I don't have someone who can watch him on Fridays. That's not even touching on the now-reduced hours."

The woman was still unmoved. How many people had she already told this to today?

"I'm very sorry. We're doing what we can, but it is what it is. Ava's class is going stay open at least...we hope. Unless someone else gives their notice..." The woman's face took on a dark and nauseous expression. "I'm supposed to be the director, not a teacher. But I'm in the classroom every day. It's not sustainable. And the reduced hours are to give me some time during the day to do my director responsibilities."

Gee, wonderful.

"What am I supposed to do with Theo on Fridays?" Her heart was going to pound a hole in her chest. Even her freaking fingers were going numb.

"I'm sorry, I don't know. I prepared a list of other daycares in the area. We're not recommending any one over another for obvious liability reasons, it's just informational, but maybe that will help?"

Blackness started creeping in the side of her vision.

*Breathe. Breathe. Breathe.*

"When is this effective? Both the Friday thing and the reduced hours."

The director just handed her a stapled packet of papers and smiled gently. "End of this month. Again, we're very sorry, but there was nothing we could do."

Two fucking weeks away?

Megan could taste vomit.

"We just don't have the staff; I'm sorry."

"Yeah, me too." Megan closed her eyes and tried not to take it out on the director. "Can you get a statement typed up about the closing classroom so I can submit it to the office manager at my work? They're going to want to know what's happening."

The words tasted like fucking ash on her tongue. She shouldn't have to have a formal fucking letter from her daycare for her bosses to believe her.

"I can refer you to an FMLA—"

"Just a letter is fine, thanks."

Fucking bitch.

It wasn't really her fault.

But it helped to blame *someone*.

But blaming her wouldn't make Megan's upcoming life any easier.

She stomped out of the daycare center and to her car, unable to stop her mind from, once again, going in one million different directions.

What would work do?

Would there be rate changes for Theo's classroom?

Would she be able to find a new daycare that had five-day coverage and was open till 5:30?

Would a new daycare have a spot for Ava so Megan could have one drop off and not two separate daycares to visit in the morning?

How many minutes outside of the city was this new daycare going to be? Did any daycares even have openings? How many minutes would that tack on door morning commute? How much earlier would she have to wake up in the morning to bring the kids to school and then get to work? What would that do to the afternoon traffic for when she was picking up the kids from school?

Breathe. Breathe. Breathe.

Her headache was full-fledged by the time she finally got into the office and sat down at her desk. Mechanically, she loaded up the programs on her computer and jumped into work, only to realize several hours later that she had forgotten to track her time on her timesheet.

Billing in six-minute increments fucking sucked.

Therefore, she had to go and recreate her entire day as best as she could so the billing would be as accurate as possible.

God forbid her Realization and Billable Hours goals be influenced by a missed timesheet day.

Fucking fuckers.

She glared out at her computer as she tried to recreate the past few hours, her headache still pounding at her despite the ibuprofen she had taken.

"Megan?" a disembodied voice said through her phone speaker.

"Yes?"

"Danny Parker for you on line one."

Megan closed her eyes and rubbed her temples, cursing the tumbling in her chest and the burst of excitement that swarmed her.

The man was a breath of fresh air. All happy and sunshine.

Where she was a grump. Especially right now.

She just wasn't sure she was up to his fighting weight today. Fighting his teasing flirtations was hard enough, doing it while managing a headache and stressed about daycare?

She'd be goo in his hands.

And men like Danny should *never* know how gooey you are for them.

Toddler gymnastics was an absolute blast with him the other day. He didn't even seem phased by the various stares of adoration the other parents were laying on him.

In fact, at one point when a bold single mom tried approaching him for a picture, Danny had handled it like a champ and extricated himself with grace and finality. When he came back to Megan's side to play with her and the kids...Megan couldn't stop the skip of her heart.

It was such a cliché.

But him ignoring his fans so he could give her and the kids his undivided attention? What a weird, empowering rush of victory and satisfaction.

Emboldened by the memory and rallying herself for the upcoming burst of energy, she picked up her phone. "Hello, this is Megan." No need to let him know she knew who was on the line.

Why did her chest feel tight while waiting to hear his voice?

"Hey there, Meggo-my-eggo"

Did he want to eat her? Yes, please.

"Hi...Dan the Man."

"Weak, Ms. Lowell."

He was right, she needed a better nickname. She paused. Were they the nickname type? Was *she*?

Megan sank deeper into her chair and rested her head back against the headrest. "I'll find a better one. What's up?"

She could hear the smile in his voice. "Don't sound so happy to hear from me."

She grinned despite the heaviness still on her chest. "Sorry, just a crappy morning and you caught me at a bad time."

Immediately, his voice became alert. "Are the kids okay?"

"Oh." Megan sat up at the concern in his voice and immediately felt bad for worrying him. "Yeah, totally. They're fine. I just had some unwelcome news from daycare this morning on top of messing up something at work. That's all. Nothing horrific." To his way of thinking at least.

"What happened?"

To anyone else, Megan would tell them to go pound sand-it wasn't their business.

But coming from Danny? She found herself wanting to share with him. It felt...odd. But nice.

"Nothing life or death. They're closing Theo's classroom on Fridays and cutting back all their hours. Soon. At the end of this month actually. So I've been scrambling trying to find a new place that will take them with the hours that I need. I've called out to a bunch of local daycares but a couple of them have quite a few non-compliance reports and sanctions."

"Damn, girl. You work fast. All that just this morning? And non-compliance and sanctions? What does that mean?"

"Yeah, you know, the state keeps track of licensed childcare locations. So they'll drop in for audits to make sure the providers are being safe and following the rules. If they have any violations, it gets logged with the state for parents to access." She pinched her lips and frowned. "Our current daycare has been cited for being under ratio many times over the years. It's not ideal, but they were the only spot with two openings once Theo came along."

"Woah. This is legit. I had no idea daycare was so tightly run. I just thought people like my mom could just watch whatever number of kids they want and that was that. I didn't know they got freakin' audited. Damn, darlin'. So there's no openings anywhere?"

"Not really. Every place I've called so far has taken my name and number and said they'd get back to me. Two places have already called back and said that they have a waitlist a billion children long. And I already know there are some daycare centers that I wouldn't send my kids to even if my life depended on it. I'd quit and become a stripper first. I bet there's a market for middle aged strippers." She trailed off weakly, trying to turn it into a joke.

Danny's soft chuckle danced down her ear and to her neck.

"You were wearing socks last night at gymnastics so I didn't see your feet, but you might not need to resort to the pole."

Megan blinked and stared blankly at the wall. "My feet?"

"Yeah."

"What?"

"There's a big market and feet nowadays if you have photogenic ones. I figured everything else about you is gorgeous. Your feet are probably too. How well does this CPA gig even pay? You might be able to make it just on your feet pics alone and not have to worry about daycare."

Laughter erupted from Megan before she could stop it. She stared back up at the ceiling and wiped tears from the corner of her eyes,

How long had it been since she had laughed that hard?

"You know, that might solve my problems. A couple of feet pics here and there and I can just keep the kids home with me. Not a bad idea, Parker."

"As I've told you before, I'm an overachiever. You call, I'll answer. You ask, I deliver. Boom. Sexy feet pic solution."

Megan could picture his blinding smile coming out from beneath his thick but short beard.

Yes, he certainly was.

"So, who else knows you're a 'feet' guy?"

"Shh, it's our secret."

She smiled again and dipped her head. Fuck, at this rate, her cheeks were going to get sore from all this smiling.

"Anyways, sexy feet pics aside, I wanted to let you know that my mom finally heard back from her lawyer about getting her trust and will documents together. He said he wouldn't talk with you without written permission from her and I figured that would probably take too long for your eager-beaver time schedule."

"You figured correct."

She turned her head and stared out the big window, for once feeling nothing going on inside her head except the sound of Danny's voice and his quiet chuckles.

"So, I'll bring those over tonight."

Megan sat straight. "I'm sorry, what?"

"I'll bring those over to your place tonight."

Megan looked quickly at the phone and put it back to her ear. "The documents from your mom?"

"Yeah. I also got some presents for the kids that I want to give them if you're okay with that."

Why was her mouth suddenly dry?

"Danny, you don't owe them presents."

"I know but we're friends, or at least we're getting there. I saw something and thought of them, so I bought it. That's what friends do. I'm helping you out with finding Theo's dad. You're helping my mom. Friends do stuff for each other. And I wanted to do this for Theo and Ava. What's the harm?"

'What's the harm' indeed?

It felt too much like something a boyfriend would do, and Danny was definitely not a boyfriend.

"I'm just a little worried about what message that sends to Ava."

There was nothing but silence on the phone.

Shit.

"Danny?"

"Here," he said after a moment. "What message do you think it sends?"

How could she feel judged and not judged at the same time? Shit.

"I, uh...."

The silence felt pointed.

"Yeah, that's what I thought." She could hear the amusement in his voice. "Anyway, the daycare thing isn't necessarily the end of the world. Not just because of the foot pic potential. But because my mom would probably watch them for you. She's been going stir crazy at home lately. She loved playing with them this weekend. I bet she'd take them in whenever you needed to. Gives her the grandbabies that she'll never have, ya know?"

Her mind wouldn't sit still. Was she still upset about daycare? Was she terrified of having him see her house that night when it was deep in the mid-week mess? Was she relieved that Danny's mom might actually be a viable option for her and the kids? Was she concerned that Ava would interpret something more from Danny's presence in her life? Would Ava notice when he was gone?

And there was the crux of it.

Shit.

"Danny. I appreciate your thoughtfulness with the kids, and for helping me out with Mission Find Theo's Daddy. But I'm worried what it's going to do to Ava when you go from being around to being...*not* around." She paused to let that sink in. "I know she's only two and half, but she's bright. She doesn't talk much, never has, but she notices things. If she gets attached to you, she *will* notice when you're gone."

"Who says I'm leaving?"

Megan blinked. "What?"

"Who says I'm leaving? Why can't we be friends even after our mission is over? Especially if my mom is watching your kids? Hell, your friends are married, or soon to be married, to my friends; why can't we remain friends?"

Well, when he put it like that...

"Yeah, but you've always been very clear about kids—"

"About how I didn't want them. Not that I didn't like them. That fucking article," he grumbled under his breath. "I love kids. Fuck, I play with Kenny's and Brandon's all the time. But just because I don't want my own toxic bloodline to continue doesn't mean that I don't like kids. And," he paused, "in this world, can't we all use as many friends as we can get?"

Megan closed her eyes and took a big breath.

Yeah, she could use a friend.

Her girls were great, but they had their own lives. Their own dramas.

Sure, Danny probably had his own dramas, but she hadn't heard a peep about any of them.

A friend that was just *easy?* It sounded like fucking heaven.

Megan turned her head to look at the picture of her kids. If Theo's dad turned out to be a shithead, they could do a lot worse than Danny Parker as a fun uncle.

With a deep breath, Megan closed her eyes. As Danny's voice rumbled in her ear, she ignored the hollow ache in her heart that wished for more than friendship with Danny 'the overachiever' Parker.

# CHAPTER SIXTEEN

# September 7, Wednesday
## Danny

Later that day, Danny left a session with Jen for some pre-hab work when he heard the Spartans' Head Coach, Offensive Coordinator, and their kicker talking in a small classroom by the pre-hab rooms.

He didn't want to do this, but he couldn't think of a better time. Theo, and Megan, needed answers. And it was unlikely to get easier with time.

As he approached the open door, he almost collided with Coach Mitchell. The head coach gave him a silent nod and pushed by no doubt already late for his next meeting. The large, brooding man was so overbooked at the time it was a wonder he could keep his head on straight.

When Butch saw Danny in the doorway, the offensive coordinator urged him in and eagerly started talking about the new play he had worked up. Butch detailed every move and scenario, while Will Martin, the team's kicker, nodded along and occasionally interjected with enthusiasm. They were so caught up in explaining the new play that they didn't even question whether Danny had time to discuss it.

Danny had to give it to them; it was good. It was a systematic breakdown of the other team so the individual units would collapse on the field over the course of a series of plays. By bringing chaos to the units one at a time, the confusion would cause the entire opposing offensive line to crumble.

A thrilling concept that Danny was eager to try to implement.

But not what he was there for.

"Butch, hold on a sec," Danny interjected, trying to find a pause in the conversation.

The men didn't seem to hear him, now both standing at the whiteboard and scribbling X's, O's, and arrows everywhere.

With a lighthearted laugh, Will whistled low. "Oh man, once we pull this off, my fantasy points are going to skyrocket! Finally, we're capitalizing on our versatility." There was silence in the room, and Will followed up quickly with, "Not that I do any fantasy football. That would be a big conflict of interest..."

But the shift in the atmosphere was already there. Butch's enthusiasm waned, replaced by a silence that was overly heavy.

Danny shifted awkwardly, for once not really knowing what to say to ease the tension.

Butch gave a gruff grunt and coughed into his hand, giving no regard to the fact that he was coughing all over the marker he was holding.

Danny cringed, hoping it got disinfected by the cleaning crew.

But with the interruption, Danny seized his chance.

"There's something I need to show you guys." He dug into his pocket and pulled out the photograph he had printed. He was sick of handing over his phone. The number of times he had settings changed on him when he got it back was ridiculous. Not to mention the sheer number of dick pics when his teammates decided to run off with it.

Danny watched Butch and Will as they stared at Starla's picture. "Do you recognize her?"

Butch was still; his expression guarded. "I don't think so. You got girl problems, Danny?"

Boy, that was a weighted question.

Was Megan a problem? Absolutely not. Was she asking him to help her find answers to a problem? Absolutely yes.

Even so, Danny hesitated. Butch didn't stand for distractions on his team. If a guy had even a hint of a drama in his life, he was met with a 'Butchervention.' It only ended when Butch got what he wanted: a trade order placed by management, a replacement order issued *to* management, or the problem was suddenly *gone*. He didn't 'do' distractions with his players and he made sure those problems miraculously found ways to be 'not problems' anymore.

He demanded that his men were focused on football, or they weren't playing football.

At least, not for his offensive line.

How management allowed his iron fist to go unchecked was still a mystery, but no one could deny the results. They won games. The morale was shaky though, and decreasing with every year and questionable trade.

Will interrupted Danny's hesitation with a puzzled expression. "Wait a minute." Danny tensed. "I know her! I've seen her before."

Hope flickered in Danny's chest as he eagerly leaned in, his heart racing with anticipation. Will wasn't the *greatest* guy, but he certainly wasn't the *worst*. Everyone had their demons. And having Will as a dad wasn't as bad as it could have been. At least, Will wasn't the type to fight for custody or anything.

"Have you two ever...you know, hooked up?"

Butch tensed and looked at Danny. "What kind of fucking question is that?"

It *was* a little awkward...but Danny powered through, keeping his eyes on Will.

Will scratched his head, his brow furrowing. "Hmm, I'm not entirely sure. We spent some wild nights together; she always had the best blow...." He trailed off as if remembering where he was and who he was with. "I don't think we ever hooked up though." Will paused and dug back through the archives, scratching absently at his chin. "Yeah, no. We never hooked up." He said it with confidence.

Danny's shoulders loosened. Another two down

He was running out of 'acceptable' options. Guys he would honestly be relieved to find out they were Theo's dad. Now he was getting to some of the ones that were 'the best of a bad situation.' If it got down to the lower dregs of the roster...maybe he'd ask Megan to abandon ship. No dad would be better than some of those assholes.

With Will's somewhat embarrassed look, and Butch's severe, disapproving frown, whether at Will's extracurriculars or Danny's invasion of privacy, Danny said his goodbyes and left the room.

He was getting closer to the end of the line. They'd either find Theo's dad...or they wouldn't, but at least the search would be over.

He just hoped that it would end in a way that wouldn't wear any more at Megan's soul. The woman already had enough guilt and pressure on her, she didn't need to add yet another thing.

Hopefully, their outing on Saturday would help lessen some of that stress he saw lining her shoulders. After all, Danny knew all about having a good time and for one night, he had mama bear away from her cubs.

# Chapter Seventeen

# September 9, Friday
## Megan

"How do you *accidentally* agree to a platonic date with Danny Parker?" Julie squealed, clapping her hands at their crammed booth at Victor's Diner.

Several familiar and not-so-familiar faces turned to look at them and Lexie indolently waved them away, choosing to focus her laser silver eyes on Megan.

Megan couldn't stop her grin. "To be fair, I didn't try too hard to talk him out of it." At the resulting squeals, her grin transformed into an all-out smile.

Chloe, the most reserved one in their group, smiled softly from across the table. Her expression was a tad more tender and understanding than the others. Something in her eyes made Megan think Chloe knew exactly how excited Megan was for this date despite her sarcastic tease. Not just because it was The Danny Parker, but because Megan actually *liked* him.

Even if it was a platonic date, her stomach had been nothing but butterflies all week.

She literally lost three pounds in the span of the week because she kept forgetting to eat.

"I can't remember you looking so...excited," Rose said with a curious expression.

"All right, all right, we get it, she's happy. Move on," Lexie cut in, clapping her hands. "You girls are thinking too short term. We need to think long-term."

As their heads swiveled to her in question, Lexie started digging in her backpack. Grandly, she slapped a pen and pad of paper on the counter. She clicked the pen dramatically before leaning forward and leveling the women with a look.

"Is '*The Real Housewives of Springfield*' too on the nose?" Lexie declared and dove back into her ridiculous cartoon backpack looking for...something. She quickly gave up and looked toward the women again.

"Or, how about the '*Spartan Wives*?'" Jen said, catching on immediately, leaning forward from her place where she was sitting cross-legged on the bench seat.

"Oh, God," Megan groaned, dropping her forehead on the table, barely missing her small plate of fries.

"What about '*Springfield Spouses*?'" Rose said.

"Oh boy," Chloe muttered and winced in sympathy to Megan.

*Bitches*. All of them. Except Chloe.

Megan leveled them a tired look.

"*The Spartan Sluts*?" Julie giggled and then sighed dramatically. "What does it take to become one? Because...I volunteer as tribute? The horses don't give me much of a chance to get out and about." Julie ran a horse farm and free time was nonexistent. Like being a single mother. Julie rarely even had time to make book club meetings, so tonight was a rare appearance.

The only reason Megan was able to come was because they were all paying Rose's nanny extra to watch all the kids together at Rose's.

Rose pinched her lips as she tried to find another catchy TV show name that encompassed their knack in landing the hunks of the Spartans. "*Spartan Sweeties*?"

"*Spartan Heartens*?" Chloe threw her name in the mix.

Betrayal!

She was a bitch too!

Megan cut her a look and Chloe smiled huge and unapologetic, clearly getting into the spirit.

"I'm not even going on a real date with this guy, and I'm already being included in the *Spartan Wives* TV show?"

"Another vote for *Spartan Wives*." Lexie jotted something down on the pad in front of her.

Odin's beard, that girl was a handful. God bless William.

"Okay, okay, enough. I'm just going on a platonic date with him. He's not exactly marriage or daddy material." Amidst their cries of protests, Megan raised her voice. "Not that he's not great, he is. But we all know Danny. Either personally or through the media. He has been quoted time and time again saying that he never wants kids." She waved a hand down at herself. "Hello? Two kids already out of the oven, with a desire for more." At a sound from Jen, Megan rushed to clarify, "With the *right* guy who *also* wants more kids. Danny is not that guy."

"I'd like to point out that men and women change their minds a lot when love enters the picture," Chloe said, channeling her inner sage.

"Just because Kenny decided he actually wanted to get married doesn't mean Danny is the same. The similarities end at football and the Y at the end of their names."

"True, they don't even play the same offensive position," Lexie added with a snotty sniff.

Jen started laughing. "Bitch." She bumped Lexie with her shoulder and the two cackled together.

Little witch sisters, both of them.

"Sure, laugh now, Lexie. You won't think it's all that funny when Jen realizes you and Ryan have more chemistry than all of them combined, and she starts to play matchmaker."

Silence.

Shit.

Well, maybe not 'shit.' The two had been dancing around each other for so long it was making Megan dizzy. Maybe this would finally put that ball in motion.

"Not every woman wants to settle down and have kids," Lexie bit out, her normally carefree face serious.

"Oh?"

Chloe ducked deeper into her seat and Julie's eyes darted back and forth between them like she was watching a tennis match. Rose sat back with a semi-entertained look on her face, clearly eager to heat Lexie's blustering.

Lexie bit out. "Ryan is gorgeous, we all know that. But we also know he is overly mature, too serious, and fun-sucking *fun suck.*"

"Nice," Megan said.

"Hey, that's not nice." Jen came to his rescue. They had formed a friendship when she started working for the team, and she and John had dinners with Ryan weekly. He was basically her surrogate brother and there was no way that she'd let her surrogate sister lay shit on his surrogate brother.

Shit.

Maybe Danny was right. Their group was getting incestuous.

"What? I'm not saying someone out there wouldn't be into that overly-serious, no fun ever attitude. But do you think for one minute he'd go skydiving? Swimming with sharks? Spend all night dancing? Hell, no. I need a wild man. Scratch that, I don't need a man at all. I'm free and happy."

Jen stuck out her sharp chin and visibly bit her lip to stop herself from getting into an argument in front of everyone. However, her expression and crossed arms screamed, 'we'll talk about this later."

"I think Ryan would go skydiving," Julie mumbled from around her straw.

Gah!

Chloe and Rose pinched their lips together and shared a silent look.

"Well—"

The bell above the diner's entrance dinged and the door blew open, interrupting Lexie's retort.

And in walked the gods.

Not really, but it was akin to a holy moment.

Kenny McCarthy, Brandon Catcher, John Costner, Ryan Cole, Michael Dillon, and Danny Parker swooped into the dinner, effectively removing any free oxygen from the small dinner.

All the men were dressed in their workout gear, smiling and roughhousing with each other as they pushed in.

Dear heavens above.

Megan wanted to drool, but it was a rainbow buffet of delicious men. Anyone call for an icy blonde? What about a midnight sip of water? A medium smoky blend of yummy goodness?

All of them at once? Fuck.

"John!" Jen hopped up from her seat and rounded the table, all too willing to bring the men's eyes to them.

Shit.

It felt electric, having that many attractive men staring you down. Hell, it should have been illegal for them all to be in the same city. Riots were held over less.

As the men made their way towards the women, Megan could practically feel Danny's eyes on her.

God, could he stop looking so happy all the time? It made her all too conscious of her weary demeanor. She used to be fun, damnit.

As everyone made their greetings, Megan was aware of two things. One, that she and Danny were simply staring at each other, and two, Lexie and Ryan were doing everything but.

"Hi," Megan said softly, cocking her head to the side to take in his worn workout clothes. "You need to ask for a raise." She nodded down to the hole in the corner of his workout shirt.

Danny looked down and gave her a crooked grin. "If it ain't broke, don't fix it."

It definitely wasn't broke.

All long and thick and muscular. Sweet cherry tomato, the guy was stacked.

And, if she wasn't mistaken, she could see the outline of the tip of his penis through his shorts.

Holy Hera.

Immediate heat hit her cheeks and she ripped her eyes away and back to his, praying with all her might that he couldn't tell what she saw.

He was looking at her with a confused expression, but thankfully didn't seem to know why she was suddenly a blushing virgin.

"Yeah, well..." She gave a small cough to clear her throat. "At least buy new sneaks. Those things look ready to give out on you."

Puppies, unicorns, show ponies, penises.

Shit!

A small grin tugged at his mouth. "These bad boys? Have had these suckers for seven years. They still have more life left."

"Seven?"

"Seven. I might buy expensive, but it lasts. And I take good care of my shit."

Clearly, just look at the man's body. It was a freaking temple.

"Your podiatrist okay with that decision to wear old soles?" Megan snarked, trying to keep the banter up, no matter how weak it was, because her nose finally started smelling him and it was divine. Combine his signature leathery smell with the just-worked-out look and those gym shorts and she was ready to buy herself a gym membership just so she could ask him to train her.

"My massage therapist isn't but she's particularly anal about stuff like that. She's big into preventative maintenance and wearing *appropriate gear.*" He used finger quotes in such a childish way that Megan smiled up at him, forgetting not to let him see how charmed she was.

"Perdón, Mr. Pissy Parker?" Jen barked from where she was curled up against John. "Your massage therapist has degrees and studies to back up her claims, as well as years of experience. I've told you about the soles of shoes breaking down over time and how—"

John placed a loving hand over his fiancé's mouth and gave Danny and Megan an apologetic look. He then pulled her close and whispered something in her ear. She stiffened for a moment before settling into him, putting her whole weight into his tall frame.

Clearly whatever he said was worth stopping her bitching at Danny.

Danny shot Megan a hilarious and beleaguered look that had her fighting back another damn smile.

Man, he was tempting.

"You ready for our hot date tomorrow night?"

"You ready for me to need to be home by seven?"

"Nah, talked with Mom already. She said she has the bedtime routine covered. You're all mine, darlin'."

All his?

Pinpricks broke out on her skin. She prayed he couldn't see them.

"By the way, I'm surprised to see you. Where are the kiddos?"

Ryan sidled up next to Danny and interrupted. "What's this I hear about you going on a date with Danny?" Ryan wore a sad puppy expression that had her rolling her eyes. "You said no to me when I asked you on a date!"

Two different figures around Megan stiffened at the mention of that.

Oh. Interesting.

Danny looked a little... not himself. His normally friendly face had taken on a darker edge. A more dangerous edge.

Hot damn, that was....

Megan fought back shivers and tore her eyes away.

Only to land on Lexie, who looked like she had eaten something sour. When she saw Megan looking at her, she directed her eyes to the conversation happening next to her with Rose and Brandon.

"You asked her out? When?" Danny's voice had a new barely-there growl.

Mama likey.

Ryan shrugged. "Don't know. Couple months ago? Right after Ava had a daddy-daughter gymnastics day at the Y. I filled in and went so Meg could stay with Theo." As he finished speaking, he took note of Danny's dark expression and walked it back, his face taking on a somewhat surprised expression. "Also, it was just a friendly date invite, to get her out of the house. She works too hard. But she said she didn't have care for the kids. Oh look, Kenny needs me." And just like that Ryan fled across the table where Kenny was catching up with Chloe and most definitely *did not* need him.

"Ava has daddy-daughter days at gymnastics?" His expression seemed...bothered. And clearly confused as to why it bothered him.

Megan shrugged. "Yeah, they try to do things like that. She had a daddy-daughter dance as well. Brandon volunteered for that one. Said his boys weren't the dancing type and he wanted to go. It was cute." She couldn't stop the smile that spread at the memory. Ava had painstakingly picked out the perfect dress for that night, and seeing her dance with one of the biggest offensive linemen in the football league smiling down at her? Magical.

What would she look like dancing with Danny?

Megan stopped the thought before it could develop.

"When's her next daddy event?"

Oh boy, dangerous butterflies were starting to spring to life in her belly.

"I don't know off the top of my head, but I can check when I get back home."

"You do that." The command in his voice had her cocking her head at him.

*Yes, daddy*, her inner slut purred.

"Megan?" Ryan braved the storm that was Danny Parker and joined their conversation again, this time from safely across the way.

"Yes?"

"I keep meaning to ask you, do you want the number of my CPA to see about job openings? I know your current gig is a little...tough."

"Yeah, that's just what she wants. More stodgy old men that judge her for being a mother and expect her to pretend her kids don't exist. You can keep the contact's name of your good ol' boys' club CPA and his, I'm assuming, sexist and misogynistic views. She doesn't need boring people in her life, she needs people with personality."

Lexie just couldn't fucking help herself.

Ryan froze and then turned towards Lexie, moving robotically.

Megan's head jerked back at the venom in Ryan's normally affable face. It was like watching Danny's face when he saw his dad pull up in front of his mom's house. Something they still hadn't spoken about.

"One, I didn't ask you, Princess. Two, just because you like to play Russian roulette with your life doesn't mean that someone who doesn't court that type of risk is automatically boring, three, my CPA is a woman in her thirties just outside the city, and four, she runs her own firm, is incredibly successful, and one of the most empowered and intelligent people I have ever met." His mouth clamped shut and his nostrils flared as he took a heaving breath in through his nose. The friends were silent as they watched him struggle to get control of his emotions. He opened his mouth to say more but then shut it and shook his head.

Ryan dismissed her and turned back to Megan, who now had Danny's hand resting on her chair back. "Do you want her number?" His tone was carefully modulated but you could tell that he was close to losing it.

Megan nodded but otherwise kept her trap shut.

Ryan nodded and turned back to the others. He didn't even let his eyes rest on Lexie who was now looking at him with regret and rebuke. "I'll text it to you. Her name's Emily Ashford and she's totally great. But I gotta head out. Stuff to do." He gave vague nods goodbye, walked to the to-go counter, grabbed a bag, and left without another word.

"I—" Lexie began. She wasn't one to let silence linger.

"Just don't," John, of all people, bit out.

Lexie had known John since she was basically a kid, so his curt words caused her to jerk back and her face to pale.

"Enough, Lex. You're always at his throat. God knows why. Just cut the shit. The guy's been through enough."

What did that mean?

Megan looked up to Danny and he twisted his lips and shook his head, his blue and hazel eyes somewhat sad as they met hers. He gave her a gentle squeeze on her shoulder and Megan's skin prickled at the contact.

Danny's assurance was enough for her. She didn't need to pry. She had enough people's secrets floating around her head. By nature of her job, she knew all sorts of dirty laundry. If Ryan wanted people to know what was going on with him now, or what happened in the past, they'd know.

As the group wrapped up and said their goodbyes, Danny stayed by Megan's chair.

Before he left with the guys, he turned back. "You were okay that I texted and didn't swing by with the docs on Wednesday, right? It sounded like you were a little panicked at the thought so I just thought that maybe—"

Megan couldn't reassure him fast enough.

"Oh god, yes. Very okay with that. If you ever see my house, it needs to be after a deep clean. So maybe in like...five years?" She gave him a hopeful look.

He laughed hard at that.

Much harder than he should have, considering she wasn't joking.

He gave her a soft squeeze on the area where her neck met her shoulders and beamed down at her.

He was still letting out soft chuckles as all the men left with their to-go dinners to bring back to the stadium.

But before he officially left the small diner, Danny paused at the door, almost as if sensing that Megan was watching him leave. "See you tomorrow, darlin'."

The bitches at the table loved that.
Fucking hell.
Even so, she couldn't stop her smile.

# CHAPTER EIGHTEEN

# September 10, Saturday
## Megan

Megan spent the next day at Nikki's dining room table, poring over documents and tracking numbers on spreadsheets. All while Danny and Nikki ran around the house chasing after Ava and giving endless snuggles to Theo.

It was a shame that Danny was notorious for saying he never wanted kids because the guy would be a hell of a father.

In her more fantasy inclined moments when she'd get distracted by his attentiveness, while looking at Danny holding her two kids she could almost pretend what it would be like to have a partner like him in life. Someone who reminded her to laugh and let go. Someone who reminded her to eat or schedule a doctor's appointment.

Heck, just someone to talk about the day with.

He had an optimism that was refreshing and so different from the people Megan spent ninety percent of her day with.

When watching Danny with the kids, she could almost make her fantasy real by looking for similarities between them and Danny. Which only served to make her imagination run even crazier.

If they were an item, if they could make it work, if Danny changed his mind...you know, the small details...what would her and Danny's children look like?

Megan packed away the various documents and stood, arching her back and leaning into the stretch.

Feeling a tingle of awareness spread, she turned her head and saw Danny's eyes zeroed in on her chest.

The shiver that coursed through her was trouble with a capital T.

"Checking for ticks?" It was easier to be snarky than to embrace the arousal and flirt like a lady, damnit.

His eyes flashed to hers and the wicked grin lit his face.

"Might not be a bad idea. They've been bad this season. Here, let me take you into the bathroom and I'll give you a more thorough checking." His eyes dropped down to her chest. "I might see one that I need to inspect closer."

A blush burned her cheeks, and she crossed her arms. "It's chilly."

His smile widened. "Of course."

Nikki bustled in with a homemade puree pouch for Ava to munch on while they colored at the table.

"My green machine mix. A guaranteed win." At Megan's aghast look at the congealed green mixture in the reusable pouch, Nikki explained further. "Trust me. And I put a bunch in the freezer for you to take home later to give her throughout the week. I know you said you had a hard time getting her to eat greens...I'm sorry, are you cold? I can turn up the temperature."

Nikki belatedly took in Megan's crossed arms and 'cold' posture. "I'm good, thanks."

"Yeah, Megan is really good."

Megan shot him a look.

Irreverent punk.

He simply shot her a wink in return.

Somewhat adorable irreverent punk.

Not to be distracted, Nikki continued. "The next time you come I can make sure that it's warmer. Sorry. Menopause has been a bi...bear." She hesitated as she corrected what she was about to say.

"Language, mother dearest," Danny chortled out.

Nikki sniffed delicately. "Just need to get used to having little ears around again. I'm still loads better than you, mister."

Megan chuckled. What she wouldn't give for that kind of connection with someone. Anyone.

Nikki still had a guilty look on her face though and kept looking back at Ava like the little girl was going to start singing Morisette's 'I'm A Bitch' at any second.

"Don't stress about it. It's hard. I slip all the time. Everyone at work swears like a sailor, so it feels weird to *not* swear. Then when I get home I have to change gears. I find myself slipping frequently." Megan gave the kids a soft smile. "Luckily they haven't noticed yet."

"I bet you don't slip nearly as much as you think you do." Danny was studying her closely, his normally jovial face somber as he watched her.

Awareness spread again.

Megan stayed silent but gave him a shrug in response to his assessment.

"And I bet you beat yourself up over every little slip too."

Another shrug. He didn't need confirmation, he already knew.

If anything, his face got even more sober.

Why did that make her heart squeeze and her sinuses burn?

Ava looked up innocently from the table, interrupting the heavy air. "Is Nikki my new school?" It wasn't quite that coherent, but Megan was fluent in broken-Ava-toddler-speak so that's how she interpreted it.

Megan felt eyes on her but instead squatted down to Ava at the table.

"No honey, we haven't figured out our new school situation yet." She never was able to figure out baby talk. It felt like doing the kid a disservice to babble and not use real words. Megan's mind just didn't work that way.

Hearing Ava try to use complex four syllable words that adults used?

Worth it.

"I want to go to Miss Nikki's," Ava said with a little wine.

Crap

Megan looked up to give a wince to Nikki only to stop at the woman's joyful expression.

"Oh, I would love that," she gushed. "Are you looking for a new school for them?"

Megan cut her eyes to Danny and he shrugged. "Hadn't gotten around to talking about it yet with her."

She narrowed her eyes on him and then turned back to Nikki.

"Daycare is a little bit of a hot topic right now in our household. They reduced their open hours and have closed Theo's class on Fridays at a minimum. The director suggested that more closures will be coming if the staffing situation can't get figured out. So I'm looking for alternatives so work doesn't ki—" She stopped, all too aware of Ava's eyes on her. She'd rather not introduce the concept of 'killing' to the three-year-old, "—clobber me for missing more time."

Nikki clapped her hands and reached down and scooped up Theo from Danny who was on the floor with him still. "That could be fun, little man. Fridays with Nikki!" She squeezed his cheeks and he gave a semblance of a grin back at her. Nikki tossed out a hip expertly, set Theo on it, and turned to Megan. "You don't need to decide right now. Just think about it. But I would absolutely adore watching your children whenever you needed an extra set of hands."

"Told you."

"Quiet, you," Megan piped back to the handsome and smug peanut gallery. "I promise I'll think about it," she assured Nikki.

The generosity of the offer made her stomach squirm.

But it wasn't like she was able to not give it some consideration.

Rock and a hard place and all that.

Without meaning to, her eyes cut to Danny. It wasn't like he had a horse in this race. But somehow it still felt like he did. He had been there both times that Megan had come with the kids, but it wasn't like he was going to be able to do that during the week. How would Nikki fair when it was just her and no Danny to spread the childcare workload? Ava could be exhausting, god love her.

Danny sensed her hesitation. "Again, no pressure." He stood and approached his mom. He then plucked Theo off of his mom's hip and put him on his own. Danny then turned to address Megan. "But, like I've already said, I agree with my mom. I think it would be a good break for you to not have to worry about daycare closures, staffing issues, having to pack lunches and snacks every day—"

Before he could continue, Nikki interrupted with an outraged gasp.

Megan's heart dropped and she swiftly started inspecting the children.

Oh god, what was wrong with the kids? Was Ava choking?

When both were visibly fine, Megan gave a confused look to Nikki, asking why she was gasping like someone had poked out an eye with a pair of scissors.

"They don't even give the kids snacks?"

Jeesh, that was all? It was hardly a capital offense.

"Uh, yeah? Most places nowadays make you do lunches and snacks, I think."

"Not at Nikki's," the older woman declared solemnly. Oh shit. She patted herself on the chest. "At my place, I will feed them, and they will love it. One less thing for you to worry about and it can be a learning experience for both to learn how to be in the kitchen. There are lots of ways to make it interactive and fun."

Shit, the woman was a teacher right down to her core. She must have been the absolute shit in her prime.

"Don't let her fool you, she wasn't this always put together."

Both women's eyes flew to Danny, who was watching Megan with a somber look again. Nikki looked ready to fight him about that until he continued, refusing to move his eyes from Megan's.

"She's supermom but she's not *supermom,* if you know what I mean. She has her strengths and she has her weaknesses, just like any other parent. Yeah, she loves doing arts and crafts and can make food from scratch, but it wasn't always like that. Especially when I was younger and required so much more time and attention. I don't remember what pieces of artwork she put on the walls, or whether she made homemade mac and cheese or if she used store brand. I just remember her being there and caring." He was giving her a heavy look that had her equal parts embarrassed and *seen*.

How did he know her so well?

"So don't compare yourself to her. She has all day long to make purees and freezer meals. She has years of training and experience on how to deal with kids. Parenting isn't a competition. And if it was, you're winning. Your kids are happy and healthy. That's all you need, Meg. Don't be someone you're not. If you're not the homemade puree and mac and cheese mom that's one hundred percent fine. You're you. Neurotic, adorable you."

Megan blinked.

Her normally loud mind was quiet.

How did he *know*? How did he see her so *easily*?

Nikki was now looking at Megan with a sad expression that had Megan's hands squeezing tight into fists.

Okay, enough of that.

Megan swallowed the burn in her throat and avoided Danny's probing eyes as she squatted next to Ava.

"Time to go, baby doll. We need to go home and get the house ready for Nikki to come over and play with you and Theo there."

Megan slid Ava off the chair and pushed to a stand, her thighs burning.

When did Ava get so heavy?

Still avoiding Danny's eyes, she said, "I'll definitely think about it. I could use the help. Obviously. And hey, maybe Theo's dad will turn out to be a total stud and have a connection to another daycare, or a nannying service, or something." She shrugged as if it wasn't a big deal. "You never know."

Or he could legally fight her, win, and take Theo from her, thereby rendering her need for Friday care moot. And completely breaking her heart and soul in the process.

Breathe. Breathe. Breathe.

"That's all I ask. I'm up at five-thirty every day. You can drop off the kids pretty much as early as you want and there's no rush at night. You can pick them up pretty much anytime. Except for Mondays, I have bingo."

Danny nodded seriously. "Don't interrupt her bingo time, for anything."

Megan felt the burn start again in her sinuses and willed herself not to cry.

Swollen eyes wouldn't be a fun look for her upcoming "non-date" date with Danny that evening.

But even so, she reminded herself that even though Danny and Nikki *felt* long-term, people very rarely stuck around and answered when you needed them. So, even though they were ingraining themselves in her very everyday life with an ease that was scary, Megan could feel herself tightening up, preparing herself for the day they'd eventually leave.

And she'd be back to being alone.

# CHAPTER NINETEEN

# September 10, Saturday
## Megan

Danny and Nikki followed Megan to her apartment. Not having to bring the kids and their stuff up and down their stairs solo was a game changer.

No wonder people got married.

After Nikki was happily settled in with the kids, Megan zipped into "comfy" clothes per Danny's instructions and ushered him out the door, uncomfortable with having him loose in her home.

God only knew what he'd get into.

Somehow, someway, he'd naturally stumble upon a missing vibrator or something.

The universe was funny like that.

As they made their way back down the stairs, Danny rubbed his hands together eagerly. "Are you ready for this?"

Megan rolled her eyes and gave him a small grin. "What did I let you talk me into?"

Danny's smile widened and he threw her arm around her shoulder tugging her close. "Trust me, you're gonna love it"

The smell of leather drifted over to her and once again she found herself wondering how expensive his cologne or body wash must be to offer such an authentic leather smell.

He walked her down to the car, all while telling her stories of the kids' morning while she was working on Nikki's project.

He left nothing out: funny things Ava said, a cute face Theo made, Ava's favorite food she made.

"I'm serious. You really should consider my mom to watch both kids."

Without pausing a beat, he walked around to the passenger side of his SUV and opened the door for her.

She shouldn't have been surprised based on his relationship with his mom and his general disposition, yet somehow butterflies still curled, deepened in her belly at the kind gesture.

"That's a lot to ask of her," Megan said as she climbed up in the seat.

Megan waited until he made his way around the car and into the driver's seat, before continuing their conversation. "I would be taking away your mom's Fridays, on top of interrupting her schedule in the middle of the day.

"A few weeks ago, you mentioned how much she loves to get espressos with her friends on Tuesday afternoons, and how she likes to hang out at the bookstore on Fridays. I'd be taking that away from her if I did take her up on her offer." Megan rolled her lips together and looked out the window. "Plus, what if she decides that the kids are too much work for her and cancels on me? I'm not saying she will," she hurried to say. "But what then? I'm out of options again."

"Hey." Danny's soft call had her looking back at him. "One hundred percent honest right here, right now." His soft blueish green eyes almost glowed in the afternoon sun shining through the windshield. "My mom's no pushover, except sometimes when it comes to my dad." His face took on a sour look for half a second before smoothing out. "If she said she was willing and eager, then she is. She's sometimes honest to a fault and she would never lie to make you feel better. If she didn't genuinely enjoy spending time with your kids, she wouldn't have offered. The fact that she'd rather watch your kids and go hang out at a bookstore or get coffee with friends says a lot about what she thinks about your kids." He paused and reached out a hand and tapped her nose. "And what she thinks about *you*."

"What if she's just offering because she feels bad for me?" Her voice sounded small. And pathetic. But she couldn't stop herself from asking.

"Why in the world would she feel bad for you? You're a badass. But even badasses can use a hand now and then. My mom knows that firsthand."

Almost as if he knew she needed the mental space, he was silent for the rest of their car ride.

About five minutes into the car ride, he turned on a soft country music station and put it on low. Danny sang under his breath, his long strong fingers tapping on the steering wheel as he bobbed along to the music.

Megan caught herself watching him drive.

He did it with the same way he did everything: with confidence and no hesitation

He wasn't reckless but his brakes definitely got a work out, and the guy had a need for speed.

"I have something I've been wondering, and I didn't know if we were close enough to ask," she said. "You seem to enjoy playing with the kids..."

"I spent my whole life helping my mom with her various daycares and babysitting gigs. So, yeah, I like kids."

Megan chewed on her lips. Why the hell not? They were friends and he was trying to get his mom to be her babysitter. Not only that, but he was also trying to find her son's biological father.

She shifted so she could face him better in the car. "You've been quoted, on multiple occasions, as saying you never want kids."

"Is that a question?"

"Why don't you want kids if you enjoy them so much?"

Danny's face was still and his fingers stopped tapping on the steering wheel. He shot her a quick look before putting his eyes back on the road, clearly chewing over what he wanted to say.

Megan could wait out a toddler sitting on the potty. She could wait out Danny.

But he didn't make her wait long.

As he threw on his blinker and slowed to turn, he shot her a quick look. His face did not have quite the same free and easy expression as it normally had.

"I love kids. I think they're great. In another world, I might even have been a teacher." He shrugged. "But to be frank, my dad's a shithead." His straight nose curled and distaste as he said it. "I'm much better off being a fun uncle, rather than a deadbeat dad."

She gasped. "What in the world would make you think you're going to be a deadbeat dad? Have you *seen* you?"

He threw the truck in park and looked over to her, his face a little torn. "I don't know. Genetics?" He chewed on his lip before continuing. "I had a problem with alcohol a while back. By some miracle or act of pressure from the Spartans' management, the media never caught wind of it and I was able to deal with it privately. But knowing that not only did my grandfather and father have a problem with alcohol, but I did too, the similarities there were too stark. I don't want to risk it. No child deserves a drunk for a dad."

Megan inspected him, looking for signs that he was battling an addiction. "You don't look like you're a struggling alcoholic..." She was unsure how to phrase her question.

Danny let out a soft chuckle.

"A little over a year sober," he said with a proud smile but then became solemn again. "But that doesn't change facts. Any genes I have to pass on would have that tendency. Would have that risk. And I don't want any kid of mine to carry on that family legacy."

She took a chance and rested her hand on his that was resting on the center console. "It looks like you're doing all right," she said softly, smiling up at him.

His smile turned into a wolfish grin.

"I am, and I'll be doing even better in ten minutes."

Megan looked around at the nondescript building and tried not to let her lack of confidence show.

What the hell she had gotten herself into?

Was it good or bad that she took the time to shave in the shower? And why did she care?

# CHAPTER TWENTY

# September 10, Saturday
## Megan

"Are you ready for this?" Danny asked.

"I don't even know what *this* is," she reminded him

Danny smiled big and tapped the center console twice. "I know. It makes this even better. Let's go."

He was out and to her side of the vehicle before she even realized what was happening. In true Danny fashion, he had her door open and was offering his hand so she could climb out of the truck.

Megan caught a whiff of his yummy cologne as she walked by, and she had to fight not to linger and take another deep inhale of the warm scent.

Again with the car door opening—*who was this guy?* How could he open car doors one minute and look like he was undressing her in his mind the next?

She gave him a ridiculous look. "Do I look like the type of woman who would demand a guy open a car door for her?"

Danny just grinned. "When we get back to your place tonight and my mom asks you if I open the door for you, now we don't need to lie. I'm all for feminism but that doesn't mean I can't be polite."

She looked up at the nondescript building and cocked her head.

Was this the FBI headquarters? It certainly fit the bill.

Where the hell were they?

Her mind jumped back to his chivalrous behavior, which was so at odds with his horndog admiration from earlier. Danny Parker was an enigma.

"Would you open the car door for one of your teammates?"

Dani leveled her with a look that had her chuckling.

"I thought so."

Danny stopped walking and turned to look at her. "I'm assuming you're just giving me shit just to give me shit and not because it really bothers you, but I do want to be sure, so please confirm."

His expression was somber, and Megan felt a twinge of discomfort. Even though she felt like she had known him forever rather than a few weeks, they really didn't know each other well enough for her to be busting his chops like this.

She reached out and touched his arm quickly before pulling it back. "Yeah, you're right. I'm sorry. I'm just teasing. Actually," she paused and chose her next words carefully. "I actually kind of like you opening the door for me. At work, we're always opening the doors for clients and letting them go first. Clearly, I'm a feminist," she paused. "Or maybe feminist isn't the right word..." She tucked her hair behind her ear. "Maybe I am an equalist? Is that a thing?"

"I think the term is still feminist," he said with a soft smile.

Megan rolled her eyes. "Whatever the term is. I'm a person who believes in equality for all." She looked up at his pretty blue-green eyes. "I'm sorry for teasing. It was very sweet that you opened the door for me—"

"And I will never do so again."

"*And,*" she chuckled, "you can absolutely do so again. *And* I look forward to it."

As they stared into each other's faces, Megan felt her small smile slide off her lips. Instead, she found herself wondering how in the world she got mixed up with someone like Danny, and wondered at how the strange attraction between them even developed. They couldn't be more opposite.

Sure, she had seen him at various events throughout the years, just by being a friend of Lexie and the other book club babes. But she didn't think she and Danny ever actually exchanged words. She always admired him, and some of the other player hotties, from afar.

She loved that he was a brief distraction in her otherwise heavy world. She was doing her best but her neurospicy tendencies had been bumped into overdrive since Theo entered the picture. She was slowly losing herself. Losing her joy. Depression was looming and she was spiraling. And Danny wasn't long-term, she knew that. But looking at him now? It felt so easy being with him that she could trick herself into forgetting that. She could trick herself into believing that he was long-term. That he was endgame. That he would have a 'come to Jesus', realize he was in love with her, and they'd all live happily ever after.

Her friend Emma wrote a romantic suspense novel with a similar premise years ago. Maybe it wasn't that far off.

Megan bit back her scoff. A girl could dream, as long as her feet were still planted firmly on the ground.

She knew he wasn't the type of guy that would play Daddy to Theo and Ava, but she was *lonely*. Having Danny around gave her a sense of peace. A reminder to not take life so seriously. He gave her a glimpse of the person she used to be before the kids came along, her cousin died, and her money and time got tight.

It was like he saw her beyond the identity of just being a mom or an employee.

Heck, it was like he saw her beyond her just being a woman.

It was like he saw her just for *her*.

The crankiness, cynicism, forgetfulness, neurotic-ness, borderline obsessive tendencies, and the anxiety-riddled mess that she was.

She hadn't hidden her snark from him on a single occasion and rather than being put off by her rough edges, instead, he saw it, processed it, and rose to the unintended challenge of smoothing them out. Or at least just gliding over them without getting cut.

Danny coughed slightly into a fist and fidgeted.

"I, uh," he stuttered in a way that was very unlike him. He shifted his weight on his feet and nodded towards the black metal door next to them. "You ready?"

Megan rubbed her hands together, fighting off the blush that their momentary stare-down had caused. "As I'll ever be." She rubbed the palms of her hands on her pants, hoping she was dressed appropriately.

'Dress comfy' wasn't a whole lot to go on.

"Ladies first?" he asked with a wicked grin.

She rolled her eyes at his attempt to display his chivalry bone once again. Yet even so, she fought a giddy grin as she walked by him when he heaved open the weighty door.

Immediately, she was accosted with a smell so exclusive that it brought a smile to her lips.

It was so distinct, that a person only had to smell it one time and it would forever be imprinted in any person's memory bank.

Puppies.

She looked around with wide eyes, searching for the source.

Danny took her hand. "Come with me."

Electricity shot through her hand at the contact. It felt so comforting, so right, that Megan firmly gripped his hand back, giving it a small squeeze.

They made their way through a second doorway, and as it opened, the sound of puppy yaps filled the air.

Odin's beard.

There were puppies everywhere.

Where in the hell were they?

# CHAPTER TWENTY-ONE

# September 10, Saturday
## Megan

Heaven. This was heaven.

Puppies and dogs of assorted sizes ran around the warehouse sized room, tumbling over each other, chasing tails and spinning in circles. The room was filled with chaotic barking whines, and baby itty bitty adorable puppy growls. Sections were walled off with short walls and fences, separating some of the dogs, but each space was a healthy size.

Megan shot wide eyes at Danny. "You're joking." She breathed out, looking back at the cuteness overload in front of her.

She noticed him grin out of the corner of her eye.

"Phew. I was debating whether or not I should ask if you had a dog allergy before bringing you here. But looks like we're all set as you're not demanding we leave and buy some allergy meds immediately."

A lone puppy that was not confined to the back room chaos came over to explore Megan's shoes. Megan immediately dropped down and let the puppy smell her fingers.

"Hi, Sweetie Pie," she said in a high voice.

"What are you up to, Delilah?" Danny also dropped down and mimicked her falsetto as he rubbed at the puppy's floppy ears.

Immediately, Delilah opened her puppy jaws and started to gnaw on Danny's fingers.

The guy didn't even wince.

They were approached an exhausted yet happy elderly employee of this little piece of heaven in the city.

Danny pushed to stand and Megan followed suit only through a sheer force of willpower.

If she had her way, she'd been sitting on the ground with puppies climbing all over her and nothing would get her to move for the next fourteen hours.

Man, the kids would love a dog.

"Daniel Parker. I've told you a million times. Do not let her gnaw on you. It sets a bad precedent for the puppies." The older woman gave him a chastising look and then turned to Megan; the disciplinarian look now completely gone. "Welcome! You must be Megan. So great to meet you." The woman held out a hand for Megan to shake and Megan quickly tried to wipe the puppy drool off her fingers.

The woman waved and shook her head with a small chuckle. "Like I'm not covered in dog gunk all day long." She gripped Megan's hand in a firm shake. "I'm Trish Jenkins. I'm in charge of the center."

Megan looked around letting her appreciation show. "What exactly is this place?"

The woman gave a huge beaming smile at Danny before looking back at Megan. "This is the result of many years of hard work." She paused and gave a wry look to the football stud next to her. "And Danny's foolish generosity."

Danny barked out a rough laugh and crossed his strong arms on his chest. He gave the woman a tired yet amused look. "Mrs. Jenkins. I told you time and time again. This place wouldn't run without you, my initial contribution was nothing compared to what others have done."

She gave him the look a grandmother might give her grandson, "And what have your second, third, fourth, fifth, I could go on, contributions done? Are those *also* nothing?"

Danny rubbed the back of his neck and Megan's eyes caught on his biceps.

Yum.

As if he caught her looking, his eyes darted over to her.

Feeling unusually bubbly and happy, Megan gave him a cheeky smile. In a change of roles, he rolled his eyes and looked back at Trish.

"It's a good cause and the least I could do."

The woman looked unimpressed with his dismissal but let it go, turning back to Megan. "Well, as you can see, Mr. Patron Saint Parker won't accept any credit, but we're a puppy rescue center. We rescue animals for puppy mills and other abusive situations. Similar to a humane society, except we only deal in dogs. Danny helped us get off the ground and since then he comes a couple times a month to visit with the dogs." She leaned toward Megan. "It's important the dogs get exposed to a variety of people so they can adjust to life better when they're adopted. Big, little, tall, short, female, male. Danny even drags in his teammates occasionally—"

"I don't like to think of it as 'dragging,' per se..."

Trish continued, ignoring him, "As such, our puppies get adjusted to large, sometimes loud, men. It helps the adoption process when they aren't scared of the men in the households."

"I bet," Megan agreed, now looking around with a different perspective. Sure enough, there were a variety of things throughout the space that might spook another dog, but left in an innocuous place where the dogs could inspect when comfortable? What a great tactic.

"Anyway, I'll let Danny show you around and teach you the ropes. Let me know if you need me."

As they entered through the half wall door, Megan asked Danny quietly, "Do I need a waiver or anything?"

"Shh."

Rule breaker!

The air filled with the sounds of excited barks and playful yips. The atmosphere was warm and inviting, if a bit stinky, with adorable puppies in their various play yards in the huge space.

Her heartstrings pulled.

Megan and Danny found a spot in a quiet corner and plopped down on the ground.

Megan immediately removed her jacket and tossed it behind her. She slipped her phone out of the pocket to make sure she'd felt it if Nikki needed her.

Danny's long, muscular legs stretched out in front of them, the jean fabric clinging tight to his leg muscles.

Yeesh, that fabric needed to be commissioned by NASA.

He gave her a cheeky grin when he caught her staring.

She elbowed him and fought her blush. "Shut it, you. It'd be like walking into the Sistine Chapel and not looking up. It's impossible *not* to look."

He didn't say anything, but a smile grew bigger.

She rolled her eyes at him before looking across the room at the cautiously exploring puppies.

A lone, brave pup caught their scent and his head pointed in their direction.

"Here they come," Danny sang under his breath, leaning forward slightly.

And just like that, a herd of puppies trampled over to where they were sitting. They were immediately engulfed with little limbs and puppy breath.

Megan was swatted by tails, paws, heads, and ears. One puppy went so far as to prop his front paws on her chest and breathe heavy puppy breath up into her face.

Even as stinky as it was, it was still adorable.

She didn't have enough hands! She wanted to love them all!

Megan scrambled to make sure she was touching each puppy and doting affection on each one with silly inane baby talk.

Apparently, she couldn't figure out how to baby talk human children, but puppies? *That* her brain allowed.

She vaguely registered that Danny was doing the same thing next to her.

His big hands made the puppies look twice as small.

Some were so tiny they couldn't even climb up on his legs.

Her breath caught in her chest as she saw him cautiously reach around the more boisterous puppies and extend a slow finger towards one of the more reserved puppies. The puppy gave a slow smell, a timid lick, and then looked up at Danny with gorgeous, mismatched eyes.

"She's a beauty," Megan said softly under her breath so as not to spook the little Australian Shepherd puppy that was now exploring a little bit closer to Danny.

Danny matched her quiet tone. "Don't get me wrong. It's impossible to not adore every single puppy here. But somehow winning over the reserved ones, the quiet ones, the ones who have been burned before, the ones who are scared to trust to trust me...getting them to trust me...those ones feel like the biggest wins."

Thinly veiled, Mr. Parker.

A puppy tumbled off his thigh and bumped into the skittish one. The movement sent her flying back toward Danny's feet. She took a couple of quick steps away before venturing over to investigate Megan's shoes.

Megan felt a tingle shoot down her spine.

She turned to see Danny watching her.

"Am I the puppy?" she asked with a raised brow.

Danny leaned towards her slightly, careful not to disturb any of the romping dogs. "Only if you want to be," he said in a low voice.

More tingles danced, much lower in her belly this time.

His eyes danced down her body and came back up to her own. He continued in that low, sexy voice, "Do you want to roll over and let me rub your belly just to give it a trial run? I know how much you live trial runs."

She bumped her shoulder in him to distract herself from the butterflies flying south for winter. "Cut it, you."

He chuckled and leaned into her. "Come on. Keep it going. It's fun."

He gave her a pouty face and she rolled her eyes, once again biting back a smile.

"Fine," she grumbled. Megan leaned toward him and raised her brows, "but if you expect me to kick my leg for you, you'll be sadly mistaken."

A wicked gleam showed in his eyes and his smile deepened.

Apparently her flirty dog pun skills were weak given how entertained his face became.

"Oh, my dear little accountant...your leg won't be the only thing that starts shaking when I get my hands on you."

She rolled her lips to the side before leaning back slightly and giving him a haughty look. "Careful. You said 'when.'"

He continued to let his hands dance amongst the puppies around them. "I guess I did."

She didn't break eye contact. "Hey. We're *friends*. I have kids. We don't want things to get messy."

His expression turned into downright saucy trouble. "Promise?"

She shook her head and looked down at the puppies climbing around her lap.

"Danny—"

He leaned in closer, his voice dipping to a husky whisper that sent shivers down her spine. "Megan, we're playing. We know what we're doing, and we're just enjoying each other's company. If it bothers you, we'll stop. But you're *fun*. You challenge me and don't let me get away with shit. It's just...refreshing to be with you. Teasing and flirting, or not. Just say the word." His fingers brushed against her hand ever so slightly, igniting sparks that raced through her veins.

Who would have thought that he would have found *her* refreshing? That was his role to her.

Megan met his intense gaze, her heart racing in her chest. She cleared her throat, her voice coming out softer than she intended. "It's fun."

A mischievous smile tugged at the corner of his lips. "Good, because I have to say, even in this room full of adorable puppies, my attention seems to be gravitating toward a certain someone." He shot her a wink.

Her cheeks warmed. "Flattery will get you everywhere, Danny Parker."

He chuckled, the deep sound resonating in the air around them. "Don't I know it? I think my coaches have wanted to choke me on more than a few occasions over the years." He paused while remembering something. "Man, there was a time about a year and a half ago that I was really causing some problems for Butch. Thought the guy was going to put a hit out on me just to get my drama-filled ass off the team. Luckily, we're fine now, but man...that time was a bitch."

Megan laughed softly, basking in the warmth of their banter. "Hard to think of you not getting along with anyone."

He leaned in even closer, their shoulders almost touching. "I think I was 'getting along' with too many people, and that was the problem."

Their gazes locked, a charged energy passing between them that felt both exciting and dangerous. Megan's heart raced as she held his gaze, the puppies around them becoming background noise to their silent exchange.

Danny's fingers brushed against hers again, this time intentionally, and a jolt of electricity seemed to travel from her hand to her core. "You know, this platonic date night of ours might end up being the most memorable date I've had."

She swallowed hard, her voice barely a whisper. "It doesn't seem very fancy. And it won't end in sex, so either my conversation skills are much better than I thought, or your previous dates have seriously sucked balls."

He tilted his head, his lips dangerously close to her ear. "Maybe don't use the phrase 'sex' and 'suck balls' in the same sentence. Makes me question whether I was a sex addict or just a drunk. And then it makes me want to take you home just to find out"

Megan's breath caught, her pulse pounding in her ears.

"But we're just friends, so I can't. So no more naughty words, Miss Meg."

She could feel the warmth of his body, the magnetic pull between them impossible to ignore. In that moment, surrounded by playful puppies and suppressed desires, Megan realized that this platonic date might be the beginning of something much more complicated, and infinitely more exciting and forbidden than expected.

As the puppies continued their adorable antics, Megan and Danny shared a charged silence, a thousand unspoken words hanging in the air. It was a moment suspended in time, a moment that held the promise of something new and exhilarating, and still, impossible.

After a few minutes, they began teasing and talking anew, discussing the kids, Starla, football, and the team. Once the banter got back on safe ground, the time flew. An hour passed, and Danny leaned back slightly, stretching his back. "Ready to move on to phase two of our tour of puppy paradise?"

Megan nodded. "Absolutely."

She never could have dreamed that in five short minutes, Danny would be getting an up close and personal view of her nipples, and that she'd be forever thankful that she took the time to shave.

# CHAPTER TWENTY-TWO

# September 10, Saturday
## Megan

They entered a rather stark room with several drains on the floor as well as some big dog-sized tubs, and hoses coming from the ceiling. All the while, the puppies still danced around their feet.

Megan couldn't help but stop and give them loving pets every couple of steps.

"Am I going to be able to get you out of here when we're done?"

Megan chuckled and looked up at him. "I don't think so. My boss might even have to move my desk here. I'll work remotely from now on."

She gave another head a pat and he laughed. "Would you get any work done?"

Her low chuckle answered that question.

Megan turned to look at Danny and stopped short, her breath catching. Danny had shucked his shirt, tossing it on a nearby stainless-steel table and was now just standing there in jeans and sneakers. The edge of his boxers sat higher on his hips than the jeans and the brand should have been paying him endorsements...if they weren't already.

Megan felt like a cartoon character who needed to pull her jaw back shut.

"Can I help you, Miss Meg? I'm not a piece of meat, ya know," he teased in a drawl. With attitude, he cocked out a hip and crossed his arms on his beefy chest.

Megan literally shook her head to try to knock some sense into her brain.

The guys she had been with in the past were not necessarily athletically inclined. They were more of the intellectual nature than physical.

Sitting at a computer and using spreadsheets and software did not give a man a body like *that.*

To cover her embarrassment, "God, do you ever leave the gym?"

Danny looked down at his pectoral muscles and thick arms across his chest and, ridiculously, his boobs started bouncing. "Oh, these old things?" He flexed his pecs back and forth.

Tingles danced in Megan's belly, up her chest, into her throat. Even her head felt light.

Man.

When was the last time she had felt so unburdened and carefree?

Being around Danny was light and fluffy. Airy.

It was like he injected oxygen into a closed room.

Megan took a deep breath and rolled her eyes at his still flexing chest muscles. And without meaning to, she reached forward and placed her hand on his chest and gave him a small push.

"Braggart," she teased with a laugh. She felt the hard, sleek muscles of his chest flex as she made contact.

This time the butterflies didn't travel north, and she felt her lower stomach squeeze at the thrill.

Quick as a snake his arm shot out and he wrapped his hand around the wrist of the hand that was poking him. He held it there, just an inch away from his chest. They stayed there looking into each other's eyes. Their only contact was his hand on her wrist and Megan felt her breath grow heavy.

"Another rule," He growled. "No naughty words from that delectable mouth, and no touching when my shirt is off, and your eyes are heavy with sex like that."

She squeezed her legs together.

Danny always seemed like a good ol' boy. Someone always looking to have fun.

But once again, she was reminded that people were rarely only what they seemed.

Just because Danny was always happy and friendly it didn't mean that he couldn't be serious.

And judging by the look in his eyes as he stared down at her, and the slight wandering of his thumb on the inside of her wrist...she was thinking his thoughts had taken a very serious turn.

"I like rules. I have never met a rule I didn't like. So I can follow them. Promise. Starting now." She tried pulling her hand away, but he didn't release it. Instead his thumb kept burning a path of fire along her skin. One that shot straight to her center.

His intense expression didn't change. The easy smile didn't pop back onto his face and the  hungry look was still there.

Waiter! Bring them water!

Megan couldn't shake the low and heavy feeling sitting low in her gut.

One by one, his fingers released.

Danny jerked back to the tubs and roughly twisted a couple nozzles to get the water flowing.

Holy Hera.

He said in a gravelly voice, "If you have a shirt on underneath that, I would suggest you strip down to your lowest layer. Otherwise, you're going to get very wet, very sudsy, and very, very hairy in a minute."

Megan looked down at her comfy t-shirt and made a pro/con list in her head.

On one hand, she really didn't want to spend the rest of their evening together in a wet and dirty shirt.

But on the other hand, she really didn't want to just wear her cami tank top in front of Danny.

Not when he stood there in front of her with all those deliciously tanned muscles exposed.

Crap on a cracker.

She felt Danny approach and his hand entered her view. He raised her chin with his pointer finger. "What's up? Talk to me. Why do you look like I kicked a puppy?" His voice was low and soft, but still had the hint of the arousal that was in his eyes earlier.

"You work out a lot," she said quickly and he blinked. "I have two kids at home. I work sixty hours a week." Again, he said nothing and just watched her closely. "I don't go to the gym." He just cocked his head, and she moved her hand up and down referencing his godliness. "I don't look like you."

"Good, because I'm not gay and I wouldn't want you to look like me."

"That's not what I mean. I'm just not fit and tan and sexy."

He chuckled and shook his head dropping his hand from under her chin. "Oh, my dear Meg. How wrong you are. Lose the shirt, darlin'. We got some puppies to clean." He then paused and looked toward the doorway. "Miss Jenkins might have an extra one you can wear if you are feeling really uncomfortable."

She could only imagine what the little old lady had for an extra shirt. It was fine. She was just being finicky.

Quickly, she shook her head. "No, it's fine. I just wanted you to be prepared for what you were about to see. It's a mom-bod, not a superhero bod."

Danny chuckled again but didn't say anything more as he turned and twisted more knobs and pulled more soap bottles from the shelves.

Megan quickly pulled off her top shirt and tossed it on the same table Danny had put his shirt on.

When she turned around, she immediately heard a clang as one of the soap bottles fell to the floor.

Her eyes darted from the puppies scattered on the floor to where Danny was standing near the tub. Megan saw his eyes locked on her body, his expression frozen, his eyes wide.

"Danny?"

He shook his head and visibly tore his eyes from her chest and made eye contact with her.

"Meg, my little kitten." He growled, even lower than he had earlier. "There was nothing in the world that you could have said to 'prepare' me for *that*. Fucking hell, woman. I think I just had a stroke. Do you not own a mirror?"

She looked down at her skintight cami. It wasn't something she wore by itself. She didn't have the body type or the confidence. But she loved having them on under her shirts, so when she was playing with the kids and her shirt rode up, her skin wasn't exposed. Something about the air on her skin between her shirt and her pants was a big 'ick' for her.

So his appreciation? It was nice. And clearly not staged given he was still staring. Megan felt the heat bloom in her cheeks and spread down her neck and chest.

She knew she wasn't a troll. But still. That was nice.

Danny gave a rough cough and clapped his hands. "Okay, let's get started."

For once, America's Guy seemed at a loss for words.

As they brought the first puppy to the tub, Megan dipped her hand into the soapy water, creating a cascade of bubbles. She splashed some playfully towards Danny, her wicked chuckle mingling with the sound waiting barks by their feet. "Oops! Sorry."

Danny, finally out of his stupor, gave her a long, assessing look.

"I'm a professional athlete, Miss Meg. You think I can't handle a little competition?" Danny retaliated, scooping up a handful of water and flicking it towards Megan, the droplets landing on her cheeks and hair. "Careful. You might regret provoking me."

With more random splashes and teases, they worked on the current pup, letting their conversation ebb and flow naturally.

Megan grinned mischievously as she playfully splashed some more water towards Danny. "You know, this reminds me of bath time with my kids. Except, it's a lot more fun to not have to worry about cleaning up after."

Danny chuckled, his eyes sparkling with amusement. "Well, I'm glad I can offer a more entertaining bath experience. Does Ava wriggle like this in the tub or is she calm and easy?"

"Oh, god, no. Not calm and easy," Megan replied, shaking her head. "One time, she decided to use an entire bottle of bubble bath. I was sitting right next to the tub giving Theo a bottle and didn't even notice. I swear it looked like a foam party gone wrong. I had bubbles up to my waist."

Danny grinned. "Sounds like a nightmare for you, and a blast to me. Did you join in on the foam party or shut it down?"

Megan smirked, recalling the memory. "My inner anxiety was going nuts. But she looked so damn happy I stuffed down the unease and played for as long as I could. We ended up having a bubble fight in the bathroom, and by the time we were done, we were all covered in bubbles. I had to call over our friends Mickey and Benji to help deal with the aftermath, but it was worth it for the laughter." Megan paused, her hands resting on the small, wet pup in front of her. "She still brings it up sometimes when we're cuddling before bed."

Megan's heart squeezed at the love she felt for her little princess. How could you love someone so much it hurt? How was that even healthy?

Their eyes locked again, a shared understanding passing between them. Megan's voice softened as she continued, her words laced with emotion. "You know, there's something liberating about letting go, embracing the mess, and finding joy in unexpected moments. Like this." She dripped some bubbles from her hands. "Though, it's much easier to do in an environment you own, or don't have to worry about cleanup maintenance."

Danny nodded, his gaze intense and focused. "Sometimes, life's best memories are made in the messiest of situations."

"When did you become a sage?"

"I think it's the cannabis-infused soap." He nodded toward the doggy shampoo that had a leaf on the outside that very much indeed looked like a pot leaf.

"Fun marketing," Megan remarked as she inspected the bottle and rubbed her hands through the fur of the wiggling puppy.

"Mrs. Jenkins takes donations of dog shampoo from anywhere. This place had a disgruntled employee that printed a bunch of...inappropriate labels and attached them to the bottles. You should have seen the bottles from a few weeks ago. NSFW."

She smiled and held his contended grin.

Man, he was just so...easy.

As they moved from one puppy to another, they always found moments to douse each other with more water and suds.

Megan couldn't help but notice the way Danny's wet skin glistened in the light, his muscles flexing with every playful motion. Every time he grazed her wet, slick hands with his own, it felt like she was touching an electric eel.

Probably not the same sensation, but damn close.

Their bodies continually brushed against each other, sending jolts of desire through Megan's veins. She could feel the heat emanating from Danny, a silent invitation that was impossible to ignore. Their laughter mingled with stolen glances, and their eyes held lingering gazes that spoke volumes.

Forbidden, impossible, not allowed.

At one point, Megan bent over to reach a spot on a particularly wriggly puppy and the water splashed over her back and chest. She felt it as Danny's eyes followed the droplets as they traced a path down her skin, a trail of temptation.

Once she stood straight again, she tried to ignore the chilly wet that was drenching the front of her thin cami. Across from her, she'd frequently catch Danny's eyes lingering on her wet chest, a mixture of pain and desire etched in his handsome face. It stirred something within her, a boldness she hadn't felt in a long time. As if the wet and chill wasn't doing the job enough, having his eyes devouring her, had her nipples pushing hard at the fabric of her tank.

God, they were starting to ache.

They wanted to be *touched*.

Every time she rubbed against them with her elbows or bumped them against the edge of the tub, her arousal grew. God, why did her and Danny have to be off limits? He'd fix that ache in a matter of seconds. He'd be down for a quickie in the bathroom. She hadn't had a public bathroom quickie in years, but fuck, it had to be like riding a bike.

And with the way Danny was staring at her, all hot and heavy, he wanted to be that bike.

Megan did her best to ignore her growing ache. It wouldn't get her anywhere and it would only cause trouble.

As the bath time fun continued, their playful banter gradually shifted into a more intimate and charged conversation. The puppies provided the perfect distraction, but the chemistry between them was undeniable. Their words and gestures carried a hidden promise, a hint of what could be, but never would.

As the last puppy on their waiting list was bathed, Megan found herself standing face to face with Danny, the air thick with...something.

Their eyes locked, and Megan's heart raced, her breathing shallow. In that moment, they both knew this puppy bath had become much more than just a platonic friendly date activity.

It was a line crossed.

The sound of the puppies' excited barks and the distant hum of the rescue center faded into the background as they found themselves closer, their lips inches apart. The world around them ceased to exist as their bodies leaned into the charged silence...

A bump at their feet caused them each to reluctantly pull away, a mixture of disappointment and hunger etched on their faces.

And the night wasn't even over yet.

# CHAPTER TWENTY-THREE

# September 10, Saturday
## Megan

"You clearly love dogs, so why don't you have one again?" Danny forked some spaghetti into his mouth and washed it down with some water.

The restaurant was cozy, the aroma of various pastas dishes filled the air as Megan and Danny settled into their booth, their laughter and conversation flowing effortlessly in a continuation of that from the puppy rescue center.

Megan's heart still fluttered from their playful puppy bath adventure earlier, but she couldn't help but they were walking a tightrope between friendly flirting...and not.

"I'd love a dog to have around. If not for myself, then just to teach my kids to be comfortable around them and how to care for them, but it's not in the cards. I don't have the time, energy, or frankly, the money, to devote to a dog right now. Maybe one day."

She twisted her lips to the side and tried to suffocate the sadness that was creeping into her heart.

"When I was growing up, my neighbor had this incredible dog," Megan began, her voice tinged with nostalgia. "His name was Max, a golden retriever with the biggest heart. He was always so gentle and loving."

Danny's eyes sparkled with interest. "Oh, yeah?"

A wistful smile graced Megan's lips as she continued, her voice filled with fondness. "They never seemed to care that he spent most of his time with me. Max was my confidant, my partner in crime. Whenever I had a bad day, I would go home, make a peanut butter sandwich for him, grab him from their place, and we would walk in the woods together. He never judged, was always happy to see me, and never abandoned me. He was the epitome of loyalty. You called; you just knew he'd come running. He'd never not answer your call."

Danny leaned forward; his face soft.

Megan's gaze turned distant; her eyes clouded with a hint of sadness. "Until one day, he didn't. The rumor was that someone left a bucket of antifreeze out, and Max got into it. It was...devastating. I remember feeling so helpless, so heartbroken. Losing Max taught me how fragile life can be and how much I longed for a dog of my own, but circumstances never allowed it."

Danny's expression softened, a hint of compassion in his eyes. "One day, you'll have that dog for you and your kids. You'll get there."

Megan's sad eyes locked with Danny's, her heart heavy with longing.

Danny nodded, a contemplative expression on his face.

Megan reached across the table, her hand resting gently on Danny's, a silent gesture of gratitude.

"Man, I know how to kill a mood." She tried to chuckle but it sounded forced. Probably because it was.

Danny did that thing of his where he was watching her closely, like he was trying to figure something out. Goosebumps erupted.

"A peanut butter sandwich, huh? A real gourmet meal for your bestie."

She smiled and took a quick sip of her water. "Don't even. I'm sure it's probably ten shades of terrible to feed that to a dog, but I was a kid and didn't know better. My cooking skills haven't improved any, either. My idea of cooking dinners for the kids is to heat up a freezer meal and dole it out into little cups. And it's usually something that can be reheated and served later for lunches. There's not much I know how to make from scratch.

"Starla and me," she paused, taking a deep breath to steal herself. "We had a lot of ramen when we first came to the city."

Danny's eyes turned soft. "Don't put yourself down. Meal prep is still meal prep. Whether you're doing it by cooked meals, baking your own bread, or whether you're buying the bread at the store and making your own peanut butter sandwich for their—"

"No peanut butter allowed. It has to be Sun Butter."

Damn, she interrupted him again. She needed to stop doing that.

"Sun Butter?" His face turned disgusted. "I guess we didn't really deal with peanut allergies with my mom's kiddos. Gross."

"My thoughts exactly."

Danny chuckled and rubbed his chest. "So, yeah, sounds like you're a pro at sun butter sandwiches now. Though," he hesitated, "are you sure it was the antifreeze and not your ever-so-thoughtful meals?"

Silence.

Nothing but silence in her head.

Oh god.

She looked up at him in horror, her mouth hanging open.

At her aghast expression, he quickly course corrected. "I'm teasing! I'm sure it wasn't sandwiches. Jesus, fuck, sorry! It was just a joke." He finished with a wince.

Holy shit. Had she killed her best dog friend?

Well, now it was doubly good that she didn't have a dog. She'd probably kill that one too.

Holy Hera.

Danny stared intently at his plate, dragging his fork in the food there.

She then looked down at his plate, and chuckled at the fact that he had rolled all of the peas from his complex platter to the side and was eating around them.

"Does your mother know you really don't like peas?" she asked with a grin.

He stilled and then looked up at her. "I like my mom's peas," he said with a completely straight face.

Megan cocked her head at him, unsure whether she should call him a liar or whether his mom's peas really were just that good.

"Hey, Megan?"

She looked up and stilled at the sober expression on his face.

"You might not have Max anymore, but you have me. If you call, I promise, I will always answer. I give you my word. No trial run needed. If you need me, I'll be there." He seemed to be waiting for her confirmation, so she swallowed past the lump in her throat, blinked away the burn in her nose, and nodded.

"No trial run needed," she agreed.

# CHAPTER TWENTY-FOUR

# September 13, Tuesday
## Megan

Megan had just finished loading her shopping cart with 'appropriately shaped pretzels' when her phone rang. She glanced at the screen and saw Danny's name flashing. It had been a couple of days since their non-date date, and she still smiled whenever she thought about it.

With a mixture of curiosity and anticipation, she answered the call.

"Hey there," Megan greeted, her voice filled with warmth.

"Hey, there yourself," Danny replied, a hint of excitement in his voice. "I've got more good news. Maybe. Depends on how you look at it."

Megan's heart skipped a beat. She wasn't sure what to expect, but she knew it could be significant. "What is it?"

"Well, I finally touched base with a couple of our guys from the team that were traded within the last year, and all of them don't recognize Starla. So we're really getting down to the wire on you needing to make a decision. Most of the good ones are out of the potential pool. Now we're going to start dancing in not so good territory," Danny began, his voice slightly hesitant.

Megan nodded, even though Danny couldn't see her. She remembered their conversation well.

The uncertainty of all of this was causing all sorts of mixed emotions within her.

Part of her was relieved, knowing that none of her friends' significant others were Theo's secret baby daddy. Yet, there was also a tinge of disappointment. They all would have been great dad options for Theo. And none of them would have tried to take him from her.

She took a deep breath, trying to process her feelings. "I...I don't know how to feel about that," Megan admitted honestly. "On one hand, I'm relieved because it would have been a mess if any of our friends turned out to be Theo's dad. But on the other hand, I can't help but wonder if it would have been better for Theo to be their kid."

Danny hummed in agreement. "Yeah, I get that. But we'll figure it out. One way or another. Just a couple more guys to touch base with. There are a few good ones left I just haven't gotten alone yet. I'll work on them asap so we can figure out our next move."

Our?

Butterflies danced.

As Megan finished the call, she focused her attention on her energetic, and loud, kids. The grocery store seemed busier than usual, with people hustling through the aisles and the faint sound of chatter echoing in the background. Theo was starting to get fussy, and Ava seemed determined to touch every item on the shelves.

Breathe, breathe, breathe.

She desperately needed to finish this shopping trip and get back home.

Just as she was struggling to maintain her composure and was fighting back the panic of the aisles closing in on her, a familiar figure appeared in the aisle.

Danny, with his easy smile and contagious energy, walked towards them with a swagger in his step.

Megan's heart skipped a beat, and suddenly, the grocery store felt less suffocating.

"Danny?"

He grinned mischievously. "You didn't think I'd let you wrangle these two rascals all by yourself, did you? I could hear them through the fre—... phone."

She gave him a tired yet grateful smile. "Well, I've managed so far, but an extra pair of hands never hurts."

As Danny joined Megan and the kids, their play filled the air. He effortlessly engaged with Theo and Ava, making them giggle and forget their earlier fussiness.

Megan watched, a mix of amusement and wonder on her face.

Here was a man who claimed he never wanted to be a dad, yet he seemed to relish these moments with her children.

Together, they maneuvered through the aisles, grabbing the essentials while indulging in some impromptu snacks for the kids.

At one point, Danny playfully juggled a few apples, showing off his skills to the unimpressed children.

"Tough crowd."

"You're not kidding," Megan agreed absently, looking quickly at the available fruits so they could keep moving.

As they made their way through the produce section, Danny spotted a bunch of bananas and couldn't resist. He picked one up, holding it up to his ear with a grin. "Hello, Banana Headquarters, we've got a fruity situation here!"

Ava burst into laughter, grabbing her own banana and mimicking Danny's actions.

Danny continued the playful act, pretending to have a serious conversation with the banana. "Yes, I understand, Mr. Banana. We'll make sure to keep the bunch in line. No bruised bananas on my watch!"

Danny lowered the banana, shooting Megan a wink.

They carried on with their silly banter as they navigated the aisles, Danny making funny faces and sounds to keep the kids entertained. He'd occasionally lift Ava up, pretending they were flying over the cereal aisle or bouncing on his shoulders like little acrobats.

Other shoppers couldn't help but smile at the sight of Danny's antics and the infectious laughter of the kids.

With their playtime giggles still lingering in the air, Megan paid for the groceries and they left the store.

As they loaded the groceries into the car, Megan turned to Danny with a playful glint in her eyes. "You know, you make a pretty good grocery shopping partner. I might have to bring you along more often."

Danny grinned, leaning against the car. "Well, someone's got to keep the bananas in line and provide some entertainment, right?"

"Absolutely."

"Do you want help bringing them up to your apartment?"

Megan stilled.

Oh.

Oh, that sounded heavenly.

But she didn't want to impose.

"Uh, no, I got it."

He watched her. "Nah, just changed my mind. I have to go over that direction anyway, so I'll help you bring them up and be on my way."

Liar.

She narrowed her eyes on him and he grinned unabashedly.

After they separately drove to her apartment, Megan was exiled to the apartment with the kids, while Danny single handedly carried up the groceries. To not have to worry about what to do with the kiddos while running the groceries up and down the stairs was a welcome relief.

No matter what option she chose, she always felt guilty about it after.

As she was putting the groceries away, Danny brought in the last bag and leaned against the counter next to her.

"So, you mentioned this the other day but I forgot to follow up on this." A playful smile tugged at the corners of his lips. "You've gotta spill the beans about this fantasy football addiction of yours."

Megan's cheeks flushed, a mix of embarrassment and amusement coloring her face. She chuckled softly, shaking her head. "There's not much to tell anymore. I used to manage other people's teams. Now I'm in a couple of different leagues, but just for fun and for myself. But I might have a bit of a reputation for being, uh, very invested."

Danny's eyes sparkled with mirth. "Invested? How did you get into managing people's teams? I'm guessing there's a story behind that."

Megan's laugh was a mixture of nostalgia and embarrassment. "Well, when I first came to the city, I needed to make ends meet, so I stumbled upon these underground gambling dens. I had a knack for picking the right teams to bet on, and soon enough, I found myself managing other people's fantasy football teams. It helped me pay for college and my apartment."

Danny's eyebrows shot up in surprise, a mixture of amusement and intrigue dancing in his eyes. "There's that much money in it?"

"Well, I had scholarships and my other jobs too."

He whistled low. "The rule-breaker accountant with a secret gambling side. That's both intriguing and hilarious."

Megan's blush deepened, her eyes meeting Danny's with a mix of vulnerability and worry. "Don't worry, I've left the underground dens behind. These days, it's all about friendly competition and enjoying the game. I won't steal and use your steam secrets. I'm not like Jen's dad."

Jen's dad had stolen her personal notes on each of the players awhile back. He used her notations about injuries to place a variety of bets. One of which could have cost Jen her life.

"Not for a second was I concerned." He reassured her, turning and grabbing some stuff to put in the fridge. He opened it and came to a halt.

Embarrassment flooded her senses and she wanted to hurl.

She rushed over to him and took the gallon of milk out of his hand, quickly inserting it onto a shelf and shutting the door promptly.

They stood there awkwardly, the silence only interrupted by occasional baby and toddler babbles from the next room.

"So, that's uh…"

"Yeah."

"And you…"

"Yeah."

"Okay, then."

"Okay."

Rolling her lips together, she looked up at him, hoping he wasn't thinking of fleeing and never talking to her again.

"The organization and colors help my brain feel less overwhelmed and cluttered." She pushed out, trying to convince him not to run away from them.

Danny just stood there, looking at her, his eyes working.

Finally, he said, "It's no prob, Meg. If you need to organize your fridge, house, dresser, kitchen, whatever, to help you function better, that's not a bad thing. I just wasn't expecting a Dewey decimal system." He ended with a grin.

She gave him a small push to his shoulder and let out a breath of relief.

"It's not the…" She growled as she turned and continued to put items away.

"Do you want help, or will I just mess it up for you and make things worse?"

Her heart thumped hard at the fact that he cared enough to ask.

"I got it. You can leave, or play with the kids, or whatever. Whatever you want."

"I can stay and chat with you?"

Her heart thumped harder.

"That works." She tried to hide her giddiness.

What was she? Thirteen?

Their conversation flowed and gradually shifted to football, and Megan leaned forward on the counter in front of him, her eyes sparkling with enthusiasm. "So, how are the Spartans vibing this year? You all are playing well but something feels...off."

Danny's face lit up, his passion for the game evident in his voice. "It's been interesting. We've had some intense matchups and a few close calls, but we're fighting hard. And yeah, the team dynamics have been...intriguing lately."

Megan nodded, "It's translating a bit on the field."

"Damn, darlin'. Don't pull any punches." Danny's lips curled into a lopsided grin and he looked down at her mouth and paused there. He opened his mouth to say something and was interrupted by his phone ringing.

Megan pushed away and played around with straightening some items on the counter.

Right angles for the corners of the papers....

"Hey, Meg? I gotta get going. I'll call you later?"

She nodded and before she could react, he plopped a soft, somewhat lingering, kiss on her cheek and was out the door.

Oh.

*Friends* did that?

# CHAPTER TWENTY-FIVE

# September 15, Thursday
## Danny

Danny sat in his living room, contemplating the events of the past few weeks with a smile on his face. The playful puppy bath, their banter at dinner, and the undeniable connection he felt with Megan had left him yearning for more. He couldn't deny the attraction that simmered between them, but he understood the complications it would add. She didn't need a guy coming in and messing up her life with the kids. Especially with them closing in on answers on Theo's dad.

His thoughts were interrupted by the sound of his phone ringing, and his heart skipped a beat when he saw Megan's name flashing on the screen.

"Hey, darlin', miss me already?"

Megan's voice trembled with a mix of panic and desperation. "Danny, I'm so sorry to ask, but I'm in a bind. Theo has a fever, and Ava has a runny nose. The daycare is kicking them out, and I'm stuck in a work meeting that I can't miss. I hate to ask, but I don't know who else to turn to. Can you pick them up from daycare for me?"

Danny's brows furrowed while he tried to figure out how to get out of his mandatory game review this afternoon. " Of course I'll pick them up. No worries. I'll be there right away. Take care of your meeting, and I'll take care of the kids."

Relief flooded Megan's voice as she replied, gratitude evident. "Thank you so much. I hate to ask this of you, but I'm really in a bind. I couldn't get a hold of the girls, or I would have asked them.

Swing by the office and you can grab the car seats? Or we can trade cars?"

Danny's heart squeezed. "Megan, you're not imposing. Seriously. You call, I'll answer. I already told you that.. Just focus on your meeting, and I'll handle everything." He tacked on in a soft whisper. "You're not alone anymore, honey."

A small, choked sound broke through the phone and Danny squeezed his eyes shut hard.

Fuck. How long had she been barely treading water? And why the fuck had her girls not noticed?

After ending the call, Danny sprang into action, grabbing his keys and heading out the door. His thoughts wouldn't slow: swirling with a mix of concern for Megan's well-being and a growing sense of responsibility toward their small family unit.

He swapped car keys with Megan at her office and made his way to the daycare.

The place was a zoo. Kids running around everywhere, and no locks on the door.

There was a fucking mop with soap in a bucket next to a questionable splatter on the ground.

One that smelled very much like vomit.

Gross.

He paused as he walked by; should that be out in the play area for the kids to touch?

Actually...

Where the hell were the teachers?

He found one crouched in a corner, rocking a crying toddler while playing defense on another that was trying to hit the one he was cuddling.

Another teacher was standing in a doorframe across the way and talking back and forth between a kid in the bathroom and someone standing outside it.

And another teacher was at a diaper changing station, wiping up a mess.

And not one of them had turned to look at him.

Jesus. Anyone could just walk in there.

After introducing himself to the teacher who seemed the least busy, he asked the teacher to lead him to the kids' stuff so he could take them home. Theo was in an adjoining classroom and Ava was in the viper's den he just walked through.

No wonder she was tough. She had to be to survive in there.

The teacher looked exhausted, burnt out, and completely over it when she said they were  short-staffed.

"Short-staffed" was fucking right.

Someone was going to get fucking hurt.

As Danny loaded them into the car, Danny glanced at the two quiet children in the rearview mirror. Theo had a runny nose, and his flushed face and watery eyes reflected his discomfort. Ava looked fine, despite the goop of green dripping from her nose. Her big eyes observed Danny through the rearview mirror from her throne in the back seat.

Man, she was so much like Megan.

Nurture beats Nature once again.

As much as this situation sucked, it was somewhat good that it happened. It was a chance to show Megan that she could lean on him, that he would be there for her and her children in both the good times and the challenging ones. They didn't need to be in a relationship together for him to be able to help. To answer her calls.

Belatedly realizing that they might need some supplies, Danny made a detour on the way home. He drove to a nearby baby store, loading the kids up into a squeaky shopping cart.

Stepping inside, he was greeted by a flurry of activity and a chorus of distracted hellos.

As Danny navigated through the aisles of the baby store, his presence caught the attention of the staff. They exchanged knowing glances and sly smiles, clearly recognizing him.

As he approached a wall of highchairs, a young saleswoman with bright eyes and a friendly smile greeted him.

"Hi there," she said, her voice tinged with a hint of flirtation. "Finding everything you need?"

Danny returned her smile politely. "Yes, thank you. Just picking up a few essentials."

The saleswoman leaned in slightly, her eyes lingering on his muscular arms. "Well, it looks like you're quite the pro at shopping for baby supplies. Are you a dad or maybe their uncle?"

Danny pressed his lips tight together in a semblance of a smile. "Not mine, but mine all the same."

Maybe that would deliver the hint that he didn't need help.

Even though he kind of did.

What highchair did he need? There were frickin' fourteen thousand.

The saleswoman's playful banter continued as he ignored her and stared at the walls.

The little traitors in front of him were perfectly quiet and behaved, not giving him an excuse to excuse himself.

He looked down at them, Theo's car seat rested in the large body of the cart and Ava swung her legs happily in the front seat, looking around in awe.

*Will you two fuss? You're supposed to be sick!*

Speaking of, that was a huge glob that her tongue was reaching out to lick.

He grabbed a tissue from his back pocket and quickly wiped before she had a chance to claim her prize.

"Well, they're lucky to have someone like you. If you ever need any advice on parenting or just someone to talk to, feel free to swing by. We're here to help, in more ways than one."

Oh, she was still there.

Danny turned back to her and gave her a distracted nod. "I appreciate the offer."

Halfway through their excursion, Danny snagged a second cart and tugged it along behind them. With a cart and a half full of diapers, wipes, baby food, and other essentials, Danny made his way to the checkout. The cashier, a friendly young man, flashed him a smile. "You've got adorable kids. Are they yours?"

Before he could answer, another saleswoman, her eyes twinkling mischievously, chimed in. "You know, if you ever want some company while taking care of those kids, I'm just a phone call away. I'm great with children."

"Uh, thanks, but we're probably fine."

And then the circus began.

He tried to manage the requests for autographs and pictures as he paid for the items and tried to escape.

He generally didn't live life wanting to punch people, but when a phone was pointed at the kids in the cart...all bets were off.

As he left the store, Danny couldn't stop the fire from burning through his system. He was not an angry person.

But holy fuck, he wanted to take that phone and spike it to the ground.

Where did people get off, trying to take pictures of children?

*He* was the celebrity. Not them.

They shouldn't have to be hounded just because they were out with him.

As he thrust the items into the back of his SUV, he tried to focus on cooling down before the kids in the car started to notice that he was brooding like a spoiled bitch.

It wasn't like he was unused to that behavior.

But somehow, subjecting the kids to that invasion of privacy...

He wanted to rip some heads off.

He hoped Theo's dad, whoever he was, would have the same instinct. And not use it to take Theo from the mom who loved him so.

· · · · ● · ● · ● · · ·

Arriving back at his place, Danny carried the kids inside and dashed back out to the car. He lugged the bags of supplies inside and set them down on the kitchen counter. He glanced at the kids, their wide eyes taking in their new surroundings.

Kneeling, Danny spoke softly, his voice gentle and comforting. "Hey, little ones. We're going to have some fun together today. Let's get you settled in, and then we can play and have a good time until your mom comes."

The day slipped by, they did everything from play in the kitchen, be pirates in the tub, wrestle on the bed, and make a couch cushion fort.

He ordered a swing set to be delivered that weekend while Ava was taking a water break.

Theo slept through most of it...which would maybe come back to bite Megan in the ass that night, but when he texted her, she said it was fine.

As the evening sun dipped below the horizon, casting a warm glow across the room, Danny found himself immersed in a dramatic play of epic proportions. He kneeled on the carpeted floor, proudly displaying his makeshift wrestling attire—his football jersey wrapped around his head like a bandana. Flexing his muscles and striking exaggerated poses, he unleashed his alter ego, Danny the Destroyer as he battled Ava the Annihilator.

Ava couldn't contain her delight. She bounced up and down on the couch cushions and pillows, her little legs carrying her closer to Danny. She'd point at something across the room, and when he would turn...bam!

Spear!

"Any last words?" Ava exclaimed, her laughter filling the room and she clung to him.

Danny flexed his muscles, and groaned, struggling to dislodge her. "Off me, you wildcat! I will defeat you!"

He then picked her up, spun her upside down, and tackled her back onto the pillows, all the while, being careful not to whiplash her.

With their imaginary wrestling match in full swing, the room reverberated with laughter and joy. They tumbled and rolled on the carpet, laughing, and trying to tickle each other.

Girl was going be a WWE world champion one day.

Their energetic play continued, punctuated by fits of giggles and playful shouts. The room became a playground, their laughter a soundtrack of pure bliss. Danny's heart soared as he witnessed Ava's unbridled joy, her innocence and imagination illuminating the space around them.

What he wouldn't have given to have that as a kid. Instead, he got saddled with a dad who drank too much and was too easy with a belt.

As their energy gradually waned over the next hour, the room settled into a gentle calm. Ava's eyelids grew heavy, her relentless playfulness giving way to weariness. Theo, now awake and cozy in his pillow fortress, observed the scene with a watchful but still spacey expression.

Realizing it was time to transition to their bedtime routine, Danny gently scooped Ava into his arms, cradling her against his chest. She nestled against him, her small frame sinking into the safety of his embrace.

Good thing they had already done dinner, bath, and teeth.

She hugged him tight.

He tucked his chin and whispered against her hair, "Time for dreams, little champion."

Ava, her sleepy eyes half-closed, whispered back, "No leave."

"You're not leaving, we're just going to take a quick rest while your mom gets out of her meeting. Don't worry. I'll be right here."

He planted a soft kiss on her forehead and gently laid her down on the bed. Satisfied she was staying put, which was a miracle, he went back out to Theo.

It wasn't even their bedtime yet, but the little man was struggling to stay awake as well.

Sickness really took it out of him.

He cuddled Theo close, rocking him in a recliner out in the now crazy living room.

Theo fell asleep on Danny's chest and even did the same semi-snore that Danny did when he was exhausted. As he continued to rock there, soaking up the baby snuggles, and letting his thoughts drift, Danny was struck with a disquieting thought.

Was he wrong to have written off fatherhood? Had he missed his shot? His thirties wasn't a terrible time to have kids, but his body aged more than most. Just wrestling with Ava and rolling on the ground had his bad knee and lower back screaming.

But these snuggles? Heaven.

He placed a gentle kiss on the baby's blonde hair.

"You need to feel better, little buddy," Danny whispered. "You don't want to be sporting a cold when we finally track down your daddy." He paused and his stomach clenched. "He better be okay with snot." He hiked him up a little so Theo looked a little more comfortable. "If he's not, I'll kick the shit out of him."

Swearing to a sleeping infant was probably okay.

He wouldn't tell if Theo wouldn't.

CHAPTER TWENTY-SIX

# September 18, Sunday
## Danny

The Spartans' gym was buzzing with activity as Danny and some of his teammates gathered for a workout session. They were all focused on their individual exercises, but there was an air of camaraderie and light-hearted banter that filled the space.

Danny chatted with Michael while they both worked on their respective machines. The clinks of weights and the rhythmic sound of sneakers on the treadmill provided a lively backdrop for their conversation.

"Man, Megan reminds me so much of my mom," Danny remarked, a slight smile playing on his lips. "Tough as nails, but deep down, she's got this soft center, you know? Like a cinnamon roll."

Michael chuckled. "That could be sick and Freudian but we're ignoring and letting your therapist deal with that." He nudged Danny. "So you want to eat her up? But can't because of the kids?"

Danny rolled his eyes and shook his head. "I'd fucking eat her up in a heartbeat. But...I can't go there."

Michael raised an eyebrow. "If you say so."

As they continued their workout, Danny couldn't help but bring up Megan's kids to Michael. "Her kids are seriously the cutest fucking things. They've got these big, innocent eyes that light up whenever they see their mom. It's adorable."

Michael nodded, his lips pressed tight and his eyebrows high. Clearly he wasn't going to talk more about how he thought Danny should 'go there.'

"They're just cute," Danny added on a scowl as he turned back to his weights. "Fucker," he tossed at Michael.

Michael gave him a half-smile and stayed mute.

Across the gym, John and Ryan were deep in conversation, analyzing game film on the tablet in front of them. Their discussion was peppered with technical terms and strategic insights, a testament to their dedication to perfecting their craft.

Amidst the chatter and laughter, Coach Mitchell entered the gym, one of his lumbering 'assistant coaches' trailing behind him, giving off enforcer vibes. How Butch ever got management to sign off on getting one of his lackeys a job, the guys on the team would never know. He went straight up to Liam Polowski, one of the team's tight ends, and exchanged a few tense words.

Meanwhile, Kobe Richardson and Kyle Justice, sweating profusely, engaged in a friendly banter as they pushed themselves on the treadmills.

Over at the weight benches, Kenny and Brandon were sharing photos on their phones, laughing about their kids' latest antics. Their laughter echoed through the gym as they shared stories, their friendship evident in their interaction.

This was his family.

Any one of these guys, he would trust with Megan's kids.

He knew it'd be fucking complicated as hell, but why couldn't one of them have been the little guy's dad?

Liam barked out something to Butch's retreating back and Butch stilled for a moment before continuing his march out of the room.

Actually...

He hadn't had a chance to grab Liam for a Starla-vention yet.

Danny patted his pockets but didn't have her picture and had long since erased her from his phone.

Michael's face scrunched up in annoyance as he watched Liam's frustrated slam of his sweat towel.

"He's a fucking asshole," Michael grumbled, shaking his head.

Danny jerked. "Liam?"

Michael shook his head. "Butch. During the last season, it felt like he had this uncanny ability to find out about our injuries and then have us run plays that would make them even worse."

Danny furrowed his brow, thinking back.

Well, now that Michael mentioned it.

No.

No way that would fly. Someone would have noticed that by now. Michael was just pissed he didn't get as many carries as he wanted last week...

Maybe...

"Now we're all hiding injuries because of him. Only Jen gets told about that shit. Sure, Butch gets wins, but at what cost?" Michael paused, his gaze drifting towards John, who was deep in conversation with Ryan. "You know, I wish John would take over as the offensive coordinator. He's got the knowledge, the passion, and the right attitude. He's not just a great QB coach, he could do so much more for the team."

Danny looked over to watch John and Ryan working together. "Yeah, John would be great. But we've got to make the best of what we have and keep pushing forward."

Michael sighed, releasing some of his frustration. "I can't believe you, of all people, are saying that. After all the shit between you two last year? I was half convinced we were going to find you dead in a ditch somewhere with your truck wrapped around a pole and I wasn't sure whether we could say it was the alcohol or Butch's connections."

Danny shrugged. "He let it go and moved on. I can too. If the team is performing..."

"And miserable," Michael grumbled before taking a slug of water.

Danny paused. Were things really that bad? He'd been distracted lately with Megan and the kids. And his dad had been hounding him again, not that he was letting that even enter his orbit right now with the kids around.

Their conversation intertwined with the sounds of clanging weights and the rhythmic hum of the gym, creating a backdrop of determination and resilience.

The gym continued to pulse with energy, filled with the sound of laughter, camaraderie, clanking weights, and the collective determination of the team to push themselves to be the best.

He forgot about asking Liam about Starla.

# CHAPTER TWENTY-SEVEN

# September 23, Friday
## Danny

Another week later, without realizing it, Danny had become an adoptive member of Megan and the kids' lives. The time spent with her and her children had filled him with an incomparable peace and a profound sense of purpose. He actually found himself looking forward to when practices and sessions were over for the day because then he could either call and check in, or just visit.

As he stood in Megan's kitchen, preparing dinner for the kids while Megan worked late, a mixture of contentedness fluttered in his chest.

The sound of Theo's giggles and Ava's laughter echoed through the apartment, filling Danny's heart with warmth. Seeing their happy faces, he couldn't help but marvel at the love he felt for them, a love that seemed to grow stronger with each passing day.

As the delicious aroma of dinner filled the air, Danny watched Ava proudly display her artwork—a beautiful drawing of...orange scribbles.

Kid was going places. That almost looked like a person!

His heart swelled with adoration. She was a bright little star, bringing light into the world.

Theo, much calmer and constantly curious, hung out at his place on the floor on the other side of the kitchen, far from any possible kitchen mishaps. Danny scooped him up, lifting him playfully into the air, and blowing raspberries on his big belly, eliciting bursts of laughter from the little boy. The pure joy reflected in Theo's eyes was a testament to the bond they were forging.

As dinner came to an end, Danny set to work cleaning up, feeling a mixture of exhaustion and sadness. Saying goodbye every time got harder and harder. Especially when the tears started.

For the kids, not him.

Well, not him after that first time at least.

Just as he finished tidying up, the front door creaked open, and Megan stepped inside, her weariness evident in the slump of her shoulders and the shadows beneath her eyes. Danny's heart sank at the sight of her fatigue. Mama needed a hug and a bubble bath.

Megan greeted the kids and Danny, putting on a happy face while giving kisses all around.

Even to Danny's scruffy cheek.

Then she escaped to her back bedroom, lugging her work bags with her.

The woman was always working.

She shuffled back out and wordlessly, they worked together to put the kids to bed. When they were both asleep, Danny went back to the kitchen and Megan escaped to her bedroom to change out of her work clothes.

When she came back out, she was dressed in a much comfier, and sexier, outfit and her face was void of makeup.

"Any leftovers?"

"Of course." As if he wouldn't make extra for her. Psh.

As Megan filled him in on her, her body trembled with pent-up emotions. At one point, Danny was sure he was going to see tears start to fall, but she breathed through it and stuffed them back in.

Danny pulled up a seat close to her as she ranted. He listened, nodding and occasionally interjecting with sympathetic comments. "That sounds incredibly frustrating," he said, his brows furrowing in empathy.

What more could he do to help her? Maybe he could get her a lead on a new job? Maybe grease the wheels on landing her a better daycare opening?

He leaned forward, his expression determined. "You know, I might have a friend who's looking for someone with your skills. I could put in a good word for you."

Her signature lavender smell was not offering any calming effects at all. He was starting to wonder if lavender ever actually soothed his high-strung lady or if it was just positive thinking and hope on her part.

Vodka would do it though...

He mentally shook himself and forced his thoughts to reroute.

"Hey," he said gently, reaching out to touch her hand. "You're doing an amazing job. It's not easy, I know. But you're strong, capable, and you got this."

She met his gaze, her eyes reflecting a mixture of gratitude and vulnerability. Without thinking, he closed the distance between them, his lips gently pressing against hers in a tender, reassuring kiss.

Their bodies remained close, and Danny's thumb brushed against the back of her hand. "You're not alone in this, Megan," he said softly. "I'm here for you, no matter what."

Megan leaned into Danny's embrace, releasing a deep breath. Danny could feel her pulse beat rapidly in her neck and a faint blush tinged her cheeks.

Slowly, he brushed his thumb along her cheek, his eyes locking with hers. Megan gave him a small smile before leaning in for another, longer, lingering kiss. Danny's hand shifted to the nape of her neck, gently twining his fingers through her silky-soft blonde locks.

Soft and warm...

Heat simmered between them as their kiss deepened, their tongues dancing.

Fuck, she tasted good.

Their bodies shifted and he took charge. He wrapped his free hand around her back and tugged her off her stool and to the area in between his own legs on his stool.

That was better.

The kiss got heavier. Danny explored Megan's mouth, learning the taste and feel. What caused her to moan or her fingers to clench. Tingles raced down his spine and he had to stop himself from letting out a groan of pleasure. What would those full, soft lips feel like on other places?

*Focus. One thing at a time.*

With their bodies now flush, Danny tilted Megan's head to change the angle and deepen the connection. Her fingers embedded themselves in the short beard on his cheeks and gave a slight tug. The warmth radiated throughout his body, tingling and driving him to increase his explorations.

Fuck.

Her hips gave a little thrust into his when one of his hands started wandering and his balls tightened.

Double fuck.

A small little whine erupted from Megan's throat and Danny forced himself to pull back, knowing where this was headed and how complicated it would make everything. He broke the kiss and kept his eyes closed to prevent distractions and calm his rampaging libido down.

He didn't get a chance.

Immediately, he felt her hands go to the hair in the back of his head and he felt himself pulled back to her hungry little mouth.

Fuck. Fuckity. Fuck.

Was this really happening? Did they want this to happen?

"Meg?" He tried to pull away to get a read on her. "I'm not sure—"

"Are you always this chatty before sex?" she panted out, trying to pull his neck back to her hungry lips.

Wait.

"Woah, Meg. I don't—"

"Agh!" She ripped away and stared at him in frustration. "Do you need a written invitation? Work sucks. Daycare sucks. I have no time to date. I'm a shell of a person. I'm a CPA, a mom, and a friend. But I want to be a woman! For one night, can I just be a woman?" Her voice took on a pleading edge and her eyes shined bright.

"Yeah, baby. You can be a woman," he said softly, his thumb creeping up to rub at the apple of her pink cheek. Danny pulled her in for a more leisurely exploration. Partly to show Megan that she was more than numbers, kids, and friendship and partly because, fuck, did she taste like heaven. And he had spent a lot of nights the last few weeks wondering exactly how she would kiss...and more.

His tongue danced with hers, sending jolts of electricity throughout his body.

Fuck. He wanted her. All of her.

He stood and backed her down the hall, not taking his lips from her. Whatever he could touch, taste, lick, bite. He wanted it all.

When they finally got to her bedroom, he kept his awareness enough to shut her door quietly so the kids wouldn't be disturbed.

Then he was on her again. He lifted her shirt up and enjoyed the feel of her creamy, smooth skin.

Fucking hell she was stacked. Thick ass and thighs, trim but soft waist, and her tits.

Fuck.

Without wasting more time, because who knew when one of the kids would wake, he ripped her thin bralette up and over her head and stared.

Megan's breasts were a work of art and he pushed her back onto the bed so he could fully worship them.

His balls clenched and wanted their own play, but he ignored them to focus on her pleasure. Megan writhed and arched into Danny's grasping hands and touches. When his mouth enclosed over the rosy nipple, her knees rose and squeezed his sides, letting out a sexy little moan.

Oh, he would be hearing that on repeat in his shower.

He rolled the nipple in his mouth, testing different pressures, sucks, and flicks to see what made her gasp and pant.

"More."

*When Megan asks, Danny delivers.*

He switched breasts, enjoying the slide against his whiskered chin. Megan's gasps and wriggling told him she was okay with the burn. That brings a smile to Danny's face. Yeah, little miss accountant liked a little stinging pleasure, did she?

When her hands dug into Danny's pecs and tugged at his shirt, he didn't complain. Before he could enjoy Megan's exploring fingers, her nails dug into the hairs at the nape of his neck and yanked him up her body for a filthy, scorching hot, greedy kiss. He moaned into her mouth as sparks shot to his cock.

Yes.

They ground hard against each other, completely wild for each other, desperate to touch everywhere all at once. Danny tore his mouth away with a ragged breath and started to travel south, needing Megan to cum all over his face, fingers, or dick.

Any. Fucking. Way.

The sounds she was making were otherworldly and he was looking forward to hearing them multiple times.

He only got as far as pressing wet, open-mouthed kisses down her soft, plump tummy before she wiggled out from under him.

What?

He looked up at her with heavy, confused eyes?

"I want to taste, too." Her lips were swollen and her cheeks were red from the beard burn.

Actually, there was a trail of red all over her body, showing exactly where his lips had been.

It was fucking sexy as hell.

Yet...

Danny took a beat and reached out, trailing his fingers over the red burns on her nearly white skin. "Is this okay? Does it hurt? I can go shave it. Won't take five minutes." Probably more, but he didn't want her to be in pain.

She grabbed his arm and pulled it to her pussy, rubbing his fingers against her. "Does that feel like I'm in discomfort?"

He took charge and twisted his hand so he could do his own teasing. Her hand fell away and she let him.

"No discomfort." He grunted when her hips bucked hard against the palm of his hand.

With surprising speed, she rocketed up and kneeled in front of him, grabbing his cheeks in both hands. She looked deep in his eyes, her own half lidded and hungry. "And if you even mention shaving your beard to me again..." she leaned forward and rubbed against his cheeks, her eyes barely open now, "I'll never speak to you again."

He tossed her onto her back and she let out a quiet squeal. "Sounds good, darlin'. Now what's that you mentioned about sharing a meal?"

Without breaking eye contact, she opened her legs wide. "I've changed my mind. I'll play with my food after." She bit her plump, red, lip and arched her back. "I need to be eaten first."

Thank. Fuck.

Danny darted forward, spread her lips with his thumbs, and dove in. The reaction was immediate and intense. Megan's hands entered Danny's hair again, firmly keeping his face right where she wanted it. Not that he was fighting the forces.

He should have known she'd be a powerhouse in bed.

Thank fuck.

He lapped up her sweet, tangy arousal, using the tip of his tongue to lightly tease at her entrance, then dragged upwards, pressing slightly firmer as it passed over her clit. Danny alternated between fast and deliberate with light and precise, seeing what Megan liked best.

He sure as fuck didn't dally though. He wanted her to come hard and fast, but not so fast that it took it out of her.

They had a lot of time to make up for.

After only a few minutes, Megan bucked hard into Danny's face, moaning loud, and it took most of his athletic ability to keep at it instead of rutting into her like an untried teenager.

He lapped at her slowly as she came down and he made sure to rub his beard into her-she moaned extra hard when he did that. Hell, he was never washing his face again. He wanted her smell on him, on his lips, chin, cheeks, every day, all day.

He wanted to be running a fucking route in the Superbowl and catch of whiff of her sweetness still on his beard.

Once her body relaxed, he climbed over her and settled in. He rubbed back and forth against her folds. Not entered, just coating himself in her, and causing her to give small bucks when he rubbed just right.

She went wild when Danny kissed and nibbled at her throat and jaw, also pinning Megan's arms above her and causing her nipples to scrape deliciously along his chest. Still keeping her arms pinned, he made sure to lean down and rub his rough beard over her taut nipples. As she arched up into it, his balls tightened further.

Yeah, they'd play with that more later too.

The road to her second orgasm was a short one. He hadn't even entered her yet and she was jerking and shaking under him. It took all his self-control not to join her. The idea of slipping in during one of her hip flexes was tempting but he needed to check in with her first.

When she was panting and quiet, he leaned in close and brushed more soft kisses against her lips.

"I don't have a condom, Meg. Do you have one or do you want to rawdog it?"

Her legs tightened around him in response. "I'm clean. and on the pill." She paused. "Though, to be fair, sometimes I do forget—" She gasped as he rubbed against her clit again. Those slow strokes against her outside were going to result in him coming on her in a spectacular fashion but he couldn't stop his hips from grinding against her soft, smooth, wet.

"Yeah, so I'm good. Inside now, please." She gasped, matching his hip thrusts. His cock would get right there, almost about to slip in, and they'd flex away.

Fuck, they'd have to try edging with each other at some point.

But playtime was over.

Time for the real fucking to start.

With one flex Danny popped past her entrance and they both sucked in deep, long breaths. Fuck, she was so tight, gripping him perfectly, firing nerve endings everywhere and causing uncontrollable aftershocks.

Fuck. He hadn't cum upon entering a partner in years.

Not since high school.

Megan was going to wreck him. And he couldn't wait.

It took some effort but he refocused, and even helped her focus. He ran his rough beard against her tits again, causing her hips to thrust into Danny's. Perfect. He flexed in answer and hit home balls deep. Megan's head fell deep into her pillow and her eyes widened a fraction at the intensity. She writhed and wiggled, looking for more or something and Danny used all his reserve energy to start thrusting.

Hips slowly built into thrusts. In and out, in and out. Megan latched onto Danny's shoulders and dug in. Just when it looked like marks would start, her hips reared up and started meeting him at every down thrust.

Dirty, filthy, hardcore thrusts. His ears rung from the intensity, ringing from the grunts and groans filling the room. His senses were reeling from the overwhelming and exquisite amount of goodness surrounding him. Soft skin, spicy pussy, Megan's lavender scent. This was heaven.

Megan gave soft, sweet grunts and squeaks with every perfect thrust.

Danny's beard continued rubbing against Megan and their sweat-soaked chests only added to the brutal scratching.

Danny switched his angle and Megan's whole body shuddered. Found it. Megan's nails started embedding into Danny's shoulders and his cock got impossibly harder.

Fuck yeah.

The slap, slap, slap sounded out and their grunting shifted up in pitch and frequency. Danny dropped his forehead to hers, looking her dead in the eyes and their combined, building orgasms pulsed through them. Fuck, she was so hot. Beautiful. Stunning. Firecracker in and out of bed-

Fuck. Fuck. Fuck.

He came hard, stars lighting behind his eyes and Megan's walls clamped onto Danny, hugging him through it, and lighting new sensations throughout his sensitive-as-fuck cock.

As they came down, they lay connected and breathed in sync. Catching their respective breaths and forcing their heart rates to settle to something more within healthy zones.

Instead, their heart rates rocketed the more they remembered tonight.

What the fuck just happened?

And how soon could they do it again?

# CHAPTER TWENTY-EIGHT

# September 25, Sunday
## Megan

Megan sat at the kitchen table in Nikki's house, the weight of her recent discoveries heavy on her mind. She had spent hours meticulously combing through financial records, meeting with Nikki's 'advisors', and piecing together the evidence of Danny's father's deceit. The realization of the extent of the theft left her feeling a mix of anger and sadness.

As she looked up from the paperwork, she caught sight of Danny walking through the front door, his face lighting up with a radiant smile as he spotted the kids. The conflicting emotions within Megan surged anew.

She hadn't seen him since Friday night, or should she say, Saturday morning. They spent all night exploring each other and getting as 'not platonic' as possible. If there was an inch of skin on each other's bodies, it was thoroughly licked, touched, sucked, flicked, pinched, bit, or more.

The kids had interrupted any possible 'morning after' talk and he'd been busy all yesterday with going over game film and prepping for that night's Sunday Night Kickoff.

In terms of priorities, as much as she'd love to talk to him about what they did, she really needed to discuss Nikki's situation with her finances.

Though...should she burden him with the truth about his father's betrayal? Would it be better to shield him from the pain, especially considering his strained relationship with his dad? Maybe she could get away with just telling Nikki?

As soon as she thought about it, she knew it wouldn't work. Nikki would fill him in. Plus, it wasn't her place to try to influence his relationship with his shitbag father. Some of the stories he shared with her about him... Fucking hell. The guy was a monster. He made Megan's and Starla's family look somewhat normal.

She didn't understand how Danny allowed him to come within one hundred feet of him. One night, when she had Mickey and Benji over for dinner, Danny stopped by. When they were knee-deep in a game of cribbage, Danny made an offhand comment about how his dad literally broke his right arm when he was younger, so he'd learn to better use his left. He had never told his mom the truth of how he broke it. Aghast, she made a comment that Mickey should give the number of his 'fixer' to Danny to take care of his father. Danny looked intrigued and horrified that a hair stylist would have the contact information for someone like that, but after hearing how it came about, the horror was replaced with rage and savage satisfaction.

Her thoughts were in a whirlwind as Danny approached, his smile easy and not at all conflicted, which, considering what they did to each other not even thirty hours ago, was a miracle.

Megan, on the other hand, her mind was still grappling with the aftermath of their intimate encounter.

Was it just a one-time thing, a fleeting moment of passion, or was there more between them?

Why hadn't Danny reached out after their passionate encounter? Sure, he had work, but not even time for a text? Did he regret it? Was it simply a physical release for him? The doubts and uncertainties gnawed at her, making her question her own actions and choices. Typical.

How did this affect the kids? Their friendship? She was basically done working on this project for his mom, so at least there was that.

The desire to discuss their relationship, to gain clarity on what they meant to each other, weighed heavily on Megan's heart. She'd barely been able to focus on anything else.

As she watched Danny greet the kids and his mother, making his way to her, Megan couldn't help but admire his steadfastness.

You called, Danny would answer.

Always.

Swallowing her apprehension, Megan decided to prioritize the fraud. Then they'd tackle the sex talk.

"Little monsters! I have presents!"

Megan quickly gathered the documents and made her way to the living room, where she found Danny standing in the doorway, his broad shoulders filling the frame. He looked dashing in his casual attire, a black T-shirt and jeans that accentuated his athletic physique.

Ava's eyes widened, and she clapped her hands excitedly. Theo simply smiled, reaching out for Danny.

Danny stood up and opened a bag he had brought with him, revealing two sets of jerseys neatly folded inside. "You guys can each choose either a cheerleader jersey or a football jersey with my number on them," he explained, holding them out for the children to see.

Megan watched as Ava unhesitatingly pointed to the football jerseys. She couldn't help but chuckle at her decision.

Obviously, Theo just sat there curled in Nikki's lap on the floor.

Danny laughed, ruffling Theo's hair affectionately. "We'll start with the jersey but if you change your mind when you're older, then we'll talk."

Nikki, who had been observing the interaction with a wide smile, chimed in. "They certainly take after their mother. I'm so excited you agreed to come to Danny's game tonight with the kids. It'll be so fun. I promise."

Megan hesitated, her mind racing with conflicting thoughts. The idea of attending a football game, being a part of Danny's world, both thrilled and intimidated her. But she really needed to tell Danny about his father.

But the look of joy on both Nikki's and Danny's faces gave her pause. The bad news could wait until after the game. Danny didn't need to be focused on that and possibly get himself injured.

She'd tell them after the game.

# CHAPTER TWENTY-NINE

# September 25, Sunday
## Megan

That night Megan stood outside the towering stadium, her grip tightening around Ava's small hand. She had opted to carry Theo in her baby carrier, hoping it would free her hands up for whatever her anxious mind had conjured up. Both kids were wearing their new jerseys. Nikki walked beside them, sporting her own 'Parker' jersey, and radiating confidence and excitement as she chatted about the upcoming game.

As they approached the entrance, security personnel began their routine bag checks. Megan nervously handed over her diaper bag, purse, and cooler bag for Theo's bottles, all of which were stuffed to the brim. The thorough inspection only heightened her anxiety, what if they told her she couldn't bring one of the bags and she had to trek all the way back to her car?

Ava was already getting restless...

Maybe this was a bad idea.

"Mommy, I wanna see Danny!" Ava babbled out, her high voice tinged with impatience.

Megan flashed a reassuring smile, although her own doubts gnawed at her. "We'll get there soon, sweetheart. Just a little more waiting, okay?"

Theo squirmed in the carrier, his chubby fingers reaching out for the colorful jerseys worn by passing fans. Megan shifted slightly, hoping the change in perspective would distract him from the noise and commotion around them.

Did she double check that she brought the infant headphones?

As they navigated through the crowd, the atmosphere grew rowdier. Megan's heart raced when a group of drunken fans stumbled past them, hurling vulgar insults at supporters of the opposing team. She instinctively pulled Ava closer. Did she remember the toddler headphones too?

Everything felt like it was closing in on her. Trapping her. She felt too hot.

Her neck prickled. Someone was looking at her.

Everyone was looking at her.

Breathe, breathe, breathe.

She took a moment to close her eyes and center herself. She got there...barely.

A sigh of relief escaped her lips when they reached the entrance to the family box. The noise of the crowd muffled as they stepped into the corridor, and Megan felt a wave of calm wash over her. This was the sanctuary Danny promised, a place where her children would be safe and comfortable.

Inside the family box, Megan found herself surrounded by friendly faces, though their curious gazes didn't escape her notice. The players' families, along with other prominent figures, turned their attention toward the newcomers.

Nikki, ever the gracious hostess, introduced Megan and her children to the others, beaming with pride. "This is Megan, and these are her beautiful children, Ava and Theo. They're here to support Danny today."

Warm smiles and greetings filled the room.

Man, she wished Rose or Chloe came to these. At least it would be a friendly face.

But Megan's worries began to dissipate as the welcoming atmosphere enveloped her and her children.

As the game began, the noise from the crowd outside gradually faded into the background, replaced by cheers and chants of support.

The family box provided a sense of protection, shielding them from the chaos of the stadium.

Megan glanced at Ava, who was now enthralled by the action on the field, her little face painted with expressions of awe and excitement.

Perhaps bringing her children to the game wasn't a mistake after all.

As the game progressed, Megan struck up conversations with other families in the box, sharing laughter, stories, and the occasional gasp at a thrilling play.

•‌•‌•‌•‌•‌•‌•‌•‌•‌•‌•

As the game progressed, the atmosphere in the family box was electric. Megan cheered alongside the others, her eyes glued to the field where Danny showcased his exceptional skills.

Megan's heart skipped a beat as she watched Danny take a hard hit. Time seemed to slow down as he fell to the ground, and the stadium held its breath in collective concern. The cheers faded into worried murmurs.

Megan's grip tightened around Ava's hand, her eyes widening with fear. She leaned forward in her seat, her heart pounding in her chest as she waited for him to get to his feet again.

But as Danny remained on the ground, taking a moment to recover, Megan's fretful thoughts intensified. Every second that ticked by felt like an eternity.

"Get up, get up, get up." She said it quietly so as not to freak out Ava or Nikki.

Nikki understood the risks of the game, but it didn't make moments like these any easier to bear.

Finally, Danny stirred, slowly rising to his feet.

It was probably only a handful of seconds, but it felt like eternity.

A collective sigh of relief swept through the family box, Megan included. She released a breath, her body relaxing slightly.

Nikki, who had been holding her breath beside Megan, placed a comforting hand on her shoulder. "Gets me every time. Never gets any easier. The day he picked up a pigskin is the day God decided I was going to die young," she whispered, her voice filled with conviction.

Theo was learning chess. It was decided.

Danny's passion for the game was an integral part of who he was, and she had to find the strength to support him, even in the face of potential dangers. But that sure as shit didn't mean she had to watch her own kid get rocked on the field like that.

As the game continued, Megan's eyes remained fixed on Danny.

·  ·  ●  ·  ●  ·  ●  ·  ·  ·

Later that night, a soft knock resonated through Megan's front door, drawing her attention away from her book. Surprised yet delighted, she rose from the couch and approached the door, a mixture of curiosity and nervousness fluttering in her chest. As she opened it, she found Danny standing there, a warm smile on his face, holding a smoothie and a plate of Nutella crepes.

Megan's eyes widened, and a blush tinted her cheeks. "Danny, " she said, her voice filled with a mix of delight and nerves. "Hi there."

"Hi yourself." Danny stepped inside, his gaze focused on her. "I remembered how much you love Nutella crepes so, here they are," he explained, his eyes twinkling with affection.

Megan's heart skipped a beat as she welcomed him into her cozy living room. They settled on the couch, the sweet aroma of crepes filling the air. The tension in the room was palpable as they both savored the moment.

"So, how was the game from your perspective?" Megan asked, breaking the silence, her voice laced with genuine interest.

Danny's face lit up as he began recounting the highlights, his voice filled with excitement. He animatedly described the crucial plays and the electric atmosphere of the stadium. Megan listened intently, captivated by his enthusiasm, but her nerves intensified with every passing moment.

As Danny paused, Megan took a deep breath, her fingers twirling together. She knew it was time to broach the topic that had been weighing on her mind. She mustered her courage and met Danny's gaze.

"Danny, I have to ask," she started, her voice wavering slightly. "What are we?"

Danny's expression softened. "Honestly? I don't really know. Friends. Good friends. Good friends that want to...do stuff. A lot of stuff. A lot of dirty, sweaty stuff." He trailed off as his eyes wandered down her body which was once again in just a small cami.

Megan nodded. "Yeah, I know that. But...are we anything more, or no?"

Danny leaned closer, his voice gentle. "I...I don't know," he admitted, his tone sincere. "The connection I feel with you, the way you've become such an important part of my life, it's undeniable. But we also have the kids to think about."

A mix of relief and vulnerability washed over Megan as she took in his words. "I don't want to confuse them or risk losing you. For me, or for them."

Danny reached out, gently clasping Megan's hand. "I love you guys. You would never lose me. No matter what. So, maybe, we can trial run? Explore things a bit more? I believe that we owe it to ourselves to explore what we could be, to see if this connection between us could grow into something more. Or if it will fizzle out with time."

Fat chance of that.

Her expression had him laughing and leaning forward, stealing a quick kiss from her lips. "Yeah, I don't expect any fizzling either, but I know how much you like trial runs."

Megan's nerves began to ease, replaced by a glimmer of hope. She looked into Danny's eyes, searching for sincerity and finding it in abundance. "I do indeed like trial runs."

Danny smiled, a mix of excitement and tenderness in his gaze. "I think I need another trial run tonight. I'm worried we fizzled out. I need proof that we didn't."

She climbed up in his lap and pulled off her tank, sitting astride him in just her small pajama shorts. "Yeah, I think things fizzled for me too. Better try to see if you can get it restarted there, Wonderboy."

Danny's smile turned wolfish. "As my lady requests." And he dove in.

# CHAPTER THIRTY

# September 28, Wednesday
## Megan

Megan sat on the worn couch of Nikki's living room, engrossed in a playful game with Ava and Theo.

"Trot, trot to Boston. Trot, trot to Lynn. Better watch out, or you might, fall, in!"

Laughter filled the air as the children giggled and squirmed with joy, loving the sensation of almost being dropped.

Danny's mother, sitting nearby, joined in the fun, her face glowing with happiness and love.

Given that Megan had just broken the news of Nikki's ex-husband's fraud to her a few days earlier, it was a miracle the woman could smile. Danny had fumed so hard, he needed to get out of the house to cool off. Nikki had just retreated to her room for a handful of minutes, and came back out, completely composed and ready to move on.

A total boss.

Megan's playful antics were abruptly interrupted by a loud, forceful bang at the front door. The sound reverberated through the room, shattering the tranquility like a lightning bolt.

Megan's heart skipped a beat as the door swung open without their welcoming call, revealing Danny's father, consumed by a tempest of rage and resentment. His eyes blazed with anger, his face contorted with an unsettling mix of fury and intoxication.

Megan instinctively stood, a protective instinct kicking in as she positioned herself between the children and the volatile presence before them.

The man had good reason to hate her.

She discovered that he never submitted the divorce documents. He and Nikki were technically still married and all of their 'advisors' were in on it. He still had access to all of her accounts, and basically moved money around so frequently there was a hope that she'd never have the time or energy to see what was going on.

Her inattention to the small line of her statements that said "withdrawals" also didn't do her any favors.

It also didn't help when most of her paper documents were altered to show incorrect numbers before being put in her mailbox.

Steve was thorough, she'd give him that. She had to request online access and see the source docs before she realized what was happening.

Luckily, she and Danny convinced Nikki to contact an attorney, even though she desperately just wanted it to be done and over with.

Looking at his face now...guess he just found out he was cut off from those accounts.

Steve was closed off from all of their accounts, retirement and savings, the mortgage, the car, everything. Danny pulled every string he could, he even asked Butch for help on some things. Fuck, Butch even made it so Steve was banned from his normal haunts like the casino, some betting dens, and even most of the local bars.

The man was blackballed.

When people felt backed into a corner...they could be unpredictable....

Unpredictability with a history of getting physical? Sounded like a recipe for disaster.

Megan's hands trembled with a mixture of fear and anger, her voice shaking but firm as she stood and faced him. "Steve," she stated, infusing her voice with a steely resolve. "You need to leave. Now."

Steve was beyond reason, lost in his own fury. He pointed a finger at Nikki, his voice booming with accusation. "This is all your fault! You've ruined everything!"

Nikki, her eyes flickering with defiance, stood her ground. "Nu-uh, no way. I will not be blamed for your crappy ways. Leave my house *now*. Before I call the cops."

The room became a battleground of words, a cacophony of anger and threats.

Megan's anger grew steadily, fueled by the toxic vitriol spewing from Danny's father's mouth and the way he berated Danny's mother. Steve got so loud that even unflappable Theo started to cry. Ava clung to Megan's pant leg in fear at the violent yelling.

She wished she could retreat with the kids to the other room, so they'd be safe from this, but she also didn't want to leave Nikki alone. Who knew what Steve would do?

Her protective instincts intensified as the sounds buffeted her from every direction.

Steve's screaming, Nikki's requests for him to leave, Ava and Theo crying, the pulls at her pant legs.

Everything just...overwhelmed her senses. She wanted to cover her ears and crawl out of her skin.

It needed to stop.

"That's it. I'm calling the cops." Megan's voice bit out.

Just as Steve turned and took a menacing step toward Megan, Danny burst into the still open front door, his eyes wide with concern as he took in the scene unfolding before him. Clearly, he heard the yelling from the driveway. He took in his father's threatening step and Megan's determined stance, and the rage that took over Danny's face was truly terrifying.

"What the hell is going on here?" Danny's voice thundered. He moved swiftly toward Megan, positioning himself between her and his father.

His father's gaze shifted to Danny, a mix of hatred and defiance etched on his face. He took a step forward, his voice dripping with venom. "You think you're better than me, don't you? You always have!"

Theo's particularly piercing wail intensified at that second, adding to the craziness and without breaking eye contact with his father, Danny bent and picked Theo up from where he was sitting on the ground.

Steve's eyes narrowed at his son's movements. Suddenly, his head jerked, looking at the baby in his arms. His red and sweaty face turned confused, and then contemplative as he stared at Danny.

Was he realizing what he was missing out on by being a complete jackass?

Danny was such a forgiving person; he'd probably fucking forgive the asshole for everything and welcome him back with open arms if the man would make half an effort.

He turned to Megan, "what'd you say your name was?"

Woah. Multiple-personalities much?

Against her better judgment, she gritted out her answer from between clenched teeth. "Megan Lowell."

"From Lowell?"

Funny.

Like she had never heard that one before.

"No. Winchendon. What of it?"

"I know a couple of Lowells there."

Megan blinked and looked at Danny in confusion. What the fuck was this? He was trying to get to know her now? Was he deranged?

Danny looked equally confused as he stared at his father, absently bouncing Theo on his hip.

Steve looked at the kids before looking back to Megan. "They don't look like you."

The room stayed silent.

"I was asking about you down at the bars – before they turned into fair-weather-fuckers – turns out those two aren't even yours kids?"

"They're mine in all the ways that count–"

"What the fu- heck were you doing asking about Megan?" Danny looked like he was going to blow for an entirely different reason now.

Steve just kept his beady eyes on her, making her skin crawl. "Word is they're your cousin's kids. How do their dads feel about you not giving them back their kids?"

Megan's stomach roiled and a chill sluiced down her spine. She felt Danny stiffen and absently she was thankful he was holding Theo, he would be less likely to assault the man for his not-so-vague threats."

"Their dads aren't in the picture. The adoption was iron-clad. You need to get sober and get counseling, but first, you just need to get out. Now." Her face felt like it was on fire but her cheeks felt frozen, a suffocating feeling gripped her lungs and she fought to maintain a steady breath and not let a panic attack claim her now.

"Is that why you're here shacking up with Danny? Using him? He's got enough cash to support you. Hell, he has enough to support you, his mom, and still have some leftover for his dad." Steve thumped himself on the chest. "That's what you do for family. You get it. You took care of your cousin's kids. Danny needs to step up and take care of his family. Bad shit happens when you don't. Shit has a way of coming out of the woodwork when you don't.

Danny's eyes blazed with a mixture of anger and disappointment. "Our relationship isn't based on money. I'm not a fucking money tree. Especially not yours. You need to leave. Get help. But we can't enable you any more. You hurt, Mom. You were always a dick to me...but her?" Megan sensed Nikki stiffening. "That's just...unforgivable. You truly are just a manipulative, lying, and selfish prick. So before I take care of my father that would involve a phone call to the police...Leave. Now."

The room fell into a heavy silence, the air pregnant with tension and unspoken emotions. Theo made some small noises but at least wasn't crying anymore.

Steve stared hard at Danny, his face twisted with rage. Then he turned those angry eyes to Megan. "People do crazy things for survival. To pay the bills."

"It was never for the bills, Dad." Danny's soft, defeated voice broke Megan's still-racing heart.

"Kicking a man when he's down and has an addiction. Mighty big of you son. I hope one day you feel the same sense of loss that I have standing here, knowing I lost my only son."

Danny didn't even respond.

With one final, contemptuous glare, Danny's father turned on his heel and stumbled out of the room, leaving behind the sharp stench of vodka.

Well, things couldn't get worse than that at least...

# CHAPTER THIRTY-ONE

# October 3, Monday
## Danny

Danny had been searching for Liam for days, struggling to find a moment when his teammate wasn't surrounded by the drama that seemed to be swirling around him lately. The guy's personal life had gotten...complicated. Hence why he was the latest on Butch's shit list.

But today, luck was on his side. He found Liam sitting on a chair in Jen's pre-hab rooms, staring at his phone with a distant expression while he waited for his turn to be worked on.

"Hey, Liam?" Danny's voice was cautious as he approached.

Liam glanced up, his small crystal blue eyes meeting Danny's for a moment before he blinked in surprise. "Danny, hey. What's up?"

Danny took a deep breath, his heart racing. Maybe this was it. He berated himself for waiting this long to track Liam down for this. "I need to ask you something. Can we find a quiet place to chat real quick?"

Liam frowned but stood anyway. "Sure, man. Let's go to one of the empty classrooms."

As they walked to the nearest empty classroom, Danny's mind raced. He should have done this weeks ago. Maybe it was as simple as just asking one of the nicest guys on the team.

Theo would be fucking lucky with Liam for a dad.

They shut the classroom door behind them and Danny cleared his throat. "So, I need to ask you something. For a good friend."

Liam's eyebrows shot up in surprise, and he stared at Danny for a moment before giving him a funny look. "Okay?"

Danny nodded, his heart pounding. "Yeah, my girl Megan has a son she adopted from her cousin, Starla. Starla left a note to Megan that her baby daddy was a guy on the Spartans." He handed over her picture, which was well wrinkled at this point. "Do you recognize her? Have you ever seen her before?"

Liam leaned back, his eyes narrowing as he pulled the photo into the place where his eyes could see it better. Guy needed glasses but refused.

He took his time, as if sifting through a mental album of memories. After a moment, he let out a low whistle, his head cocked to the side. "Yeah, man. I remember her."

Danny's heart raced. This was it. His hands started shaking. "Yes?"

Liam looked back at the picture and then began to speak slowly, as if he was piecing together memories. "It was about a year ago, I think. She showed up at my big Valentine's Day party. She was...let's say, she left an impression."

Danny leaned in, his anticipation growing. "You guys hooked up?"

Liam chuckled, shaking his head. "Fuck, no. She was hitting on all the guys, acting wild. She even took off her top and danced on the bar by the pool. I had to coax her into getting dressed again."

Danny's heart fell. "Fuck"

Fuck, fuck, fuck.

His head felt heavy and he rubbed hard at his face. Fuck, Liam was their last 'good' option on the team. Danny let out a hard sigh. He needed to call Megan and give her the bad news. Let her decide if she wanted to give up and not risk the custody battle, or worse.

Liam moved slightly, catching Danny's attention, his expression changing. "Actually, now that I think about it, I remember thinking she was your date that night." Liam let out a funny laugh. "I remember worrying about you because your bar had gotten so low during that time of your life."

Danny's heart skipped a beat. "What?"

He didn't remember her at all.

Yet another reason he got sober.

Liam raised an eyebrow, giving Danny a funny look. "Oh yeah, she was by your side most of the night, feeding you drink after drink."

Danny's mind was spinning and he drew his eyebrows together as he tried to remember. He rubbed harder at his face like it would help him remember more from that night. The timeline matched to when she would have gotten pregnant...

Holy fucking shit.

Danny's mind spun and his stomach clenched as he tried to process the bombshell Liam had just dropped. There was a chance he could be Theo's father. Him. A dad.

No. No, it wasn't possible. He racked his brain, desperately grasping at hazy memories of that night over a year ago. But it was all a blur, lost in a drunken fog.

He couldn't be. He'd remember.

Megan's face flashed in his mind. What would that even mean?

Before he could vomit all over both in panic and shock, Liam spoke again. "But you know what? Never mind. It wasn't just you."

A cool wave of relief washed down him, making his legs and arms feel weak.

He wanted to collapse in the nearest chair and sleep. He felt like he just ran an emotional gauntlet. He needed a break.

Fucking hell, that was close. Thank God he got sober.

"She was all over Butch a ton too. I forgot about that."

Danny's stomach dropped. Alarm bells went off in his head.

Butch?

Fucking hell.

Butch was one of the last people he wanted to be connected to this situation.

He'd go after Theo hard, just from an entitled perspective, not because he wanted a kid. He'd fucking beat Theo just like Steve beat Danny, he was sure of it.

Danny's heart was racing and he couldn't stop his hands from shaking. He was a world class athlete, nerves of steel. He had won a freaking Super Bowl damnit!

And right then, he was shaking like a leaf. Like a child.

Liam noticed Danny's turmoil because he spoke up again. "Hey, man, I think I remember her taking the walk of shame the next morning. I've got security footage from that night. Closed circuit stuff. You could pull up old feeds and maybe see who she stumbled out with."

Danny's heart stopped. This was it.

"Could you? Now?"

Liam nodded, reaching for his phone. "Yeah, sure. I'll text you the code to my alarms and the lockbox with the extra key. You can run over and check."

Relief and excitement surged through Danny. "Fuck, man. Seriously, Liam. This could be it. Megan will probably want to avoid this result with a ten foot pole but at least she'll have an answer for Theo. I can't...I can't thank you enough. I wish I had cornered you sooner."

Liam shrugged, a small, worried smile on his face. "No problem, man. Happy to help. I hope you find what you're looking for."

Danny stood up, his heart pounding.

He needed to tell Megan about this.

Now.

He pulled out his phone and dialed her number, his fingers trembling with a mix of nerves and excitement.

"Megan? Meet me at Liam's house as soon as you can. I'll text you the address. I think we might finally have our answer."

The line was silent for a moment before Megan's voice came through, filled with curiosity and worry. "Really? Are you serious?"

Danny's heart raced as he replied, "Yeah, babe. I think we're about to find out who Theo's father is."

# CHAPTER THIRTY-TWO

# October 3, Monday
## Megan

Megan and Danny entered Liam's house, their hearts pounding with a mix of anticipation and anxiety. They left the kids with Nikki with promises to see them soon.

This could be it. Their answer.

They made their way into Liam's high tech CCTV room, surrounded by the flickering glow of screens and the weight of uncertainty.

As they began scrolling through the videos on their side-by-side computers, Megan's fingers trembled slightly. The room was filled with a palpable tension, an unspoken understanding of the gravity of their search. Time seemed to slow down as they navigated through the memories captured on screen.

As they scrolled through the videos, Megan's finally landed on Valentine's Day party.

She nudged Danny, her eyes glued to the screen. "Look, it's Chloe and Ryan. Was this their Valentine's date disaster they always laugh about?"

Danny chuckled distractedly. "Oh, man. I remember this party now, the day after was the day I finally decided to get sober. I told you about that night. I woke up naked in Liam's guest bedroom with pool floaties all over me. I went to my first AA meeting that morning."

Megan's small smile faded as her eyes scanned the footage, her attention momentarily diverted. Danny's innocent remark hung in the air, something about them making her skin prick.

Her heart skipped a beat, her mind racing to connect the dots on the screen in front of her.

A jolt of recognition zapped through her and she cocked her head as she kept her eyes fixed on the screen.

Was that?

Jen's dad was at the party?

Megan's mind scrambled. Was that before or after Jen told him to get lost?

Megan's stomach fell as she watched Jen's father exchange something with the Spartans' offensive coordinator. Everyone knew Butch liked to gamble and drink. So it wasn't a surprise they knew each other. But what the fuck did they trade?

Megan's eyes bulged as she finally saw Starla enter the frame. Her fingers involuntarily flexed at the image of her cousin, being wild and seemingly happy. What had she gotten into?

She was never Sister Theresa, but she was Megan's friend. Once upon a time. Her suicide still hurt.

Megan's mouth fell open, and she swayed slightly in her chair as she watched Starla stumble heavily into Butch, grabbing at his crotch and breathing into his face. Butch gave her a pinched smile and looked down at her, giving her a once over.

They exchanged a few words, the video recording didn't have audio, and then Butch passed a small baggie to Starla.

Oh god.

Megan's whole body started to shake.

Darkness started closing in and her body felt too hot.

In horror she watched as Starla turned around, not nearly as seemingly drunk anymore and looked for someone in the crowd.

Her face turned laser focused when she found what she wanted at the bar.

She stumbled over, losing her steadiness with a practice that had Megan's eyes bulging and a tightness form in her chest.

Then, Megan watched as Starla, her cousin, her roommate, her friend, the mother of her two children, emptied the small baggie into Danny's drink before climbing up on the bar and stripping off her top.

If Megan wanted to Google it, she wondered if she'd find that the length of Starla's little strip tease was the same length as what it would take for a roofie to dissolve in a drink.

She slowly rotated her head to Danny, who had his own eyes glued to Megan's screen, his eyes huge and a green tinge to his skin.

The room fell into an eerie silence as the weight of the revelation hung heavy in the air. Megan's mind raced, her thoughts swirling with a mix of horror, anger, and concern for Danny.

Danny's face was pale, his eyes wide with a mix of shock and confusion. The gravity of the situation began to sink in. In slow motion, the pieces of the puzzle began to align, and a sick feeling settled in the pit of her stomach.

"Danny," she finally managed to say, her voice quivering with a mixture of disbelief and concern, "Danny, I am so—"

Danny's voice cracked; his throat constricted. "I need to go." Immediately, he thrust himself away from the desk and rushed from the room, letting the door slam shut behind him.

# Chapter Thirty-Three
## October 3, Monday
## Megan

Danny abruptly rose from his seat and rushed out of the room, leaving Megan bewildered and alone as panic surged through her veins.

What the fuck had just happened?

What did they just see?

She sat frozen, her mind racing.

The weight of the situation pressed down on her, suffocating her with a mix of fear and confusion.

Frantically, Megan scrambled to her feet, her heart pounding in her chest.

Breathe, breathe, breathe.

Step one: She needed to find Danny and offer whatever support he needed.

Step two: Freak out after.

She searched the whole house, not finding him anywhere. When she checked the driveway, his car was gone.

Fuck.

Immediately, she dialed his number, only to be sent straight to voicemail.

Again.

And again.

And again.

Tears welled up in Megan's eyes, threatening to spill over as a sense of helplessness washed over her. She knew she couldn't let her distress overshadow her responsibilities.

The image of her kids, eagerly awaiting her and Danny's arrival, flashed in her mind, reminding her of her obligations as a mother.

Nikki had bingo that night. Megan didn't have the option of just leaving them and trying to track down Danny. That wouldn't be fair to Nikki. It was the one request Nikki made of Megan: that she and the kids not disturb her bingo nights.

Fuck.

Then again, her son had been raped. Not that Megan could tell her that. It wasn't her place.

But it was a damn good excuse for having Nikki miss bingo.

Then again, he *left*.

Maybe he wanted space.

Danny had shit to deal with, trauma to process. He didn't need Megan chasing him down when he clearly wanted to be alone. And she couldn't necessarily drag her kids along.

She paused... technically, Theo was his kid too.

Her skin felt too tight and her headache was severe.

She didn't watch the rest of the video. Maybe Starla just drugged him...

Which was bad enough.

But maybe she slept with someone else?

Or maybe that wasn't the night she conceived Theo?

Desperate hope made her mind suggest increasingly unlikely possibilities.

Then again...why was she involved with Butch? Was the Butch baggie the same thing Jen's dad passed over?

Fuck, her head hurt.

Her chest spasmed and she rubbed at her temples.

Would Danny want him full-time? Would he fight for him? Or would he avoid him like the plague?

*Breathe, breathe, breathe.*

With a heavy heart, Megan put her phone away. Danny would call her back when he was ready. Probably. Maybe. Hopefully.

Every step felt heavier than the last as she made her way back to the computer. She needed to send the video footage to herself. And any other angles.

And...

And watch the rest of the night.

Did Starla and Danny enter the same room?

How could her cousin do this? What was she involved in? What was that wad of cash in the envelope from? Was she paid to hurt Danny? To violate him? What else had she done? Anger, no, rage, surged in her. It was such a violation. Such a...there wasn't a word for the hatred swirling in Megan.

To hurt another person like that...it was unforgivable.

Unforgivable.

Under the rage, betrayal and sadness churned, but the more Megan thought about it, the more they were wiped out in the need to unleash her fury. Starla needed to pay.

But...

Starla was dead.

And that was another question.

Why?

Was there something more nefarious there than just an overdose? Suicide not because of depression or post-partum? But maybe from guilt? Maybe a murder that looked like an overdose?

What the fuck was going on?

She needed to know if Danny was okay.

But no. He wanted space. So, she'd give him space. But in the meantime, she'd get more information.

She pinched her lips and closed her eyes tight before bracing herself and opening more video files.

They needed confirmation.

They needed to know whether a DNA test should be done.

Though...thinking of their similarities...she didn't think it was necessary. Thinking on it now, she was amazed she hadn't recognized the similarities between them sooner. Theo looked just like Danny when he was a kid. Nikki always commented on it when they were looking at pictures. They all just always discredited because Danny said he wasn't his.

Holy fucking shit.

She raised a trembling hand to her lips and tried not to cry.

Her cousin had raped Danny.

# CHAPTER THIRTY-FOUR

# October 3, Monday
## Danny

That night, Danny sat alone in his shell of a house, his mind a storm of conflicting emotions. Despite the wide range of children's toys now covering the floors, it still felt hollow.

He fought the urge to vomit. Again.

The weight of the revelation bore down on him, threatening to choke him in its suffocating grip. He reached for the bottle of vodka he had just bought after fleeing Liam's house, his trembling hand hovering just inches away, tempted to drown his sorrows and numb the pain.

A sliver of rationality seeped through the fog of despair. The bottle would only be a temporary escape, a band-aid over a festering wound. And would ruin a year of sobriety.

Apparently a year that he was a father and didn't even know it.

Just a sip. He could stop after a sip. Or two. Surely, he deserved it?

His sponsor's hard-ass voice echoed in his head.

Fuck.

With a mix of self-control and sheer willpower, he lowered his hand and looked away. His eyes roamed on the toys scattered around and he started to hyperventilate.

Fuck.

As he took them in, his heart squeezed, and his stomach roiled violently.

He'd already been sick multiple times already. The violation, the crime that had been committed against him. He felt the acid build in his throat again and he swallowed hard, trying to breathe through the growing nausea.

He ignored the persistent buzzing of his phone, letting Megan's calls go unanswered. He couldn't face her, couldn't bear to confront the truth that lay in the depths of his shattered soul. The mere thought of discussing it with anyone seemed impossible at that moment.

He thought about calling Michael and telling him what the fuck had just happened. But when he tried to dial his number, his hands wouldn't move. He convulsively swallowed again and fought the urge to shower and scrub every inch of his body.

Danny felt like he was drowning, smothered by the overwhelming weight of shame and anger. Which only served to enrage him more, especially because he knew he had nothing to be ashamed about.

*Fucking* Starla did. She should be ashamed. But she couldn't feel anything because the fucking rapist was fucking dead.

He wanted to roar. Throw things. Break something.

Preferably her neck.

But the bitch was already dead, so it would serve no purpose.

None of it made sense. Was it just any player she was after? Did she mean to get pregnant? What part of this was planned, and what part was unintentional?

The fact that she committed suicide right after Theo's birth...was it guilt? Was it an accidental overdose?

"Fuck!" he yelled out into the quiet house. It echoed off the walls and left him feeling even more empty.

He didn't want kids. He never wanted kids. Was Theo going to end up an alcoholic? Or worse, a shithead like Starla? There was nature and there was nurture. Was Megan enough to save Theo?

Danny stilled.

Fuck.

Theo was his son. His fucking *son*. Was he going to leave him with Megan? Was she going to tell Theo?

Sure, Theo was just a baby now, but as he got older...was he going to think of Danny as 'Dad?'

The room felt stifling and sweat started to drip on his neck and forehead. Frantically, Danny jumped up and started to pace.

Should he ask for custody? Take Theo on weekends? Or maybe during the week? Or off-season? What about Ava? Theo adored Ava. And Megan...Danny couldn't take Theo from Megan...

But...Theo was his son. He wanted to spend as much time with him as possible. He had already missed so much.

But he never wanted kids.

His fingers started to go numb, and he clenched his hands roughly trying to bring back the feeling in them.

The walls were closing in as he paced back and forth, his footsteps echoing in the silence.

Embarrassment coursed through his veins, a searing reminder of his vulnerability and violation.

He knew that he shouldn't feel ashamed, that he was the victim in all of this, but the societal stigma and ingrained notions of masculinity gnawed at his soul.

What fucking *guy* gets raped?

Anger surged within him; a fierce flame fueled by a sense of betrayal. How could this have happened to him? He just wanted his brain to stop working! To be silent so he could process this without a million different thoughts and feelings hitting him at every second.

He threw his phone against the opposite wall where it gave a sickening thud and crashed to the ground. A small dent formed in the sheetrock.

He couldn't even muster up the energy to care he'd have to fix that later.

His eyes locked on the vodka bottle again. It would help him forget...just for one night.

Just one night.

He'd go to a meeting tomorrow and come clean.

But just for one night, he could use a little help. It wasn't every day a person realized they were raped.

# CHAPTER THIRTY-FIVE

# October 4, Tuesday
## Megan

The next day, Megan was scribbling notes frantically in the margin of the financial statements in front of her as her manager quickly outlined the various issues presented by the management team of their client.

A knock at the door had them all pausing and looking up in surprise.

Her bosses exchanged annoyed glances, clearly disapproving of the interruption.

The receptionist looked uncomfortable but moved past it. "I'm sorry, but it's an emergency call from Megan's daycare."

Megan's heart skipped a beat. Without a second thought, she stood up, her stomach tightening with worry.

As she walked to the door, her boss called out from behind her. "This is a mandatory meeting; we'll pause until you're back. We need all hands on deck for this one."

Ignoring the judgmental glares, Megan rushed to her office to answer the call.

The daycare director spoke in a high, panicked voice. "Megan, we're so sorry, but something is wrong with Ava. She has a 105-degree fever, is lethargic, and can't stop vomiting and having diarrhea. We have no idea what's happening. We've called 911 but you should get here, or to the hospital as soon as you can."

Megan's heart stopped in her chest and her mind raced with fear. She disconnected, grabbed her purse, and hurried from her office.

Belatedly, she realized she needed to tell her team, so she sprinted to the doorway and popped her head. "I'm sorry, but I need to go, it's an emergency."

"It always is," some dickhead muttered in the corner.

Megan barely heard him, she was already turning toward the hall to leave, but her boss's words did catch her attention.

"If you leave now, Megan, you can start looking for another job. We can't have you at sixty percent. We don't pay you sixty percent and we can't keep doing this song and dance. Your absences are affecting the company and your personal life is interfering with your professional responsibilities. You had an 'emergency' yesterday too. You've already received verbal and written warnings. Enough is enough."

She froze, her body already in panic mode was struggling to process his threat. Was that even legal?

"This is why women shouldn't be CPAs," another douche chimed in from the other corner as before.

Already feeling overwhelmed and terrified for her daughter, Megan's eyes welled up with tears. The mix of frustration, anger, and worry overwhelmed her, but she thought of her sweet little daughter in an ambulance, and decided enough was enough.

"Fuck you all," she said before turning and rushing from the office.

She had a daughter to worry about, not these assholes.

Her mind raced as she raced to the daycare to pick up Theo and bring him to the hospital.

She considered leaving him there until closing. But if Ava was really sick, there was no way she was leaving her side to get Theo. And Danny still was MIA. Panic gripped her, and she questioned whether she should call Nikki for support, unsure if it was appropriate given the circumstances. Not that Nikki knew...presumably.

The unfamiliar face of a new teacher greeted her, causing her concern to skyrocket.

"Where's Ms. Johnson? Is she not here today?"

"No, she's out sick. I'm filling in for her."

Megan's heart sank further, doubting the competency and qualifications of the new teacher. Staffing shortages once again rearing their ugly head. If it was a choice between competent staffing or a closed daycare for the day...was there really a question?

Close the fucking daycare.

She scooped Theo up into her arms, grabbed the bare minimum of stuff from their cubbies, and rushed back to her car, determined to get him to the hospital where Ava was being treated.

With Theo in one arm and her phone in the other, Megan frantically dialed Danny's number again, hoping that he would answer this time.

It went straight to voicemail.

Mother trucker.

She rolled her lips together and debated calling one of the girls, they'd be here in a heartbeat...but they had their own kids. If what Ava had was contagious...

Why would Danny turn off his phone?

He promised to be there for her. Even if they weren't romantically involved, he promised to be a friend. A constant. He promised not to let her down.

He needed to return her calls!

She angrily swiped at her eyes.

Fuck him then.

It always boiled down to herself anyways. She didn't need a man, she didn't need a friend, she could do it solo. Always had.

Her skin was getting hot and black spots popped into her vision. The steering wheel creaked under her grip.

*Breathe, breathe, breathe.*

As she arrived at the hospital, Megan clutched Theo tightly, rushing to the waiting room. She anxiously waited for updates from the doctors, her mind consumed by fear and doubts.

Did she hug Ava goodbye this morning when she dropped her off?

Probably.

But what if she didn't? What if she was so distracted by Theo or talking with another parent or teacher that she forgot to give Ava a hug and a kiss?

What if it was one of the mornings Ava ran off happily and Megan didn't want to rock the boat by calling her back just to say goodbye.

*Dear god, Megan couldn't remember if she had hugged her daughter goodbye this morning.*

She was going to be sick.

Oh fuck, what if she was the reason Ava was sick? Did she give her bad milk that morning? Spoiled deli meat? Did something she packed go bad? What if Ava climbed up on the table this morning when Megan was out of the room and ate some of the flowers Danny had given them? Were the flowers poisonous? Megan frantically searched for her phone so she could look up which flowers were toxic.

Just then the doctors came into the waiting room where Megan was jittering, bouncing a bobbling Theo on her knee.

She rushed to greet them, plopping Theo on her hip.

"Ms. Lowell, we're running some tests to be sure, but it looks like Ava may have gotten into some button batteries at school. We're working on removing them now and seeing the extent of the damage. When she wakes up, she'll be pretty out of it. But once we get her situated, you'll be free to visit her. We want to keep her overnight for observation but if everything checks out, you may be free to go home tomorrow."

Megan had sent her daughter to *that* daycare.

She *knew* it wasn't ideal and sent her *anyway*.

*She* did this to her.

To her baby.

She choked out a sob and covered her mouth with her free hand.

She almost killed her baby by putting her job first and not being willing to fight for a new daycare spot.

She could have lost her baby girl.

The feeling surged over her. The disgust. Self-loathing.

She was an awful parent.

Megan let out another strangled sob and collapsed down in the chair, not even caring if it was a little hard on her tailbone.

She deserved to be hurt.

To hurt as much as her poor baby.

She gasped for breath as tears ran down her cheeks.

How could she have minimized the problems at her daycare so much that she didn't see the warning signs? Was she so prideful that she made herself blind to the obvious? She could have prevented all of this by changing daycares or taking Nikki up on her offers to watch the kids full time.

She did this.

Megan did this.

Megan squeezed her eyes tight and practiced her deep breathing, trying not to have a full-on panic attack in the waiting room in front of the other patients and their families.

A small sound rose to her and she looked down. Theo was staring up at her with a small frown on his round face. A chubby hand reached out and pulled on her lower lip.

God, it could have been Theo. With his age...maybe it would have been even worse.

*Get it together, Megan.*

She took some slower, deeper breaths and made sure to arrange her features in a more pleasant arrangement so as not to freak out Theo. Poor baby boy didn't need both his sister and his mother admitted to the hospital.

She stilled.

What if child protective services were called? Would they say she was unfit if they found out she had anxiety and panic attacks?

She felt the familiar chokehold settle in on her throat and chest, squeezing tight. It was like she was being crushed.

Was she going to lose her kids?

Maybe Danny could take them instead? Would they be safer with him?

Provided that he didn't ask for a trade so he could get as far away from Megan and the kids as possible. So he'd never have to see the result of his abuse ever again.

An older woman came over and gave her a small smile before slowly extending her arms into a cage around Megan. Inch by inch they closed in tighter and tighter until Megan was being squeezed firmly by the older lady. For a few seconds, Megan closed her eyes, feeling the tight embrace compress her, trap her, cocoon her.

*Breathe, breathe, breathe.*

Gradually she felt her breathing come easier and her head start to clear. Theo was still banging lightly at her leg, but otherwise didn't seem disturbed by a stranger going up and hugging his mother.

"Thank you," Megan croaked out, rubbing at her face.

The older woman nodded and gave her a compassionate smile, she patted her twice on the shoulder and said, "You're doing great, Mom. Hang in there. We all just do the best we can." Then the woman turned and walked back to where an older gentleman was sitting, his hand wrapped in a bloody towel, waiting for his name to be called.

Okay, okay.

She was okay now.

She lowered herself and Theo to the worn carpet, absently picking up a toy and wiggling it in front of him. With her other hand, still shaking from her moment of panic, she pulled out her phone and tried calling Danny one last time, a lone tear escaping and streaking down her face, the weight of the situation crushing her. Voicemail. Again.

Was he okay?

If he was, why wasn't he answering?

He promised he would.

Obviously the frequency of her calls indicated something was seriously wrong...right?

As the hour dragged on, Megan and Theo played in the stark waiting room, surrounded by the hushed whispers of worried patients and the occasional wails of sick patients. Luckily, Theo sensed the severity of the situation and sat quietly in Megan's arms, happy to munch on whatever item was pulled out of the depths of the diaper bag, crumpled and expired as they may be.

Every time the door to the ER opened, Megan would tense, ready to stand at a moment's notice if they were coming to grab her and bring her back to Ava. But after an hour, Megan's nerves were frayed.

Every time she had gone up to ask for updates, they said that they were waiting for updates from the doctor. What did that mean?

Did she ask the nurse if something else had gone wrong?

Was her daughter okay?

She didn't want to distract them if they were busy saving Ava's life...maybe she just needed to wait?

Maybe they forgot to come get her?

Her mind swirled and she couldn't stop shaking as she worked to keep Theo entertained.

She wished Danny was here. He would have charmed the whole ER department with his easy smiles, and she would have had not only answers, but they would have been invited back and brought dinner from the hospital cafeteria and toys for Theo.

The poor kid was losing interest in the small collection of toys from their diaper bag.

Hell, if Danny were here, he would have been able to convince someone to run up to Pediatrics and steal some of their toys. Danny's presence, his reassuring words, his strength, and confidence...it would have made a difference. *He* would have made a difference.

It felt like years, but they were finally invited back to sit with Ava, her heart skipping a beat as she approached her daughter's bedside.

Ava lay pale and weak, hooked up to various monitors, her little body struggling to overcome the effects of what she ingested. Megan's eyes brimmed with tears, a mix of relief and worry flooding her. Taking a seat beside Ava's bed, Megan whispered soothing words and gently stroked her daughter's hair away from her small face.

There were no words for the emotions warring inside of her. Nothing but silence, terror, and regret coating her every nerve ending. Her brain was on autopilot. It was amazing Theo hadn't protested her robotic behavior yet.

But her brain just wasn't working.

At all.

After giving lots of hugs and snuggles to her sleeping child, Megan used the room phone to call down to the cafeteria. She didn't want to leave Ava's side now that she was finally here. She ordered two full dinners and snacks to last the night for her and Theo. She didn't want to leave even for a second in case Ava woke up.

As the hours ticked by, Megan's unease grew. Shouldn't Ava have woken up by now?

She anxiously glanced at the phone, hoping Danny had called. Nothing.

Now that she was within arm's reach of both of her children and listening to them breathe peacefully into the quiet room, she took a moment to shoot some texts to her girls, filling them in.

Immediately, she was drowning in incoming phone calls and texts. As she calmed them down with brief updates, she couldn't stop herself from mentally castigating herself for her poor judgment. Again.

She *knew* the daycare was understaffed. She *knew* it wasn't an ideal place to have a child. *And she sent her kids there anyways.*

Megan should be the one laying in the hospital bed, paying the price for that. Not her little girl.

In the midst of her turmoil, a growing resentment toward Danny for his absence built in her. Anger swirled within her, questioning why he couldn't be there when she needed him the most.

She understood he was dealing with his own realization, but fuck, she called eight thousand times, he didn't get the hint it was an emergency?

Hours turned into an agonizing night, the beeping of machines and the hushed conversations of medical staff blended into a surreal symphony. Nerves and exhaustion were Megan's constant companions as the children slept.

As the night slowly gave way to a new day, Megan decided. Counting on Prince Charming to come and rescue them was a fool's hope. It was the twenty-first century; she could be her own Prince Charming. And if she ever found her own real Prince Charming, he sure as fuck was going to know to call back when he had eight thousand missed calls.

# CHAPTER THIRTY-SIX

# October 4, Tuesday
## Danny

Danny's muscles burned as he pushed himself to the limit at the gym,. He'd been at the stadium all day, hoping that the physical exertion would somehow drown out the swirling chaos within his mind.

The revelation yesterday...

He grappled with a mix of emotions—anger, confusion, and a profound sense of violation.

He didn't know what the fuck to do with it. Any of it.

He was a dad?

He was a rape victim?

He was a fucking all star athlete...and here he was...a rape victim?

And that rape gave him a son. A child he never wanted.

But now that he knew...

Theo was fucking amazing.

If he was going to be a dad, he'd want it to be to a kid like Theo.

But his alcoholism...

After hurling his phone at the wall, Danny inspected it for damage. Besides a cracked screen, it was actually okay, though it wasn't charging quite right. The cord needed to be fidgeted with to get the exact angle. But, he'd just learned some pretty suck shit, so he figured he'd deal with the issue of his phone later.

Ya know, after he figured out what he fucking felt about everything.

Danny went ass to grass on another deep and heavy squat, puffing out a steady exhale as he pushed upwards, glorying in the burn of his legs and butt. When he racked the weight, the gym's door swung open and Jen, working late, stormed in, her eyes red and filled with fury.

Danny almost felt sorry for John, wherever he was.

He paused...

Actually, he didn't remember seeing John—

Before he could utter a word, Jen rushed up to him, placed her palms on his chest and shoved hard. He even rocked back an inch.

Fuck. What happened?

"You fucker! I thought you were better than that. How could you just disappear *like that*?" She snapped her fingers. "Do you have any idea how hard it is to wait in an ER with a child while you're stressing about whether the other one is going to survive?"

Danny's breath hitched.

What?

A sense of weightlessness entered his body and black spots danced in his vision, this time, not from the weights.

He struggled to find the right words. "What?" He felt winded.

"Megan and the kids, Danny. Or did you just decide to drop them now that Green Bay decided to express an interest in you last night?"

Danny blinked and frowned at her. Danny spent the entire night sitting in his dark house, having a staring contest with the full bottle of vodka.

He had won out and not opened the bottle.

Well, that was a lie.

He opened the bottle, but he didn't drink any.

He just took a nice long inhale of the strong smell.

"Jen, I...what?" His chest felt too tight, and his face felt numb.

Jen's expression changed to confused, but her frustration remained palpable.

"Megan. We all stopped by and brought supplies and stuff as soon as we heard, but being in the hospital with two little kids..."

He gripped her shoulder, probably harder than he should have, but he felt like was going to fall over. "What? Are they okay?" He said it so fast it sounded like one word.

Luckily, she understood his garbled speech and she gave him a long look.

"Yes...now they are—"

He took a step towards her. "But they weren't? What happened?"

Fucking Jen. She usually spoke much faster than this. Why was she talking so slow?

"Danny," she said slowly, watching him. "Ava was brought to the ER earlier today. She was really sick. She ate some batteries or something...they've been in the hospital since... Hey, where are you going?"

Danny had already started moving to the door, adrenaline coursing through his veins.

He didn't even say goodbye.

He ran to the bag where he stored his keys and phone and found his phone dead. Fucking battery.

As he drove to the hospital, Danny's mind raced with a mix of fear and determination.

Given what happened last night, would he have answered when he saw her calls?

Fuck!

He slammed his palm against the steering wheel.

The car ride felt horrifyingly long, Danny's mind was consumed with thoughts of Ava and fear Megan must have felt. As he approached the hospital, he took a deep breath, gathering his resolve.

At the end of the day, whether Megan forgave him, he was the closest thing that Ava had to a father, despite the various uncles that were in her life. And it turned out that he *was* Theo's dad, so by extension, Theo's family was his family.

And maybe, if Megan would let him, maybe he could be something more to her as well...

# CHAPTER THIRTY-SEVEN

# October 4, Tuesday
# Megan

Megan was sitting in the room, her exhaustion causing her head to flop to the side when sleep overtook her. Luckily, she was able to pop back awake to keep her eyes on Ava to make sure she was okay. After watching the video at Liam's place, and spending all Monday night tossing and turning and fretting about Danny, Megan was exhausted. Combine that with the emotional trauma of learning that her negligence and selfishness essentially injured her daughter?

She wanted to sleep. Forever.

In the ground right next to Starla.

Scratch that, as far away from that awful bitch as physically possible. That her cousin would do such a heinous thing still made her nauseous.

The depression pulled at her, making her question whether she was fit for anything at this point. She clearly couldn't handle being a parent.

She was the fucking *worst*.

When she heard a commotion down the hall, she shifted a sleeping Theo to her other shoulder and turned her head towards the door. She had refused to let the nurses shut it, wanting to be able to yell to them if she needed to.

More yelling made its way down the hall.

Something about it seemed familiar.

More shouting and pounding.

Jeeze, that dude was pissed.

Megan absently patted Theo's rump and kept an eye on the door, listening to the ruckus continue. As the sound grew closer, her instincts kicked in.

Was that...

Megan sat up straighter and her heart pounded.

A moment later, Danny came bursting through the doorway, his face flushed with anger and determination. Megan's eyes widened in surprise, not quite knowing what to feel: confusion, surprise, a touch of relief?

"Danny? What's going on?"

Danny's chest heaved as he caught his breath, his eyes scanning the room until they locked onto Ava lying on the bed. His face contorted with pain and regret.

Just then, the nurses and some security personnel rushed in behind him. He didn't get to be an all-star wide receiver by being slow. Megan sat forward, careful not to jostle Theo, and waved them off.

The security guard looked furious, but the nurses took in Danny's broken expression as he stared at Ava in the bed and let Megan decide that he was an acceptable visitor.

"Ava girl—" his voice choked out, barely audible. He moved an arm like he wanted to touch her but pulled it back before making contact.

"She's okay." Megan watched him, still not quite sure what was happening.

Slowly, Danny placed a large hand on her small forehead, swiping her small blonde wisps back from her face. As they had done all night, they sprang right back to where they were, but Danny's hand kept rubbing them backward, like he couldn't stop himself from the futile motion.

"Baby girl," Danny whispered. With bright, glistening eyes, he leaned forward and placed a soft kiss to his head and then pressed his cheek to the top of her little head. He stayed there, pressed against her, his eyes shut, and his mouth pressed tight.

Megan swallowed hard and looked away, unable to keep watching and not break out in more sobs. She had just barely gotten Theo into a deep sleep.

After a moment, Danny looked over to Megan, his voice trembling with desperation. "I'm so sorry, Meg. I should have been here. I should have been by your side, supporting you and the kids."

Again, her feelings warred within her. "I get it. You were dealing with your own shit. But Danny, when there are kids in your life, you don't just get to ghost people. You don't get to retreat and hide away. People might need you. Shit might happen."

"Yeah, I get that—"

"You told me you were going to be a friend. Someone to count on." Her voice broke but she powered through. "You should have been here. Ava was in the ER, and I needed you. *We* needed you. But you weren't *here*."

Danny's shoulders slumped, the weight of his actions crashing down on him. He rounded Ava's bed to kneel beside Megan, tears welling up in his eyes. "I messed up, Megan. I know I did. I was dealing with my own demons, but I didn't know this was happening. My phone..." He shook his head. "That doesn't excuse me from abandoning you guys when you needed me the most. I know that. But I was dealing with some pretty heavy shit..."

Megan widened her eyes and looked toward the bed. "And we weren't? You said I could count on you to *be there! You said when I'd call, you'd answer. You promised.*" She couldn't hide the sob that slipped out. It felt like her throat was on fire with how hard she was choking back the tears.

Danny's light eyes closed slowly, as if in pain. He opened them again and stared up at her, those blue-green lights flashing with the tears that had collected there, threatening to spill over.

Gone was his ever-present smile.

"Honey, I had no idea. I was dealing with something, and I ran away. I'm so sorry. But I had no idea. I came as soon as I heard. I promise. I would have been here. I swear."

Megan felt her body soften as she saw the genuine remorse in Danny's eyes. Her stomach clenched and she just wanted a hug. From him.

Unable to take the distance and still feeling the sting of being alone during this latest crisis, she leaned forward and rested her forehead against his. She took in a shuddering breath and tried not to break out into tears again. "I thought I was going to lose her." She sucked in a jagged breath as she tried to control her bubbling emotions from spilling out.

Danny nodded, his skin rubbing against her, his voice choked with emotion. "Honey."

Megan pulled away and looked down at Theo in her arms. It wasn't just Ava she was afraid to lose. Though, to be fair, in a vastly different way.

"I'll fight you for him. With every penny I have, I'll fight you for him. I know you're his dad, but I'm also his mom. And—" She swallowed hard again, unable to stop the tears from spilling out and the knot got harder in her throat. So hard it hurt.

Danny just looked at her, his expression confused and torn. Slowly, he dropped his eyes to Theo sleeping in her arms, his chubby fist up on her shoulder and his cheek resting on her heart.

"All good moms should fight for their sons," he said at last.

Megan relaxed.

"Just like all good dads should too."

Her body froze so fast that she was amazed she didn't shatter. She held Theo tighter and stared at Danny while her heartbeat rapidly in her chest.

He couldn't mean...

He didn't even want to be a dad!

His hand reached out and stroked a small curl away from Theo's face and Megan had to fight the urge to pull Theo away and sprint down the hall.

Danny looked up, his face open and vulnerable, "hat Starla did was terrible, and I don't know if we'll ever know why." He squeezed his lips together and let out a tight breath. "But just from getting to know him in the capacity that I have, I already love him. How could I not want to get to know him more? Plus, I have this very promising almost-relationship going on with his mother, if she'll forgive me…"

Megan's body released and her racing heart gave a stutter step as it tried to calm down. She loosened her hold on Theo, sucking in a shaky breath.

Was this really happening?

Her emotions were broken. How could she feel everything all at once? She was going to explode out of her skin, she was sure of it.

She stared into Danny's questioning eyes and gave him a tentative smile.

The smile she got back was typical Danny: blinding.

# CHAPTER THIRTY-EIGHT

# October 5, Wednesday
## Megan

Megan watched as Danny and Ava shared a moment of laughter on the hospital bed, their spirits lifted by the prospect of being released soon.

The room was filled with a sense of relief and warmth.

As they giggled, Ryan entered the room, carrying a carefully prepared care package.

Megan smiled as Ryan presented the basket to Ava.

Ryan gave the little princess a mischievous grin and balanced the pink basket on the bed next to her. "Hey, sweetie pie. Your mom said I could bring you a get-well present. And because she still won't let me in book club, I brought our own book that maybe we can read together. Maybe we'll make our own book club." He ended on a sly wink and pulled the picture book—a book on not eating certain items. Like batteries.

*Fucking hilarious, Ryan. Jackass.*

Megan gave him a dry look that had him smothering a smile.

"I also brought a couple of other things." He presented a small teddy bear with a cast on its arm, homemade veggie chocolate muffins, and a bundle of fabric in Spartan team colors. "I figured they could use a little entertainment." He then unfurled the fabric and revealed two small jerseys...in Ryan's number...not Danny's.

Danny raised an eyebrow and grabbed the jerseys, frowning at the numbers. "Did they teach you to count at that college you went to? Think you got your numbers mixed up there, golden boy."

"Har, har," Ryan rolled his eyes, a move so like his predecessor, John, that Megan found herself raising her brows in shock. She made a mental note to tell her later. Jen would find that little nugget hilarious.

"I hope you don't expect them to wear these atrocities. They're all about lucky number thirteen."

Ryan laughed, playfully nudging Danny's shoulder. "Hey, a little healthy competition never hurt anyone. And thirteen has never been known to be lucky."

He stopped talking to make some faces at Theo, who was now balancing on the bed with Danny as a chaperone. Ryan made some weird ass sound that had Theo giggling and when Theo's pudgy fingers reached for Ryan's face, Ryan leaned in and gave them his customary nibbles. It was their favorite game whenever Ryan was around.

"If you guys need a break, I can take Theo to your mom's. Give you some time to decompress," Ryan somewhat suggested to Danny, but he turned his head to Megan to make it clear it was her decision.

Megan hesitated, torn between wanting Theo close and recognizing the need for a break. She glanced at Danny, silently seeking his input. Surprisingly, he stepped forward and softly agreed with Ryan. "You know what? It might be good for Theo to have a change of scenery and spend time with...Grandma. Might be nice for Ava to have undivided attention for a bit."

Grandma.

Woah, he really was all in.

And in front of Ryan...yikes.

Megan's eyebrows shot up in surprise, her lips parting slightly. She glanced between Danny and Ryan, who had a somewhat confused but pleased expression on his face.

A mix of conflicting emotions assaulted her but eventually she nodded. "All right, but just for a little while. I'll miss my little munchkin."

Danny leaned into her, pressing a gentle kiss to Megan's forehead. "I'll go get him as soon as you girls are settled."

Was this what it was like? To have a support system in place?

If this was truly what it was like for all her girlfriends, then they had been seriously holding out on her. This was glorious.

Maybe they just didn't want to rub it in.

A small smile played at the corners of Megan's lips.

How far could she push this? Could she get a neck rub out of this attentive, groveling new father?

"Okay, go ahead. Take Theo to Grandma's. Tell her Danny will be there soon."

After they dealt with the car seat shuffle, Ryan departed with Theo in his arms. Megan and Danny watched Ava flip through her new book, her little fingers having trouble with the thin paper pages.

Sitting side by side, Megan seized the moment to discuss something Danny wasn't going to like. "So, I uh, quit my job."

Danny's eyes widened in surprise, his brows furrowing slightly. "What? Why? What happened?"

Megan swallowed past the small lump in her throat and picked absently at her cuticles, trying to hold his eye contact but ultimately looking away. "They were a bit...dickish...about me leaving when daycare called yesterday...I reacted on impulse and sort of just quit so I could get to Ava and Theo ASAP. It's probably for the best; I want to prioritize the kids. But...it's going to be a weird transition period while we figure out what's going on with a job and while waiting for a new daycare to have two spots."

Danny reached out, grasping Megan's hand in his rough, callused ones.

He was silent for a minute, and she could feel the rage pouring off him.

After another minute of silent processing, he stuffed it back down.

At least his nostrils weren't flaring anymore.

"You know I support you, right? I want you to be happy, and I want the kiddos to be safe. And I don't know if you know this, but I'm kind of a big deal. I have a lot of money. More than I know what to do with. And that's even after I set up the irrevocable trusts for my son and his big sister."

Megan gave him a dry look. "I'm not asking you for money—"

"You don't need to, I'm offering. About time I picked up the tab for a couple of things. I have a bit to make up for. Plus, once you guys move in with me, your expenses will lessen, and it will give you more time to find something you love."

Umm, what?

Before she could say anything, he kept going. "Plus, my mom already views the kids as grandkids, knowing Theo is mine isn't going to change that. She's still going to love them both the same. And she's already offered a million times to watch them full time. So, we'll tag her into the ring for a bit once you find what you're looking for and when the time comes that the right daycare has a spot, we'll hop on it."

"Uh, Danny..."

Moving in together was a big deal and he was acting like it was nothing.

"Or hire a nanny. I'm loaded, remember. And I can talk to my CPA, whom I'll be firing and replacing with you as soon as you give me the word, but maybe he'll have a name for you—"

"Danny!"

He stopped speaking and finally tore his eyes away from his princess and looked at Megan.

"I can't move in with you!"

He blinked and looked like a freight train hit him. "Why, the h—" he omitted the word he was intending to say after a quick look to Ava, "—not?"

Megan jerked back.

"What?"

"What?" he repeated back, still looking confused.

Now she was confused.

"We can't move in with you, Danny."

"Like, I said, why not?"

Was he serious?

"Dude! It's totally too fast! We haven't even ever been a couple for real! We can't do that. We can't just jump right in without seeing if we work-"

He cut her off. "Do you need a trial run?"

"Huh?"

He gave her hand a small squeeze. "Do you really need a trial run or is that just what your head is telling you? Because I," he thumped his chest once with his free hand, "don't need one. At all. I love those two kids. I love you. I don't need a trial run to know that. The rest we'll figure it out." He leveled a look at her. "We have to. We have kids together."

She loved the sentiment...but he wasn't quite right.

"Uh, Danny...Ava's not yours."

"Isn't she?"

Megan blinked. "What?"

"Isn't she? I'm *here*. She calls me 'Daddy' all the freaking time. I know her bedtime routine, I know her morning grumpies, I know she's desperate for chocolate veggie muffins. I know her favorite bedtime stories, what she likes to sing in the car, and which princess I *always* have to be when we play pretend." He stopped and leveled a look at Megan, a dark eyebrow raised over his gorgeous eyes. "She's mine."

Megan rolled her lips and looked away, trying not to cry.

"And Meg, my sweet deluded little love, I know all of those things for you too."

Her head whipped back to him, and he gave her a lopsided grin. "We haven't played dress up yet though... We could if you wanted to. But if we're going to go there, can you at least be the princess and I can be the prince? I've been dying to get my hands on a good, old-fashioned castle. I can get one set up out back next to the playset, and we can call someone to take the kids. Then you can climb up top and let down your hair—"

"Danny!"

He gave her a small smile, tenderness all over his face.

"Danny," she repeated, softer this time. She raised a hand to his cheek and felt the thick bristles there. "I don't think I need a trial run."

He leaned forward and pressed a slow, sweet kiss to her lips. "I know you don't, darling. But I needed you to get there on your own. I know it's fast, and I know you like your pro con lists and organized timelines, and if you want, I can turn my back for a few so you can write one up, but we're *there,* honey. We might not have been officially dating, but that's only because we jumped straight into marriage. Hell, I even ignored your calls last night."

Megan glowered.

"Too soon?"

She cocked her head to the side and gave him the unimpressed look she could muster.

He looked properly chastened for point-two seconds until he gave her another small smile. "See? You're already reeling me in and making me behave. And here I am, making you take the biggest leap of faith that you've ever done." He pulled her into a big hug and took a deep breath, inhaling the smell of her shampoo. "And don't worry, I won't rush the wedding."

Megan stiffened in his arms, and he gave her a small shake.

"I said I *won't* rush the wedding. Jeez, we need to work on your listening skills. That's where Ava gets it." After a small chuckle to himself, he then added, "Plus, if we're going to have our third baby in the bridal party, then we really need to wait until you feel ready to have sex again after. I'm not *not* having sex on our wedding night."

Megan stiffened anew and jerked away and looked at him with a racing heart.

"What?"

She was choking. Dying. The world was crushing her lungs.

He just gave her one of his big, blinding smiles and pulled her back into his chest. "We'll talk later. I already got one big win today, future Mrs. Parker. We'll work on the other tomorrow."

Tomorrow?

She was going to pass out.

This was all so fast.

As she was getting ready to blast into him for railroading her, a sweet, angelic voice interrupted them.

"Daddy?" They both turned to look at Ava who was watching them quietly from her space on the bed. "Can we go home now?"

Megan turned to her. "Honey, they said it was going to be a couple of hours—"

"Sure thing, princess. Let me just go find someone." And just like that, Danny was up and out of the room, but not before pressing quick kisses to his girls.

Within twenty minutes, they were headed home...with some 'borrowed' toys from Pediatrics.

# CHAPTER THIRTY-NINE

# October 7, Friday
## Danny

A couple of days later, Danny's spirits were high as he left the stadium, the adrenaline from practice still coursing through his veins. He was looking forward to spending time with Megan and the kids that night. The day was going to end perfectly. With his family.

His father's voice cut through the air.

Wrong family.

"Danny!" Steve's voice boomed from behind the fence, his tone dripping with a mix of desperation and slurring.

Danny reluctantly approached, his mood shifting from elation to caution.

Could he just pretend he didn't hear?

As he dad walked along the chain link fence, Danny faced the facts. No, he couldn't just pretend. His dad would just make a scene or do something stupid.

"What?" Danny slammed to a halt and stared at his dad with dead eyes.

What did he do to make the man hate him so much? Why did he grow up and constantly feel resented by him? Why was he beaten by him? He was just a kid. What did he do wrong?

Steve looked worn and defeated, his eyes reflecting a deep well of despair. And a bottle of vodka. "I need some money," he muttered, his voice a blend of bitterness and neediness. "I owe it to Malachi Drexler, we all know what he does to people who don't pay up. Your little massage therapist's dad hasn't been seen around town in ages. I was going to dip into the investment accounts to repay it. One final time and then pay it back, I swear. But your little bi— cut me off." Clearly he knew better than to insult Megan to Danny. "You're my son. I won't ever ask for anything again, but I need your help."

The mention of Malachi Drexler only fueled his fury, reminding him of the dangerous world his father entangled himself in.

"You think I owe you something just because I have it? Because I'm your son? Because I made it as a professional athlete and have the money to spare?" Danny retorted, his voice tight with frustration. Danny crossed his arms across his chest, a physical barrier between them.

Steve's face twisted into a bitter smile; a mocking expression that only served to further infuriate Danny. "Yes, damnit. Like I told you the other day, that's what family is for. Without me, you wouldn't be able to run the routes half as well as you do now. You couldn't use your left arm to catch shit when you were a kid. Who fixed that for you? Me." He thumped himself on the chest. "I've been calling all week, admitting that I need help. You help family when they need you. You don't just ignore them so you can play daddy to a couple of deadbeats' orphans. Especially when we all know damn well you never wanted kids. She must be a hellcat in the sheets to get you to overlook that little complication, huh? Good thing the boy didn't get into the batteries and just the older one. Hate to know what those would do to a baby's stomach..."

How the fuck did he know about that?

Never mind, if he thought too hard about how his father heard about that...or facilitated it...he was going to commit murder. They all needed to move on. Without Steve Parker in their lives.

The thought sent a shiver down Danny's spine.

With clenched fists, Danny fought against the urge to lash out physically. He really didn't need a lawsuit right now.

Then again...

Just as Danny was about to say 'fuck it' and punch his father in his fucking nose for being so cold about Ava almost dying, a familiar voice pierced through the air.

"Danny?" Michael approached slowly, his face dark and worried as he watched the two opposite men. "I need you for a minute if you can get away."

Danny glared at his father one final time before turning his attention to Michael.

"Hey! What about the money?" His father's shitty voice called out. Fuck, just hearing him speak made Danny's skin crawl.

"Go fuck yourself. You could be dying and I'd step around you. Don't let my family's names cross your lips again, or I'll fucking end you. I don't need Malachi using *my* family as some sort of message to you. Get fucked."

Steve gave a rusty cackle. "Oh, I'll be sure to tell Malachi all about your little family. He always likes to know where he can get the most leverage. That cute little boy that looks so much like—"

"Come *on*." Michael pulled him harder towards the parked cars.

Taking a deep breath, Danny used every ounce of willpower to allow himself to be pulled away.

Otherwise, his family would be visiting him while he wore orange rather than the Spartans' navy and maroon.

The weight of the interaction and the implications in it, sat heavy upon his shoulders.

He turned to Michael. "Thanks, man. I think I was actually going to kill the fucker this time."

Michael placed a reassuring hand on Danny's shoulder, offering a supportive presence. "No problem, bud." He paused. "If I had to keep listening to him threatening your family like that, I might have helped."

• • • • ● • ● • • •

Later that evening, as Danny sat in Megan's living room, the weight of the conversation with his father still pressed heavily on his mind. Megan, ever perceptive, sensed his unease and moved closer to him, her presence a soothing balm.

"Hey, what's going on?" Megan asked gently, concern etching lines on her forehead. "You seem lost. Not that there isn't a ton to be lost in right now. Our fucking life is a *mess*." She ended with a halfhearted chuckle.

Danny sighed, his shoulders slumping. "It's my dad. He's gotten himself into some trouble and now he's asking me for money to pay off a debt to Malachi Drexler."

Megan's eyes widened, a mix of worry and surprise flickering within them. "Malachi Drexler? That's no small-time problem, Danny. He's dangerous as fuck."

Danny nodded, a heaviness settling over him. "I know. And what's worse is that my father is pointing him at us."

"What does that mean?" Megan's face now full of concern and worry.

"I hope nothing." But even as the words came out, something in them fell flat. He recognized the sensation from being on the field. Right before he took a hospital pass and was hit unsuspectingly.

Something was coming, he just didn't know what.

## CHAPTER FORTY

# October 9, Sunday
# Megan

Days later, Megan's heart pounded in her chest as she stood face-to-face with the intimidating figures of Starla's dad and Ava's father outside her apartment.

Accompanied by Danny's weasel of a sperm donor father.

That fucking idiot. That stupid *fucking* idiot! Steve tracked down her fucking family?!

Was he for real?

Her hands trembled, though she tried hard not to show it. It would make her prey to these assholes.

She could feel the weight of their hatred hanging in the air.

Uncle Brock, Starla's father, hovered in front of Megan, his foot in the doorway, preventing her from slamming it shut.

Fuck, why hadn't she checked the fucking peephole!

His eyes were bloodshot, his face contorted with righteous indignation. The memories of his violent past flooded Megan's mind, and her toes curled in her soft house slippers.

"You've got no right keeping those kids from us," Brock spat, his voice laced with venom. "They're our flesh and blood, and we're taking them back."

Megan tried to appear confident as she held the door firmly in her grip. "Starla entrusted me with their care. She wanted them to have a better life, away from the dangers of our past. They're safe with me. And it went through the proper channels. They're mine. You can't have them."

Dougie, Ava's biological father, stepped forward, a sneer on his face. "You think you're so high and mighty, playing mommy to *my* daughter. I didn't even know she fucking existed. We'll see how the courts feel about selling her out from under me. It doesn't matter if you're playing house with a professional athlete. The court will see a grieving father who missed out on a chance to see his daughter's first steps, and she'll be with me, where she belongs. Either hand over the kids to us now and we'll work on some visitation from you, or we'll go straight to the police and claim you kidnapped them. Then you'll never fucking see them again."

Megan's mind raced, panic coursing through her veins. She couldn't let these people take her children.

Brock chimed in. "We already talked to a lawyer. Stevie over there was nice enough to connect us with his. Stevie said you fucked him over too. Just like you're trying to fuck us over. Those are my fuckin' grandbabies in there. I have more claim to them than you do. Ever heard of grandparent rights?"

She hadn't. Was that even a thing?

Desperation filled her.

She needed to call Danny. And then her lawyer, Bianca.

Scratch that, she needed to call the police. SWAT. The armed forces. Someone!

"Please, just go away. Later we can set up a time to talk. You caught me at a bad time."

Her uncle Brock's anger escalated. He never did like hesitation from her and Starla. He wanted immediate reactions.

It was either perfect obedience...or punishment.

His elbow jerked as his wrist twisted on something inside his jacket pocket.

Fear gripped Megan's heart.

What the fuck did he have in there?

She looked up into his eyes and winced at the blind rage...and high she saw there.

*He's fucking deranged.*

"Please, Uncle Brock, let's just talk later," Megan said slowly, trying to keep her voice from shaking or sounding shrill.

Appear calm.

Appear confident.

Don't let them sense her fear.

"We'll talk later, just not right now. We're trying to watch Danny's game, when he comes home after, we'll both give you a call." She looked at Steve. "You too, I'm sure we can work something out."

Danny's dad was broke as fuck since being cut off and was obviously very sick of the upheaval to his life. Apparently, it was the straw that broke the camel's back because clearly the guy was out for blood. Danny's.

The hallway fell into a tense silence as Brock paused, his eyes flickering between Megan , the children playing in the room behind her, and Danny's game on the television.

For a fleeting moment, Megan saw a glimmer of humanity in his gaze, as if a faint memory of compassion fought against his rage.

But it was gone in an instant.

Dougie pushed to look around Brock toward Ava. "Come on, kid. We're going home." His smile was disgusting, and Megan felt acid burn down her throat.

Dougie pushed past Megan, knocking her into the doorframe as he passed. Megan turned with him, desperate to tell Ava to go to her bedroom, when she felt something cold rest against her temple.

Time slowed.

Woodenly, she twisted against it, just barely, and saw, and felt, Brock pressing a small gun against her head.

"Shh," he whispered maniacally. "I hear kids are expensive these days. Maybe...maybe, we'll let you buy them back to ease the burden. A little for me, for Dougie," he paused, "and a little bit for Grandaddy Stevie over there." He leaned in and blew rancid breath across her frozen face. "Your boy should have plenty left over."

"Pew, pew," Dougie laughed from deep inside her apartment where the kids were.

Her entire body screamed at her to grab at him. To claw, bite, punch, kick.

To stop him from getting to those two precious angels.

Brock read her mind and pushed the gun a little harder against her temple.

"Shh. It'll be over soon." His rabid, beady eyes stayed on her.

She hardly even registered how his hand and wrist kept tensing and twitching. Every fiber was focused on the screams of her children as they were picked up by a stranger.

She was going to puke.

Or pass out.

*Breathe, brea—*

Black spots clouded her vision and she panted hard.

Could she stop them? All she needed to do was push them out of the doorway long enough to get it latched. She could hold the alert button on her watch for an SOS call, but she couldn't do it now, they'd know she was doing it because a loud alarm would go off.

Could she...

She just needed to get them out so she could lock the door...

Could she find a way to do that and maybe take a bullet in a place that wouldn't kill her immediately?

Fuck! Why hadn't she accepted any of Jen's Krav Maga invites?

Dougie pushed by her, the kids thrashing in his arms, knocking her off balance and away from the gun.

She tensed. Maybe now was her chance...

Her wild eyes darted to the men.

What could she do, what could she do, what could-

Uncle Brock very slowly took his gun and rested it against Theo's blonde head.

She froze.

Everything.

Her body.

Her brain.

Her heart.

"Shh," her uncle whispered lovingly, like a caress. A sick, fucking awful caress.

Megan couldn't move.

"Mama! Mama! I need Mama!" Ava thrashed in Dougie's arms and reached for Megan.

Megan shut her eyes tight and tried not to do anything that would startle her uncle into hitting the trigger a little too hard with his flexing finger.

"I'll text you the amount we decide on and where to drop it. I'm sure Danny can figure out the rest. As soon as he gets us the money, you get the kids back. Easy peasy. But I probably don't need to tell you what will happen if you go to the police..."

He let that hang there and Megan blinked rapidly, still frozen there in the entryway.

Maybe this was a dream?

A nightmare?

She was going to be sick.

"I know you're real smart, Miss CPA. So, *be smart*. For the sake of those kids." Brock's breath stank like rotten mold and his sweat had a sour tang to it. "Or I'll send them back to you *in pieces*."

Every part of her being was telling her to chase after the kids, to not let them take them, but she remembered the shaky way her uncle had held the gun, the way his finger was moving restlessly on the trigger.

Did he...did he actually want to shoot her?

Brock's expression when she had given in earlier was almost...disappointment.

When younger, Megan had called the cops on him more times than she could count. Then she went and escaped with his daughter. His *property*.

There was no love lost between the two of them.

Maybe he wasn't just doing this for the money, maybe a bit of this was payback.

A way to hurt her for trouble she had caused him over the years.

Dougie and Steve started down the hall and her body couldn't stop shaking. The children's wails continued, and with every step the men took away from her, her heart shattered more and more.

They had her kids.

*They fucking took her kids!*

She should have taken the bullet. Then at least someone would have heard and called the cops. Then they would have been wanted persons and gone to jail for murder and kidnapping and never have a chance of threatening the kids again.

She'd be dead, yes. But her children would be free of them, forever.

She shouldn't have just done *nothing!*

She should have taken the bullet.

Her uncle Brock paused at the end of the hall and turned around to face her. He gave her a sick salute with his gun and then rounded the corner to follow Dougie and Steve...and the struggling kids.

As soon as they left her sight, Megan wasted no time in sprinting to her phone on the counter and frantically dialing.

"911, what's your emergency?"

"I need to report a kidnapping of my baby and toddler..." and immediately, the dam inside her broke and the meltdown happened.

Megan sank to the floor, tears streaming down her face. The weight of the encounter crashed upon her, leaving her trembling and broken.

# CHAPTER FORTY-ONE

# October 9, Sunday
# Jen

Jen's heart raced, her pulse pounding in her ears like a relentless drumbeat. The stadium roaring all around her was nothing compared to the deafening noise in her head.

She stared at the alerts on her phone, her heart beating so fast it was amazing that it didn't rupture.

She wasn't supposed to have her phone on her during the games...

But for some reason, that night she did.

Fate?

The texts and the piercing sound of the AMBER Alert notification seemed to reverberate through her entire being.

Dios Mío.

She looked up, her eyes searching desperately for someone who could help. Maybe someone on the team was best friends with the FBI, or CIA, or freaking Black Ops.

She didn't care *who*.

They just needed to save those babies.

*Now*.

Heart in her throat, her feet still frozen, her eyes locked onto John, who was engaged in a serious conversation with Ryan on the sideline. The team was currently on defense,,,

They were on defense...

Danny!

Her heart stuttered in rapid staccato and her feet started to move.

Sensing Jen's distress, John's gaze came to her and his expression darkened as he took in her sprint toward him.  She ignored his concern, her footsteps taking her right past him and to Danny.

Sweat trickled down his forehead, dampening his brow, and his eyes were glued to the field, oblivious to the tragedy taking place outside the stadium.

Jen's frenzied approach and rough clasping of his arm, caught his attention though. In slow motion, his friendly face turned toward her, only to pause.

Upon seeing Jen's expression, Danny's face took on a petrified look that would haunt Jen for the rest of her life.

Without saying a word to anyone, under the eyes of thousands, Danny Parker sprinted from the stadium to the locker room, and to his SUV.

# CHAPTER FORTY-TWO

# October 9, Sunday
## Danny

Hours later, Danny rubbed at his chest, his heart aching and his lungs squeezed tight.

This couldn't be happening.

Clenching his fists until his knuckles turned white, Danny's heart raced like a wild stallion, galloping against his ribcage. His breath came in ragged gasps, each inhale burning his lungs like fire.

Was this all his fault? Should he have paid his dad's debt and just moved on?

Should he have just bit his tongue rather than pushing his father over the edge with his rant?

Danny noticed Mickey and Benji settle against a wall on the other side of the apartment, far away from Megan, her girls, and the circulating police officers.

Danny left Megan in the arms of her girlfriends and walked stalked to where Mickey and Benji were huddled. He pivoted hard and thumped back against the wall on the other side of Mickey.

"I need his number," Danny said in a low voice, not taking his eyes off the mother of his children.

He was drowning and didn't know which way to swim.

Megan. Swim to Megan.

He needed to get back to her.

Mickey winced and shot a look at the police before looking at Danny. "McScruffy, you know I want to help…"

"Number. I need it. Now."

Benji looked like he'd rather be anywhere else than standing there, witnessing this conversation, especially in front of a bunch of cops.

"Danny…"

"Give me his fucking number!" Danny growled, ripping around to face Mickey, absolutely willing to beat the shit out of him if he didn't comply.

He'd get the fucker's number, one way or another.

The room seemed to close in on him, the walls squeezing the air from his lungs.

Benji tensed and moved as if to insert himself between them, but Mickey waved him off without fanfare.

Mickey leveled a serious look at Danny. "There's no going back. After this…well, there's no going back."

Danny dug his short nails into his palms until he felt the sting of blood.

The world was crumbling around him.

Anguish and fury intertwined within Danny's core, threatening to consume him.

Focus. Focus. Focus.

"Did you hear her tell the story? Did you hear what happened? How they pointed a gun at my kids, how they pointed a gun at my woman, how they threatened her, how they threatened my *children*?" Danny was trying extremely hard not to absolutely lose his shit, but Mickey needed to get with the fucking program and give him the *fucking number*.

Mickey and Benji shared equal looks of despair at what Megan and the kids had to go through. Mickey then gave Benji a long look, indecision, then resolve clear on his face.

"Boo Boo, can you go get us some water? Danny seems like he's in shock."

Benji, the bigger and more intimidating of the two men, simply stared at his husband, unmoving.

"Deniability, honey," Mickey whispered and then gave a nod toward the kitchen. "We need water, Boo."

With a heartbreaking sigh, the big man turned and walked away, leaving Mickey to surreptitiously pull out his phone, keeping an eye on where the cops were mingling.

As he read the number to Danny, he kept his voice low and muted.

"Pick a random name and add him under that. He only takes cash." He gave Danny another long look. "Speaking from experience, you don't ever get away from this...it stays with you...a forever skeleton in your closet...a stain on your soul...are you ready for that?"

Danny just turned and gave one final look to his destroyed woman.

Fear like he had never known clenched at his chest, compressing his heart so hard it felt like he was going to pass out. His mind was a violent, raging storm: thundering, bloodthirsty thoughts clashed against lightning strikes of doubt.

The remembered scene of sprinting into the apartment to see Megan, her voice quivering, recounting the nightmarish events to the police flashed through him like a cruel tableau.

On repeat. Like it had been for hours.

Danny's chest heaved as he struggled to catch his breath, and a brand-new wave of sobs from Megan hit his ears. She dropped to her knees across the apartment, unable to hold herself up any longer.

His control shattered like glass on the pavement.

Yeah, he was ready to take on a skeleton...or three.

## CHAPTER FORTY-THREE
# October 9, Sunday
## Danny

Hours later, Megan and Danny stood side by side on the front lawn, their hearts pounding hard. The setting sun cast a warm golden glow across the neighborhood, but their anticipation overshadowed the beauty of the evening. The massive group of friends and teammates huddled in front of Danny's house, rallying and offering their support in whatever way they could.

Danny inspected each passing car, searching for the familiar sight of the police vehicle that would bring their precious children back to them.

When would they get here?

Megan clutched Danny's hand tightly, her palms were clammy, her fingers trembling.

Danny's gaze darted back and forth, his eyes scanning the street with an unwavering intensity. Every sound, every distant siren, sent a ripple of anxious anticipation through his veins.

The sound of approaching intermittent sirens pierced the air. Danny's broken heart skipped a beat, and he looked at Megan, her eyes widening with excitement and nervousness. A knot formed in his throat, making it difficult to breathe as the police vehicle turned onto his street, its lights flashing in a vibrant display of urgency. The sirens were off now though.

Good, the kids would be less bothered that way.

The car parked in front of his house, and Megan's breath audibly caught, and stumbled a step forward, as if she wanted to run to it.

Two police officers emerged and rounded the vehicle, their expressions a mixture of weariness and determination. As they rounded the vehicle, in their arms, nestled against their chests, were the tiny figures of Theo and Ava, their innocence and vulnerability evident even from a distance.

Two steps on the grass and both Megan and Danny were running for them.

Please, let them be all right.

The police said they were. But still.

No one knew them like Mama and Daddy.

As a team, they each took a kid from the officers and cuddled them close. Both of them crying and trying not to do so in a way that freaked out the kids.

Thoe and Ava's faces were smudged with dirt, and their clothes were rumpled, but they seemed fine. Ava was already babbling away, airing her grievances for everyone to hear.

Theo had a watery and exhausted look to him, snuggling deep, as if trying to himself it was all a dream.

"Oh, my sweet babies, we missed you so much," Megan whispered brokenly, her voice filled with love and desperation.

"That wasn't a very fun trip, was it kiddos? No more trips with those meanies, okay?" Danny joined in, trying to turn the situation into something they wouldn't be discussing with their therapists in twenty-five years.

"We're here. We're here, and we'll never let anything happen to you again," she murmured, her voice filled with fierce determination. "We're going to move to The White Mountains and live off the land. Nothing like this will ever happen again."

"That's a long commute for Daddy," Danny said, still snuggling his family close in a tight group hug.

Megan's eyes flitted to him. "Then find a different job."

"You first," he fired back. Danny looked down at the kids, cuddled close. "We'll discuss it."

Danny's gaze flickered to the police officers, his gratitude pouring forth. "Thank you," he whispered, his voice filled with a mixture of relief and gratitude. "Thank you for bringing them back to us."

The closest officer, a kind smile on his face, nodded solemnly. "The circumstances are...not good. But we're glad they're safe now," he replied, his voice carrying the weight of the responsibility.

The circumstanced being that the police station received an anonymous phone call just an hour before that car matching the description of the kidnappers was spotted in a parking area for a wildlife preserve. When the police arrived the scene, the three, now *badly* beaten men were laying on the ground on the side of the car next to the woods, out of sight of the children. The children were strapped into brand new car seats, their diapers fresh, and Theo had a chewy in his fist. Ava had a *Hercules* water bottle thermos in her lap while she flipped through a book. A thermos that still had ice in it.

And the car was on...and the temperature set to *auto*.

Mickey's contact, *The Fixer*, saved Danny's children from an uncertain fate.

Unfortunately, it seemed that Danny's father had suffered a little bit more than just a little bit of bruising. The guy's liver was already shot, and after the beating he took, he was now suffering from some internal bleeding that currently the doctors were, unfortunately, trying to fix.

Threatening Megan and their kids? Danny couldn't find it in him to care that his dad was dying. He was never much of a dad anyway,

The dirt that stained Danny's normally blindingly white soul? Well worth it.

He'd make that call again in a heartbeat. Again and again and again.

If it was his soul or the safety of his kids? No question.

The police didn't need to know that though.

Danny gave them a nod of thanks.

Megan looked up at him as well, her voice hoarse from sobbing. "You have no idea what this means to us," she said, her voice quivering with heartfelt appreciation. "Thank you for bringing them back to us, for keeping them safe."

Tears streamed down her face anew as she looked down and peppered the children's cheeks with kisses, whispering words of love and reassurance.

Danny ran his fingers running through Ava's tousled hair as he joined Megan in murmuring words of adoration and relief. All the while, placing soft kisses on Theo's towhead.

Their family gathered around, their eyes glistening with unshed tears, as they witnessed the miraculous reunion. The sound of sniffles and choked sobs filled the air, a testament to the collective relief that washed over the community.

As the sun dipped below the horizon, casting a warm orange glow over the scene, Megan and Danny held their children tightly, hoping the drama was over.

And no one shed a tear for the death of Steve Parker.

Not even his son.

# CHAPTER FORTY-FOUR

# October 22, Saturday
## Danny

William's fall barbeque was always a vibrant gathering, filled with a mix of joyous chatter, laughter, and the clinking of glasses. Megan and Danny navigated through the crowd, their fingers intertwined, as they exchanged smiles and greetings with the members of the teams and their guests.

As they strolled around the lawn, Megan's gaze landed on Ava and Theo, playing happily in a pile of leaves nearby with Chloe and Kenny's twin girls: Sienna and Kyla. The little ones giggled, their tiny feet pitter-pattering on the outdoor mat as they explored their new play yard. Megan couldn't help but smile, her heart swelling with peace at the children's joyful interactions. The weeks since their kidnapping had shown no lasting trauma to the two littlest Parkers, so that was a miracle that she would be forever grateful for.

There were still questions about how the children had been found...but Danny refused to speculate.

Megan graduated in the top of her class—she didn't need him to confirm or deny anything. The important part was that the kids were home and they were safe...forever.

Megan scanned the yard as she observed the lively interactions between the guests. John and Jen were cozied up on a porch swing, swaying to the fall breeze while watching the various children run around in the sprinklers. Jen's hands were absently massaging his biceps and forearms while she chatted away. Every so often, John would cast a side eye to where William was speaking with the coaches on the team. Butch was ranting about something while Mitchell and Simon tried to talk him down.

In the corner of the yard by the pool house, Lexie and Ryan were having a heated debate with their hands flying and openly frustrated expressions. Their words weren't carrying to Megan, but she cringed when Lexie shrieked out a shrill condescending laugh and Ryan's face got red and angry.

That didn't bode well.

By contrast, by the barbecue pit stood Michael Dillon and Liam Polowski, who were clearly the lives of the party, entertaining a small group of players and their guests with their hilarious anecdotes and good-natured ribbing.

Megan could hear the laughs from across the yard.

Meanwhile, Kyle Justice stood off to the side bringing a plate piled high with food to his ex-wife who was sitting in a comfy chair by the fire pit. An ex-wife who he desperately wanted to file his taxes jointly with again. Maybe she should remind Emma about the tax savings of filing jointly...

As Megan watched Emma beam up at Kyle...Megan reassessed.

Nah, the woman didn't need any encouragement...she was already right there with Kyle too.

Megan sighed and curled deeper into Danny's side. Everything was...*good*. So good.

How was this real life?

The older kids were teaching the younger kids how to play a game of tag football and Danny chuckled.

"He's not playing football," Megan said as she watched an older boy try to get Theo to hold a child sized football.

Danny grinned as they watched the scene unfold. Theo was a master walker now, but that didn't mean he was a 'big kid'. He refused to touch the football, instead he looked at it like it was a snake, his face growing increasingly red. He didn't want a thing to do with the good ol' pigskin.

Ava, on the other hand, snatched it up and ran past the older boys before they even knew what hit 'em.

"She's not either," Megan felt she needed to add.

Danny chuckled low but shrugged rather than offering a verbal agreement.

"It's too dangerous," she continued.

Again, he said nothing, but his body vibrated next to her as the kids were all now chasing after the mischievous girl.

Chloe and Kenny approached, their happiness palpable. Their twins wandered slowly to where the kids were trying to get a makeshift football game going.

Rose and Brandon approached on Danny's other side. Their boys immediately joined the fray.

"Now *they* can play football," Megan allowed, watching the boys tackle each other roughly onto the grass.

"They're a bit wild," Rose allowed, a bright grin flashing.

"Like their mother." Brandon nodded.

As a unit, they stood there and policed the children when they got too rowdy, accepted food when it was brought around, and chatted with others who came to visit their little group.

"I'm glad we're here, Danny," Megan said, her body filled with a sense of peace. "Despite everything, we're here, surrounded by friends, celebrating your team, your family, and its milestones. It feels good, it feels safe."

Danny's gaze softened as he pulled Megan closer, his arm wrapping around her shoulders. "Still okay with no trial run?" Despite his utter confidence at the hospital a lifetime before, he always made sure to remind her that she could still back out if she really wanted. That they could do a 'trial run' of their relationship before jumping straight into it. It was unconventional...especially for her. Megan. Type A, neurotic accountant.

Yet...

She was surprisingly on board with no trial run.

It felt right.

And for the first time in a long time, she was willing to take the risk.

Megan leaned her head against Danny's chest, closing her eyes briefly as they swayed gently to the soft music playing on the speakers.

As Ryan and Kyle joined in with the kids on the lawn, splitting the group into several different teams based on age, Megan was reminded of what she wanted to tell Danny earlier before they left the house.

"Oh, by the way, I called up Ryan's CPA and left a voicemail requesting a meeting. I'm hoping to hear back shortly. So, hopefully, I'll be employed again soon."

Danny laughed and gave her a squeeze, sending butterflies through her at the affection. "You've been out of work for all of *a minute*. You're fine. Take some time off. Relax. Unwind. It's not like we need the money."

Megan just shrugged.

She liked to stay busy.

Megan grinned up at Danny. "So, Mr. Reluctant Dad, how does it feel to be in charge of a couple of mini humans?"

Danny's mouth tilted up at the corner, a playful glint in his eyes. "Well, Ms. Mama Bear... 'Pre-Megan Me' had no idea what I was missing out on, and I was foolish to run my trap without truly having a clue about what being a dad entails. 'Post-Megan Me' has hope that we'll be able to raise our kids to make good choices regarding drugs and alcohol, so they don't have to learn those lessons the hard way."

"Oh, don't get too comfortable. Wait until Ava starts with the teenage rebellion years. You might be asking me for a divorce and wishing you stuck to your guns about no kids."

Danny feigned offense, placing a hand on his chest. "Hey, Wonderboy, remember? I'm no quitter. Bring on the teenage drama. I've dealt with a decade of rookie football players who thought they ran the world. I can handle a rebellious teenager."

Just then, on the grass away from the kids, Ryan speared Kyle with a vicious tackle. Apparently, Ryan was regretting his career choice to play quarterback. The two men were quickly pig piled by a group of little bodies as the kids sensed an opportunity for a wrestling match. Some of the feistier Spartans players mingling around saw the commotion and ran over to join the fray, flopping all over each other in the middle of the lawn. Yells, howls, and screeches ricocheted through the air as they all laughed and fought for supremacy with each other...and the kids.

Luckily, the wiser kids chose to remove themselves from the increasingly intense wrestling match. Those that didn't get the hint that it had turned into an adult-only match, were scooped up and away by the various spectating Spartans families.

Men.

Megan laughed, nudging Danny with her elbow. "Well, I must admit, you do have a certain skill with handling strong-headed individuals. Maybe you'll even manage to survive her."

Danny winked, a grin spreading across his face. "Hey, I've learned a few tricks along the way. And if all else fails, we can always bribe her with those homemade veggie chocolate muffins. They seem to work wonders."

"Oh, so now you're bribing our kids with treats. You're like Oprah but you're handing out cavities."

"They're veggie muffins! Not cocaine," he protested with a laugh.

"Yeah, yeah." She waved her hand, dismissing his protest regally. "But I do have to admit, those muffins are pretty irresistible."

"Almost as much as you."

Megan rolled her eyes but couldn't stop her dorky smile.

It was refreshing to engage in banter and playfulness after a lifetime of seriousness. "You know, it's moments like that that remind me what not having a trial run doesn't feel like the end of the world. Thank you for just being...you."

Danny nodded, his expression softening. "Friendship and respect are powerful building blocks. Having the kids and associated trauma just fast forwarded everything else. Doesn't hurt that you are smokin' hot and bought the sexiest fucking Black Widow costume for Halloween. If Hollywood ever needed a stunt-double..."

Megan tipped back her head and laughed into the beautiful fall sky.

She was a far cry from Natasha Romanoff, but it didn't hurt that he saw her that way.

Strong, resourceful, capable, smart.

And don't forget sexy as fuck.

The best part? The same could be said about him.

# CHAPTER FORTY-FIVE

# Epilogue: October 24, Monday
## Megan

A few days later, Danny and Megan stood together at Starla's grave, the kids with Grandma Nikki.

The warm rays of the sun filtered through the surrounding trees, casting a gentle glow over the scene. It was a moment of reflection, a chance for closure and healing.

Danny took a deep breath, his voice filled with a mix of frustration, anger, and emptiness. "I'll never fully understand why you did what you did," he began, his words carried by a soft breeze. "Your actions caused pain and confusion, but they also led us to this moment. We have our family now, and I choose to focus on the love we've found. So, you suck. So much. And a part of me is glad that you're dead, and I don't know if I'll ever get past that. But thank you for giving me Theo." Danny looked at Megan, his face now blank and ready to move onto the next thing. "Can we be done now? How much did you therapist say I had to say before I found 'peace?'"

He clearly didn't believe they needed this closure.

Megan, and her new therapist, disagreed.

Megan gave him a weary look. "Fine, dear. You're healed. I get it." She waved at their nearby car. "Go wait for me there then while I say my piece."

"Do we have to come back and do this again?"

She broke eye contact with the stone and looked at him with another tired expression. "Dude, it's five minutes. My therapist said it might help with my nightmares."

Danny gave her a heavy look. "Your therapist is a quack. You just need to be exhausted in other ways." His eyes danced down her body as if imagining her naked. "I told you, I'd take care of that for you."

"She is not a quack," Megan defended her. She really was a lovely woman, Danny was just being a dork.

"She is if she thinks your issues are stemming from Starla. Let's go visit good ol' Grandpa Steve's grave and try out our forgiveness hat there, shall we?"

As he knew it would happen, Megan couldn't stop her rage and terror from climbing up her throat, threatening to choke her.

Her body switched between hot and cold, hot and cold, and a sweat broke out on her forehead.

Even her fingers started to go numb.

"Yeah, that's what I thought." He leaned in and gave her a kiss. "I'll do whatever you want to do, Meg. Whatever helps you or makes you happy." He pointed at Starla's grave. "But she's dirt to me. I don't care if she's found peace, or happiness, or forgiveness. She gave me Theo, who is my world, but I can't forgive her for what she did."

"I don't forgive her," Megan said it quickly, blending the words.

"I hate her." Danny blinked at Megan's words. "I hate her so much for hurting you. Taking advantage of you. It's atrocious that anyone could do that. But to know that I housed her, sometimes clothed her, made excuses for her?" She shivered. "I just wanted to stop by this one time to say... I don't know...goodbye? I never want to come back here to her again. She's dirt for me too, honey."

Danny blinked.

And then clapped his hands once.

"Good, okay, we agree." He pressed a quick kiss to her forehead and started walking back to the SUV. Without turning around, he called out, "And I know you're already fretting about what to tell Theo, and even Ava, as they get older...and my unsolicited opinion is to worry about it later." On the wind, she heard his grumbling finish, "Not that you'll listen to me."

Fuck, she loved him.

She suppressed her emotions and turned toward the stone.

She felt a knot in her throat, a mingling of emotions that she struggled to put into words. "Starla, I have so many mixed feelings," she confessed, her voice soft but resolute. "I can't forgive you for hurting Danny, ever. There's never an excuse for something like that. But I will always be grateful for the gift of our children. The beginnings of our family."

Megan squatted down against the stone and rested her hand on it for the barest of moments. She then reached into her pocket, pulled out a small white stick she had hiding from Danny, and placed it on the stone.

"I don't even care you'll get my pee on you." She paused and looked up. "But I wanted you to know."

How could she hate someone, and still feel the warm embrace of nostalgia?

Something her therapist had yet to give her an answer on yet.

• • • ● • ● • • • ·

In the coming days, life resumed its normal rhythm.

Weeks later, Megan and Danny were putting the children to bed, and rock, paper, scissoring over who would put down who.

There was an easier child...and then there was a more difficult child.

Winner and loser determined by the Gods, they then worked to get the kids down as quickly as possible so they could get their chores for the evening done.

It was remarkably different with a partner...and also remarkably the same.

Their bedtime teamwork was a stark contrast to the overwhelming exhaustion Megan had felt just months before. As they completed the bedtime routine, Megan curled up on the couch, leaving Danny to clean the kitchen and prepare meals for the week.

She finally cracked open her friend, Emma's, latest novel. A romantic suspense under Emma's new pen name. Megan was hoping that if she read it, she could finally convince Emma to join the Book Club, something the woman had been unwaveringly declining. Just as she finished the first page, her cell rang, interrupting her.

Fucking hell!

Couldn't she finish a chapter first? For once in a blue moon?

Megan tossed the book on the couch by her feet and ripped her phone from the side table, checking the number.

If it was spam or a political call, they were going to get chewed the fuck out.

Did they know what time it was?

The unknown number had her blood pumping.

"Hello," Megan barked out, primed and ready to let rip.

Apparently she was an angry pregnant woman.

She finished the call and dragged herself off the couch and into the kitchen, where Danny was making a sunbutter sandwich for Ava's next day's lunch. A small container of peas was also waiting to be loaded into her lunch box.

"So, that was Emily Ashford, Ryan's CPA. She apologized for the delay and expressed her desire to set up an interview."

Danny gave her a proud and confident smile. "Of course she did, you're a catch. I told you it would happen."

Megan's fingers itched to clean up the messy countertops.

How the man could cook and operate in a kitchen when it wasn't clean....

Megan counted the items on the far counter.

One, two, three.

She looked back to Danny who was watching her with admiration, love, patience, and understanding. "Okay?"

She nodded.

"Good, because I'm going to annoy you again."

She tensed and braced herself.

"I just got a package in the mail earlier today and I wanted to open it with you."

She waited.

Danny's smile turned blinding. "So, you go get your most toga-looking sandals, because tonight, you're being Megara to my Hercules." He grinned unrepentantly. "You promised me you'd play adult dress up, and I just got a shipment of Leia, Megara, and Rapunzel outfits that are not fit for public display. Get ready, Mama, because I also have matching hero sets."

Megan rolled her eyes.

Of course he did.

She smiled at him and shook her head.

Wonderboy was a nut.

Her overachieving nut.

Fuck, she loved him.

· · · ● · ● · ● · ● · ● · ·

*An introverted artist. A renowned athlete and ladies' man. A life-changing plane crash and a nude sketch that reveals a relationship-shifting truth.*

Click now to read the next book in the series – https://mybook.to/SSig – **Intentional Grounding** – A Steamy, Opposites Attract, Shared Trauma, Sports Romance

# Social Media Information - Ella Haines

Did you enjoy this book?

If so, please visit **www.EllaHaines.com** and sign up for the newsletter to receive additional scenes, freebies, and updates on future releases.

Newsletter signup here:
http://ellahaines.com/newsletter-for-freebies/

Also, if you have an eagle eye and caught any typos that slipped through the rounds and rounds of edits, take a moment and think if you'd like to be an ARC or beta reader for any future releases! If so, drop me an email! I'd love to have you on the team.

If you find any typos, you can let me know here: EllaHaines.author@gmail.com

# Discover More From Ella Haines

**Springfield Spartans Standalone Romances:**

Crystal Clear: A Steamy Springfield Stripper *Novella*

Offensive Holding: A Forbidden Friends-To-Lovers Stripper Romance *Novella*

Illegal Substitutions: A Friends-To-Lovers Steamy Sports Romance

Illegal Contact: A Steamy Sports Workplace Romance

Unsportsmanlike Conduct: A Steamy Single Mother Sports Romance

Intentional Grounding: A Steamy Opposites Attract Romance

False Start: A Steamy Second Chance Romance

**Springfield Cyclones Standalone Hockey Romances:**

Boarding: A Steamy Hockey Romance *Novelette*

Hooking: A Steamy Bachelor Auction Hockey Romance

# About Author - Ella Haines

Ella Haines is a lover of all things love. Raised to know that she could be anything in the world, she made the wild and crazy decision to become a neurotic accountant. Balancing trial balances and filing taxes didn't quite fill her bucket, so she started dabbling in short stories. Those short stories evolved into complex storylines with empowered women, their families and friends, and the hunky men who adore them.

# Request For Review

If this book brought you a smile, please review it on your purchasing platform (and copy it to Goodreads if you're willing and able).

This helps to spread the word about the book. Social proof to other readers is important.

*It also makes the next book come out faster ;-)*

# Praise For Ella Haines

"It kept me hooked with the angst and sweet moments" - Nicole, book review

"All the feels from the frustration, anger, pain and hurt that came flowing out from the never ending angsty-ness truly hit hard many times throughout. Putting you through the ultimate wringer in what was a super emotionally charged ride." – Maddie, book blogger

"Is it friends to lovers? Women's lit? Humorous romance? A sports romance? In the end, it's a little bit of everything." – Cat, book review

"This is a well written emotional roller coaster, which is a friends / lover's sports romance, with angst, friendships, secrets, truths, drama, twists and turns, revelations, and love, which leads to an entertaining and compelling page turner. I look forward to reading more from this talented author whose work I highly recommend." - Wendy, book review

"I would definitely pick up another book or two by this author." – Reading In the Red Room, book blogger

# Content/Trigger Warnings (may contain plot spoilers)

**Warning**:

This book will contain explicit language, kidnapping, threats of violence *(an order of a 'hit' off screen)*, and sexy times. It also has a dirt-bag family member, a character who is a recovering alcoholic, a past sexual assault, and a neurotypical heroine who sometimes has moments of overwhelm. If any of these are triggering for you – here is your warning to maybe avoid this book. Regardless, I promise there will be an HEA *(except for some people...there was a 'hit' ordered after all)*.

This book was a work of my imagination, but I did consult with professionals when writing. Any mistakes are my own and a big thank you to the therapists, survivors, medical professionals, editors, proofreaders, and others that helped me craft this story.